Developing

AFRONIA

Developing

AFRONIA

(Volume 5)

by
Chris Statham

Author Chris Statham
Poetry by Chris Statham
Cover painting by Hezdean Chinthengah
Cover design, book & e-book layout by Zvonimir Bulaja
Editing by Monthia Barton
Proofreading by Wax Ligomba

Published by **www.creativityxroads.com**

First Printing, 2021

Paperback ISBN: 978-1-9989924-6-1
Ebook ISBN: 978-1-9989924-7-8

Also by Chris Statham

The Afronia Series
Crying for Afronia (volume 1)
Escape from Afronia (volume 2)
Dying for Afronia (volume 3)
Afronia Rising (volume 4)

Other Fiction
18 Reflections and 3 Statements of Relief
Paperback Writer

Prose, Poems and Pictures Series
7 Days in One Week (Volume 1)
52 Weeks in One Year (Volume 2)

Book Cover Description

The painting is one of hope. Afronia is personified by one of her citizens about to walk up a set of stairs that is constructed of the skulls and bones of fallen patriots (this representing a violent past) to a bright new future. The nameless person is dressed in the colours of the Afronian flag, yellow representing the sun and justice; red meaning courage, revolution and spilt blood; green symbolizing agriculture and fertility; and blue representing freedom, perseverance, prosperity and the ocean. The symbol (in the middle) is of Umoja (international unity) and white is the colour of peace and purity. Ascending to the hopeful future will not be without troubles as encircling Afronia are hyenas, scavengers, individuals, governments and foreign business leaders who want to feast on a wounded Afronia and gorge on her natural resources.

To those who inspire hope

Foreword

A PASSING OF THE BATON from African independence heroes of the 1950s and 60s to a new generation of leaders in the late 80s and early 90s saw many countries move from Soviet inspired autocratic socialism to Western democratic capitalism. This socio-economic lurch was the catalyst to recent decades of an increasingly deregulated private sector led economy in which corruption has flourished and public services failed, so much so, that some countries are little better off economically four or five decades after independence.

The political upheaval on the continent, combined with the need for development in the context of population growth and urbanization, the increasing impact of climate change and growing inequality led to huge debt mountains. These were largely written off at the 2005 Gleneagles Summit. With neither donor countries nor African governments wanting to get into such unsustainable relationships again, while still there being the imperative for development, Public Private Partnerships, private equity and debt, investment bankers and other forms of Foreign Direct Investment have been the rage for the past decade and a half on the continent. With more developed economies and an increasing tax base,

African governments can invest in welfare programs, essential infrastructure projects and be better able to encourage innovation and job creation. However, working with foreign partners has led to some unscrupulous deals being struck at the expense of the ordinary citizen. *Developing Afronia* explores the national development imperative versus the ethical and economic challenges of outside money.

A Fridge Rich in Commercial Aid

Africa—
beauty all around,
the land of sugar and honey,
unblemished,
untouched since the beginning of time.

A fridge full of natural resources,
But with corrupt hands trying to eat all.
Many are jealous of what they don't have:
cameras and cars,
mansions and skyscrapers,
money.
But should Africans want the consequences?
Murder and rape,
theft and offence,
hassles and danger;
money troubles?

Does the West under develop Africa?
Is there hypocrisy of western democracy?
Is aid, a mask for economic colonisation?
for it is a pittance compared
to bad trade deals,
interest paid on sovereign loans,
remittances from family.

Aid,
a pretty face with a rotten soul.
Encouraging false aspirations
while digging a deeper hole;
the West,
ever ready to gorge on Africa's plenty.

But Afronians have not been corrupted…
yet.
Family values, community spirit,
not in the UK,
something greed is destroying in the land of colour,
laughter and duplicitousness.

Prologue

IT WAS A LITTLE BEFORE 1 AM when the first shuddering claps of thunder reverberated around Umoja City; ten seconds later a massive spike of lightening lit up the night sky. The younger animal residents of the Afronian capital let out howls of terror, the noise and night-time flashes something they'd never witnessed or heard before, Afronia having been in a devastating drought for the past three years. Harari Region in the south—a barren and desolate landscape even during good rains—had been particularly devastated.

It took over an hour of God's pyrotechnics before the first torrents of rain started to fall, but once they did, the tiny drops quickly turned into great globs that smashed onto tin rooftops in a blissful din. All but the heaviest of sleepers or those who had one too many alcoholic beverages were unable to sleep through the cacophony.

Happy at this joyful noise was President Walter Blaise and who in his eighteen months in charge had done much to bring the country back from the brink of being a failed state. He had defeated Islamic State in Sub-Sahara (ISiSS), reinvigorated the economy, but most importantly convinced all his countrymen and women, young and old, whether Hararis, Southis, Somalitreans or Wahilis to believe in his vision of a united Second Federal Democratic Republic of Afronia.

Many obstacles still lie ahead... but maybe the drought in Harari region can finally be removed from my inbox! This as Walter felt the raindrops hitting his face as he stood next to the four monkey guards at the former presidential palace on Wambule Island and which had been turned into a luxury five-star resort and conference centre. *Thank you, God, the Almighty, let these rains fill our rivers and dams so that Hararis will finally get much needed relief from the famine they have endured for so long,* he prayed before he was about to hand out the awards at the inaugural National Journalism Awards. But that hope did not last long, a devastating bomb blast ripping through the Central Post Office in downtown Umoja City and quashing what was to be a joyous event.

As dawn broke on the day after the attack of the night before, the sea was at high tide and the rain continued to pour from the heavens. Rivers leading into the ocean had nowhere to go and areas of Umoja City started to flood. Those living in riverside slums were worst affected; what little they owned washed downstream.

'Much to my surprise,' Ulrich Müller, an immaculately groomed Swiss who wore a bespoke suit and had an air of apparent ease in all that he did, said as he looked out of his window and saw the storm thrashing, *And disappointment*, he didn't add, 'Afronia is developing rather well under Blaise.' This, he stated to his visitor in the penthouse suite of the recently opened six-star Hotel President Obama.

Ulrich was the CEO of AfricaInvest, a Swiss commodity trading company which for the last fifteen years had been exporting diesel fuel to Afronia. This had been precipitated through a twenty-year friendship with Isaiah George, the former president who was currently top of the list of global fugitives. The fateful meeting between the Afronian playboy nephew of President Altimus Solomon and refined Swiss had been during a skiing, gold buying, diamond selling, whoring week-long holiday in the Italian Alps. Ever since that opportune encounter, the two had shared innumerous lines of cocaine off the bodies of multiple naked ladies, a firm bond of friendship being built. When Isaiah George fled Afronia he naturally rushed to his compadre and from where he had been living incognito as he evaded Interpol who had an arrest warrant to take him to International Criminal Court in The Hague for crimes against humanity that he committed during the Afronian civil war. Ulrich, while understanding the danger of harbouring the accused was however in Isaiah's debt, the pair having cobbled together a stupendously profitable partnership which allowed them to exploit a loophole by selling diesel with sulphur levels hundreds of times higher than European standards into the Afronian market. It had been Isaiah who had drafted the Afronian fuel regulations.

Ulrich was currently in conversation with Robert Yohan, the seventy-three-year-old former Minister of Mines and Natural Resources. 'What's next?'

'That's up to you,' Ulrich answered calmly; he was an excellent poker player.

'I'm all ears,' Yohan was not willing to give an inch, this as the wind and rain continued to lash the windowpanes.

'What if I told you… Isaiah George is alive, well and has a strong support base of Afronians and foreigners?'

'Nothing would surprise me,' Robert replied dead-pan, 'that man is a Houdini.'

'Are you talking about Isaiah?' Ulrich enquired, the term being more appropriate for Hamza Leso, the former General of the Counter Terrorism Unit, conspirator in the Lesotho Street attack, MI6 spy, lover of former President Sheila Solomon… and current boyfriend of Tamsin Solomon.

'He got out of Afronia?' Robert questioned, still unsure about the wanted man. *Why was I called to the meeting and what has that lunatic, Isaiah George got to do with anything?*

'Afronia is one on the fastest growing economies in Africa. It's even outstripping Ethiopia which has been growing at ten-percent year-on-year for the last decade.'

'Afronia had a very low base after the civil war.'

'True,' Ulrich concurred. 'But Afronia has been the darling of the west for the last year—'

'Since Blaise put Russia on the naughty step.'

'Quite so,' Ulrich guffawed, as he gave out a deafening belly laugh before changing back into a serious voice indicating that the time to talk business, rather than fool around, had come. 'As the economy grows and Blaise's vision becomes reality, there's no way that what he aspires can be financed through internal resources.'

Now we get to it.

'Certain politicians, industrialists, financiers, academics and media barons, have much interest in Africa, especially Afronia. They are specifically interested to see how the economy moves forward in the coming years.'

'Investors will certainly need to be found,' Robert neutrally agreed.

'We have similar aims… that which is in the best interests for the continent.'

And make a buck or two on the way. 'And what might that be?'

'Those who I represent believe, Africa can only sustainably develop though free market principles. Policies that reduce the chances of war and the destabilizing effects of climate change. We have concerns that Europe and North America will end up paying for chaos in Africa whether through donor aid or mass migration from the global south to the global north. We understand the benefits of political and economic union on the continent and can facilitate such discussions. And we think it's shameful how despots have not been held accountable by the International Criminal Court for their heinous excesses.'

Ulrich paused as he walked over to the window and looked out at the lightening that was still flashing in the sky. 'Africans are economic slaves to corrupt masters. Politicians and bureaucrats only display leadership qualities in the accumulation of personal wealth. African countries may no longer be colonized, but how many Africans can freely express themselves or have economic opportunities? How many constitutions are respected? Look at the civil wars that happen, the massacres in the cause of chasing money. Consider the1960s, South East Asia versus Africa. Both had a semblance of governance and economies which the colonialists had put in place, but apart from a few instances where are the African lion economies to rival the Asian tigers? And this at a time when China has not been able to buy African raw materials quick enough. The question is, why has there been such limited national development in so many African countries? The answer: nationalistic leaders got drunk with power after independence. They plundered economic resources for personal wealth and kept the masses in poverty as a form of mass control. Presidents, corrupt generals, politicians and police commissioners... are all guilty. Religion is promoted to subdue the masses and lay blame elsewhere, fate. African leaders use propaganda against their former imperial colonizers and blame economic demise on colonization, globalization and neo-liberalism. Africa is politically chaotic and economically ruinous. The average man on the street is in greater poverty and more prone to hunger and disease than under colonial rulers; the only hope for many, divine intervention. As Archbishop Desmond Tutu said in the early 1990s: South Africa had more freedom under Apartheid than many independent African countries.' Ulrich finally took a breather.

'Why Afronia? Resources?' Robert queried dispassionately; he didn't altogether disagree with the Swiss' scathing analysis.

'That plays a part when one considers the vast untapped reserves that Russia has, the growing military and economic influence of China, and how our traditional allies in the Middle-East are in the process of transitioning away from oil dependency; Europe has to keep all options for economic security available. Russia wants to see the European Union implode under the migration time bomb. Black African youth have finally seen the light and given up hope their leaders have anything other than self-enrichment in their hearts and which is the truth as to why they brace themselves to cross the scorching Sahara Desert and watery death of the Mediterranean Sea to reach the lands of their former colonial masters.'

'And so, you have invited me to talk because Blaise doesn't fit your worldview?' Robert guessed aloud.

'Partly. Blaise has done a remarkable job in bringing security to the country and the economy back from the brink, but he is a socialist at heart. We feel his state-led development agenda is not in the best interests of Afronia or the continent more generally. We are not in the business of regime change, but if he were democratically elected out of office and replaced with someone more aligned to our view, we would, as the Brits like to say, help line up the ducks.'

'Really? And the other part?'

'You have close connections with Russia and Taberia.' Robert nodded his head but stayed quiet. 'We need chaos to reign in Afronia,' the man who called himself Ulrich Müller added as he stared at the man opposite and who appeared not at all surprised, 'and then for Maduhu, with the backing of Igor Victov, to intervene.'

'So it was you who was behind the post office bomb blast?' Robert, the canny operator asked as +++ he mentally geared up for what he expected would be the negotiation of his life.

'Yes. In due course, we want you to be our President of the Second Federal Democratic Republic of Afronia.'

Chapter 1

THE DELUGE DID NOT STOP for twenty-four hours. In the first week after the heavens opened there was widespread flooding throughout the country. Fifty-nine Afronian lives were lost and hundreds-of-thousands more made homeless as straw brick houses and all possessions within were washed away. Those not adversely affected gave thanks the land becoming a little less scorched and green sprouts of hope appeared, this an analogy also for how the Afronian economy was rebounding after years of strife.

In the eighteen months since the civil war hostilities had ceased much had happened. Walter Blaise had been peacefully elected as president. The Truth and Reconciliation Commission had opened and closed. Isaiah George had been exposed as the mastermind behind the Denga Chemical Attack and financier of mercenaries; he was currently on the run. Igor Victov, the Russian President, had been unceremoniously kicked out of the Second Federal Democratic Republic of Afronia, this after his protégé, Sheila Solomon had stepped on an anti-personal landmine in the former playground of her family, Wambule Island, and which itself had undergone mass refurbishment.

In the United Kingdom, hedge funds located in the City of London had been convinced to invest in Afronia over a smoked salmon dinner party hosted at 11 Downing Street by the Chancellor of the Exchequer, Andrew Sinclair. The list of suitable investors had been drawn up by Charlie Daniels, MI6's East Africa spymaster and who understood the long-term strategic importance for the British Government of having private sector investment in Afronia.

Umoja City was no longer war torn. Battle destroyed buildings with gaping wounds from tank or mortar shells or scarred from grenades and bullets had been demolished. Double lane highways that criss-crossed the city were repaired. With Japanese and Australian funding, a Rapid Bus Transit system was under construction. The Hillview slum that had been pulverized during the civil war as Isaiah George tried to obliterate the rebels and drive all non-Somalitreans out of the capital, was once again the beating heart of the city, though now rather than housing the underclass it had been gentrified. You could once more hear the street chatter, smell aromas from artisanal coffee houses, be delighted in different dialects, taste sumptuous food and engage in chitchat in a haze of shisha smoke as you walked through the neighbourhood. And the Hillview Coffee Emporium had been rebuilt after being turned into an edifice of twisted metal and broken stonework by a Presidential Guard operated bulldozer during the civil war.

The capital, not so long ago awash with death squads and out of control inflation, was now booming on the back of Chinese, American and British money; there was barely a Rouble in sight. Estate agents buzzed through former government buildings on prime real estate; the land having been rezoned for private sector investment. A TedX conference, at which speakers had included entrepreneurs, former child soldiers and the Commissioner for a Free Media, had been hosted by Emmanuel Seid at the Umoja City Business Incubator. Football was once more played on the beaches, the youngsters' former lives as soldiers or rebels, now in the past. Culture in the form of cinema, restaurants and theatre were popping up every day. Men and women could be seen strolling hand in hand along narrow roads with smiles rather than worried frowns. On the seafront, families would amble along the promenade, swim in the turquoise waters and drink at cafes and bars. In the city centre, Peace Park, funded by a mysterious benefactor—some theorizing it was Isaiah George (whereabouts unknown)—was once again overcrowded. Shrieks of fun could be heard by children playing on the bouncy castle and swings while their parents looked on from the ice cream stands or food stalls. The Afronian capital was energetic and aspirational. It was somewhere that Altimus Solomon, the disgraced, nepotistic, corrupt father of the nation would barely recognise.

'There are two sides to Afronia,' Tigist, said to her fiancé Jacob, 'the horrible side where two million have been displaced by drought. Rural people are in search for food, water, medical care, and shelter from the unrelenting sun that destroyed their crops, their livestock, their way of life, and for many, their family as thousands die from starvation... And then there is this,' she said as she swept her arm in an arc towards the redeveloped seafront promenade and where an ancient stretch limousine jostled for business against a double-decker bus for wedding bookings.

'There are few countries with such dramatic contrasts,' Jacob agreed, as he looked at the mass of cranes and land-moving equipment. Property developers had arrived en-masse and, there were many returning diaspora, both sets of entrepreneurs expecting the economy to keep growing at a phenomenal rate.

'I only wish Jessica was here to see the new Afronia.' Tigist thought of her deceased friend who'd introduced Jacob to her shortly after the Lesotho Street attack.

Jacob lovingly squeezed his beau's hand. 'We have to find out who ordered her murder. Someone is responsible; we must get a break at some stage.'

'We're not journalists anymore,' Tigist reminded her lover.

'I know you're busy with your lounge and I'm non-stop with the business incubator, but we have to find answers… for Sam's sake.' Jacob was cognizant of how his friend had helped him after he'd lost his then girlfriend Aisha, in the Lesotho Street attack. 'Sam needs closure; it's our duty to help.'

'I completely agree, but where do we start, and should we open old wounds?'

500 kilometres to the South West of Umoja City, was Harari Region, the epicentre of the devastating three-year drought. The famine was a consequence of the longest

dry spell for thirty years, political mishandling, corruption under Altimus Solomon; these challenges had been exacerbated by the civil war. The numbers were overwhelming. 4 Million were food insecure. 2 million had left their villages and made their skeletal way to twenty-three refugee tent cities and where highly nutritious food was available for the youngest, oldest and weakest. Save the Children and Medinces Sans Frontiers—two of the dozen international Non-Governmental Organizations who had been working in the region for many months—had been pleading for further humanitarian aid as stores were running dangerously low; refugees and internally displaced were still arriving daily.

'We can't cope,' Mary and who had been working on the Taberian border during the civil war, spoke to the assembled crowd in the central tent and which acted as the public meeting space. 'We're short of shelter, stock and staff, everything,' she complained to the local and international media who had come to report on the looming humanitarian catastrophe. 'So many of the weak, the destitute, the young and old, can't make it here. Bodies are ravaged by Cholera and other waterborne diseases, but so desperate are so many to get fluid into their bodies they drink where they can find water no matter the source. Most have sold all their earthly belongings but still can't afford a donkey ride much less a taxi, and so corpses litter the roadside.'

'Conditions are very tough,' Dr Ralph Lisoyga, the Minister of Health acknowledged.

'There are legitimate concerns that if solutions are not found, and quickly, then the huge number of young, unemployed men who have lost everything… then these camps could become fertile recruiting grounds for Islamic State in Sub-Sahara,' Mary warned.

'We are developing livestock programs,' Ralph reassured those at the meeting.

'We've heard that a million times before,' an irate farmer at the back of the tent shouted. 'That's exactly what Altimus Solomon and his cronies promised, and nothing ever materialised.'

'I do not serve that president,' Ralph countered with more venom than he meant; he was fed up with being compared to the old regime. 'This is the Second Federal Democratic Republic of Afronia, and not the first. Do we have challenges? Yes. Have we solved all Afronia's problems? No… but we are trying one step at a time. Are we God? No, but rain has arrived in Umoja City and our meteorologists say it is heading towards Harari Region. Are we investing in the future of all the regions?' The minister rhetorically asked. 'Yes, we are. With me today are consultants from Stephens and Davis, experts on environmental impact studies for hydroelectric power and viaducts. The government has put out to tender a request for proposals to build three hydro-electric dams and a network of viaducts to transport water to Harari Region from the Southi Mountains so that you'll never experience such dreadful conditions again. There will be opportunities to start irrigation farming, meaning, you will have year-round income to supplement your livestock business. You have suffered, but the government of President Walter Blaise is determined to ensure the people of Harari region never hurt so much again.' Drained, Ralph sat down to muted applause.

'Promises were made before,' the unconvinced farmer spoke up, 'and then turned into the dust you see all around.'

It took three days for the storm clouds to reach the arid Harari hinterlands, but when they did, the storm was like no farmer had witnessed in living memory. If the dams and viaducts had been built, they would have quickly filled, but instead the concrete hard riverbeds were not able to absorb the downpour, the parched earth turning into deadly brown flash floods that first overwhelmed the dried up river banks and then the surrounding fields, until finally swamping the low-lying refugee camps and which had until recently been bitterly complaining about the lack of water.

'We need army choppers,' Mary pleaded while gazing to the part of the site that was perched on the downslope of the hill and where some tents had been washed away.

'Keep the kids calm,' an army officer instructed the crowd and who were looking on at the spectacle of a rowing boat rescuing a pregnant mother.

The irate farmer who had spoken at the meeting had his attention on a little girl desperately holding onto a tree trunk and crying for her mother. When she was inevitably sucked under the water, he and three heroic volunteers jumped into the water. One of them couldn't swim, but even the two who could were mercilessly consumed by the churning, gurgling brown liquid death. Four other volunteers, brothers, downstream, saw the waving arms of the little girl and dived into the river. Holding onto the petrified child they swam with all their might to a small island where they desperately held on to maize stalks until an army helicopter diverted course and rescued them, this to relieved cheering from the on-looking crowd.

As bad as the flooding was in the Harari Region it was as nothing compared to the unending torrents flowing through the capital. While there had been remarkable growth to accommodate the influx of refugees, there was not yet the appropriate support infrastructure such as roads, bridges, hospitals and schools, nor drainage. There had already been five landslides, Umoja City ringed by hills on three sides, the ocean on the fourth.

It was the worst flooding in living memory. The bridge linking Umoja City Island to the downtown area was washed away. The Umoja River delta was deemed too dangerous to put out the ferries due to all the debris. Along the Hillview Promenade, only the aerials of submerged vehicles not washed away and the roofs of shops and houses, could be seen; it was utter havoc.

'All public resources must be put to the relief effort,' Hamza advised the president. That these two men should now not only consider themselves colleagues, but friends, was a remarkable feat considering their pasts. Walter Blaise had been an anti-authoritarian member of Altimus Solomon's politburo. It had been a surprise that he had contested the first democratic elections on the back of popular support in the regions only to be defeated by Altimus Solomon who had engaged in mass vote rigging. He'd lost the second election to Isaiah George for equally dubious reasons. Finally, he had been elected, this after

Sheila Solomon—the youngest daughter of Altimus—had stepped on an anti-personal mine in the summer house on Wambule Island.

The other person in the room was the notorious Hamza Leso. He was the former General in the Counter Terrorist Unit who ordered the Presidential Square massacre when protestors had complained about the whitewash to the Corruption in the Capital enquiry. He was the mastermind behind the Lesotho Street attack before becoming a fugitive and impersonating the well-known peace activist Jimmy Ngole. He'd returned to Afronia on MI6's dime and had wooed Sheila Solomon and been the brains behind Isaiah George's rise to power. Currently he was dating Tamsin Solomon, the only surviving child of the Afronian dynasty, this the latest episode in his quite exceptional life.

Walter and Hamza were the original Afronian odd couple… but also a highly pragmatic and effective one. Since being elected president, Afronia had gone through a renaissance, partly from the goodwill of the international community who were scrambling for Afronia's natural resources and were willing to pay a high price in low interest loans and donor assistance, but equally from the president's insistence that all ministers be experts in their fields. The Minister of Defence was a rebel war hero. The Minister of Health, Dr Ralph, had worked at the Umoja City Central Hospital. The Minister of Economy, an economics professor. The Minister of Education, a seasoned teacher etc.

'Agreed,' the president concurred. 'The army has been deployed from their barracks in all our major cities. Infantry units will relieve police from civil duties. Army engineer and logistics regiments will coordinate the disaster management response.'

'Emergency teams of volunteer consultants from the British company, HydroDevelop are repairing the drinking-water supply lines that were broken by the landslides.'

'Aren't they bidding on the tender documents to run AfroWater?' the president asked about the privatization process that the Afronian Water and Sewage utility was going through.

'Yes, but we need all the help we can get; their support won't influence the decision-making process in anyway. Other bidders are also sending expert teams,' Hamza answered, remembering how he should respond to such a question, this from his last conversation with Charlie Daniels his MI6 field handler.

Chapter 2

5,000 KILOMETRES FROM the Afronian torrents, in the East Sussex village of Hazelstone, or more precisely The Prince of Wales pub, David Howells, the captain of The Eternal Hope fishing trawler, stood up. 'We need border-hunter police. Our way of life, our homes are under attack from the threat of foreigners and British liberals. Millions are trying to reach England's green and pleasant land, and I for one will die trying to stop them.'

'Hear, hear,' came a chorus of approval.

'We are proud Englishmen and the weak-willed bureaucrats at the European Union can't be relied upon to keep our borders safe. Migration is the Trojan Horse for marauding Jihadis to infiltrate our society and carry out terrorist acts. It's a proven fact,' Howells continued, 'that so-called humanitarian ships funded by Brussels' Euros, and who claim to rescue the floating from the Mediterranean, are driving the increase in boat crossings. Many of these so-called charity workers are colluding with smugglers and sharing the profits.' This was pure conjecture in the British right-wing press and wasn't factual as Howells stated

'And the politicians in Westminster don't know any better,' Derek Childs, a user of undocumented labour to catch chickens, said to a second roar of approval. 'Hazelstone is a village of pensioners, fishermen, farmers, builders and commuters—'

'And the unemployed?' a smart aleck interrupted.

'Bobby, he's talking about you!' someone shouted out the name of one of the village's true characters and who'd never earned a day's honest pay but somehow survived on a combination of fiddling the welfare system, doing odd jobs for cash-in-hand and having luck on the horses.

Fifty metres up the hill from The Prince of Wales was The George and Dragon. Mohammed Ahmed, "Mo" to friends, was holding court. 'The Prime Minister calls refugees, The Trojan Horse of terrorism. He has requested Parliament to amend human rights laws to hold asylum applicants in detention camps. Converted shipping containers are used to house the frightened and desperate as they make asylum applications via video-link. If the migrants for any reason don't cooperate, they are sent back to their country of origin… and quite possibly executed by the state… and yet we claim to be a civilized country.'

'It's a clear breach of the refugee convention.' Megan, Mo's wife, pointed out.

'Why do you think so many voted for Brexit?' a condescending Cathleen, a political activist and only child of the mixed-race couple, sarcastically queried. 'Detaining the stricken for months on end is a new low even for this Tory Government.'

'We have to do something,' Jeffrey Shields, the landlord and club captain of the local rugby team declared. 'With the refugee camp on the Taberian border closing, there is bound to be another surge of Afronian migrants to the UK.'

'Why do you say that?' Megan asked. 'Afronia is getting back on its feet, we have to keep supporting the country.'

'How?' This a question on the lips of many of the supporters of the Brits for Afronians Foundation and who had crowded into the pub for the monthly meeting.

'We need more donations,' Sylvia Toner, and who had been with Mo on his last trip to Afronia, suggested. 'We have to help more starving poor black babies.'

'What other colour would they be?' a voice articulated what many others were thinking.

'I'm only trying to help.'

'Thank you, Sylvia,' Mo, diplomatically intervened. *No matter how simplistic, often wrong-sighted and bordering on the realms of racist Sylvia's suggestions are, they come from a heart of gold... and one of the most influential members of the constituency Conservative Party and village church.* 'Any other suggestions?'

'Support Afronian entrepreneurs through making linkages with British business,' Jeffrey suggested. 'Establish a British Afronian Chambers of Commerce.'

'Very good.' Mo made a note in his pad. 'Anything else?'

'We have to change local opinion,' a voice on the car park side of the room suggested. 'If we can show that supporting Afronians can also be good for Hazelstone, we'll have won half-the-battle.'

'What do you specifically suggest?' Mo wanted details.

'We have to debunk the gumph that the brave rescuers in the Mediterranean are in anyway responsible for escalating the number of refugees making that dangerous crossing. We must keep highlighting that its predominantly worsening economic, political and climatic crisis, across several regions of Africa, that is driving up refugee numbers. We must reiterate, that coming to Europe is the last resort and, that no asylum seeker would willingly go through the violence, rape, forced labour and torture that so many endure… if it wasn't.'

And so, the conversations in the respective Hazelstone pubs continued long into the night. However, the quaint village did have some extenuating circumstances for the range of opinion, namely, it was part of a refugee experiment—this mainly due to the national profile Mo and Brits for Afronians Foundation had garnered—and had become a guineapig of a new kind of civic experiment; it would receive 500 Afronians en-masse rather than the East African asylum seekers being scattered across the country.

A first sign of the changes to come—and after years of failed applications for improvements—suddenly street lighting was fixed and, a play park of swings and roundabouts was built overnight. On the council run Beaufort Estate, where flats which had lain vacant for years, rapidly they went through mass refurbishing. It was when public signs in an unknown language (Afronian—a derivative of the Pan-African Bantu) started to appear across the village that curiosity turned into open hostility and vandalism.

Pamela Jenkins was sitting in her modest mayoral office when she got a phone call from the Home Office. 'Hazelstone will be receiving 500 Afronian asylum seekers on October 1st.'

'Pardon?' Pamela answered, not sure if she'd heard correctly.

'500 Afronians will be placed in the Beaufort Estate council flats.'

'I will need to call an emergency council meeting to see if there's a two-third's majority agreement to this proposal.'

'They are coming,' the nameless voice reiterated.

Mrs Jenkins heard muted laughing at the other end of the line. 'Is this a joke? Did David Howells put you up to this?'

'An asylum seeker coordinator will come to Hazelstone tomorrow and meet you and a Mr,' there was a sound of rustling paper, 'Mohammed Ahmed.'

'Bloody hell!' the Mayor responded, finally realizing, *This isn't a prank call.* Up until that moment the most contentious issue Pamela had to deal with had been the proposed construction of a footbridge across the Upper Woods stream and which would join the northern and southern parts of Hazelstone Woods. This project had united dog walkers for over a decade, the canines merrily splashing about in the two-metre-wide stream all times of the year as their owners had to make the five-minute detour to complete a lap along the walkway through the scenic woods.

It was not long before news of the dictate from the Whitehall mandarins turned into the hottest topic of village gossip. Phones started ringing as word spread and before the day was out an emergency meeting was organised in the church hall. Normally, such a gathering of villagers only happened for spring fireworks, the bonfire on Guy Fawkes Night, the annual cricket match against Smithwick—the next-door village—and the August Bank Holiday fete.

While the parish hall could accommodate 150 people, on this occasion there was need to erect speakers outside as double that number turned out to hear the mayor. At 6 PM, Pamela left her office and walked across the village green but before reaching the hall where the four walls were plastered with Sunday school paintings, she saw a commotion. There were not just villagers outside the place of worship but also local and national media.

'It's an African invasion,' David Howells told one reporter.

Though the melee, the grey-haired, stately, sixty-seven-year-old Mrs Jenkins, calmly strode, villagers respectfully making way to let her pass to the stage. As she walked to the microphone, two regulars of the Prince of Wales pub unfurled a large St. George flag which proclaimed: Britain for the British.

'That's the English flag,' Jeffrey Shields mocked the pair as they were escorted out, their arms held tightly against their backs by a member of the local constabulary.

'The EU is taking in 5,000 new migrants every day, 4 million by the end of 2019,' Pamela started her rehearsed speech. 'The UK will take in 80,000 new migrants by the end of this year. Most will be allowed to stay and so we must be welcoming and consider this an opportunity for Hazelstone. New business will open-up and more customers will frequent those already established. We will not permit mischief, whether by the new arrivals or by those who wish them ill will. I will not tolerate intimidation nor intolerance and have spoken to the Police Commissioner to ensure there are more community police officers during the Afronians arrival.'

'My daughters won't be safe after dark,' one voice shouted.

'Our schools and doctor's clinic are already overwhelmed and understaffed,' another pointed out.

'And what about the vigilantes who killed the Zimbabwean?' Cathleen asked, this referring to the death of the PhD student who was killed in an arson attack and for which no one had yet been arrested. 'Who's going to protect them from the racists?'

After the heated church hall meeting, Sylvia drove home to meet her husband Eric, and who had been on a strategy retreat in the Lake District for the past two weeks. Eric was a senior manager at HydroDevelop, a British water infrastructure engineering company. The Cumbrian getaway was to focus on a proposal to the Afronian Government for the design and creation of three hydro-electric dams, a national waterway for movement of inland cargo and, to catalyse an irrigation led agricultural revolution in the arid Harari region.

The World Bank was providing a loan of $575 million for the project and should HydroDevelop be successful, they stood to make an operational profit of $80 million. It was a project the company desperately wanted to win and had made Prince James—the third in the line to the British throne—a non-executive director, hoping his influence, a personal tour of some of the royal castles and, introductions to British financial movers and shakers in the City of London, would sway the Afronian decision makers to award the contract to HydroDevelop. For his part, should the proposal be victorious, the Prince was due a substantial commission and stock options.

'Through the ages, rivers have served as effective waterways that carry people and goods over long distances,' Eric, sipping a glass of red wine at the kitchen table started to evangelize to Sylvia once she had stepped through the front door; he was unaware of the soon to be upheaval in village life. 'Even in the technological age, developed countries still depend on inland water transport for moving large and bulky cargo as its cheaper, more reliable and less polluting than other options. Once operational, the dams and waterway will form part of a larger multi-modal transport network across Afronia. This web of water, road and rail arteries will transform the economy. The project is a key part of their industrialisation strategy, water being vital for engineering and manufacturing companies.'

'Very bold thinking,' Sylvia commented as she deposited her car keys in a small wicker basket near the toaster.

'HydroDevelop follows the principle of working with rather than against nature. Our proposal is also aligned with their tourism strategy and considers the seasonal changes that the rains bring; it's really quite ground-breaking.'

'That's a terrible pun,' Sylvia laughed.

'Unintended. It would be a wonderful project to work on. Our plan helps to protect aquatic biodiversity and will reduce dredging of rivers to a bare minimum. Each 85-acre hydro-electric dam will have a maximum height of 150-feet and a 13-foot diameter. There will be a 10,000-footlong tunnel, two-mile ring road and an onshore landing dock. It will generate 75KiloWatts of electricity.'

As Eric extolled the technical aspects of the project, Sylvia poured herself a glass of wine. *It's been a trying day… and to be greeted by this without even a peck on the cheek or bottle of perfume in sight!*

'If HydroDevelop wins,' Eric, continued to his wife's back, 'there's a good chance we'll move to Afronia.' Sylvia didn't say a word to this unexpected pronouncement. 'I thought you would be excited?' A somewhat disheartened Eric queried his wife when she turned around, her face showing that she was anything but thrilled at such a foreign prospect.

As conversations about the Afronian invasion—as it had been termed—was had in houses throughout Hazelstone, few of those at the centre of the divisive Westminster strategy had been consulted or had any input into the process, their fate once again decided by others.

Amongst these forgotten people was Grace. She had been trafficked by Mike Henshaw's gang, MH-16 to London. Arriving in the UK, she refused to become a prostitute. The gang-master tied her hands behind her back and to her feet for three days. She was denied food and water for the first twenty-four hours, forced to soil herself, and then once showered, raped multiple times. She had no choice but to sleep with Johns if she wanted to prevent further beatings, sexual assaults and to start re-paying her £30,000 of inflated debt in instalments as low as £20, this her price for straight sex.

Grace was one of the lucky ones. She'd been rescued during an international police operation and subsequently placed in Mo's women's hospice in Hazelstone. More recently, she'd been relocated to a flat on the Beaufort Estate, the previous resident, an Afghani, having died of carbon monoxide poisoning. Grace had been reassured the leak had been fixed during the renovation, but despite the assurance she slept with the windows open and so put on a third layer of clothes before going under two blankets.

Grace had a temporary resident permit that allowed her to reside in the UK but without the right to work. She couldn't access healthcare despite the physical and mental scars she bore. She was part of the mass unseen grey and black economy, invisible to the authorities and on the fringes of society. Like many, she was targeted by the likes of Howells and Childs who exploited the needy. Grace relied on limited government welfare payments and the altruism of well-wishers like Mo and Jeffrey. Under such grim circumstances it was not surprising that many who had escaped persecution wished to return home while others took the only option they could see, including Grace's neighbour, who two days earlier had committed suicide.

'I just want to be reunited with my family,' Sara—who'd given the tip to the police which led to Grace's rescue—said to her Afronian neighbour. 'I left my daughter in Nyala with her granny; I have missed her last three birthdays.'

'Will there ever be light again in this life,' Irene asked. 'It's humiliating to buy food that's gone past its best before date, especially fruit which is so plentiful and cheap in Afronia. I buy potatoes as I can't afford bread. I don't have money for meat or clothes. I survive on hand-outs; thank God my children are not here.'

'I hate that we can't complain. I hear that people who go to the authorities never return; they are deported or imprisoned; oh how I hate the uncertainty!' Sara confessed. 'We can't speak out as we will be detained as a troublemaker.'

'The oppression is worse than under Altimus Solomon,' Grace agreed, the other women vigorously nodding their heads.

'We are hated by the locals and forgotten by everyone else. This is a hell where no one sees nor cares about us,' Irene added. 'So many people try to rip us off with crazy prices so that we become indebted. We are wasting our best years here when we should be working, starting a family and having fun rather than living in enforced poverty.'

'This life is almost as shameful and demoralizing as when I was forced onto my back ten times a day. Maybe it would have been better to return to Afronia now there's a new president? Anything must be better than this purgatory—'

'And yet, Grace, some think we chose to come here and live like dogs; we're not crazy!' Sara, articulating what the other women were thinking. 'They really have no clue as to the horrors and persecution we ran from. If only they knew the truth of what we've been through, surely they would be more humane.'

Chapter 3

'As Umoja City goes through rapid reinvention,' Ulrich Müller started, 'I want to be your conduit to international finance.'

'That's very kind of you,' the president replied, though not for one second trusting the Swiss banker.

'The Hillview promenade is just the start of how we can help the country rebuild. We can support the construction of civic infrastructure… and stop marauding gangs taking over derelict districts.'

Is that an implied threat? How did this man get a meeting with me in the first place? I'll ask Gladys, this his executive assistant.

'Hillview was once lined with slums but is now populated with cafés. I will help you access finance for other largescale projects. Afronia needs local and international investors; I can find them for you.' The Swiss had in mind the waterfront development. The former ginnery had stood empty for twenty years after the deliberate collapse of Afronia's textile industry by Altimus Solomon. Ulrich had 130 loft-style apartments for young professionals and returning diaspora in mind. 'Imagine it's 8 AM. Commuters are going to work and tourists are finishing their breakfasts before strolling along the promenade. They smell the coffee being roasted, freshly squeezed juices being poured and artisan cheeses and meats being consumed. In the evening open spaces would hold events such as theatre, comedy, open mic sessions and concerts on the beach, with thousands enjoying themselves and lubricating the economy.'

'That sounds wonderful.'

'I would like to take this opportunity to introduce my friend,' Ulrich started to say, 'and who is also a fellow investor.' The president looked at the imposing Mr Jackson. 'Russell is a son of Afronia and founder and CEO of Ibex Investments, a social investment fund.'

'Afronia has all the natural resources any country could ask for,' Russell started, this after shaking hands with the president. 'I see so much determination to make Afronia a country we can all be proud of. There is opportunity, motivation, and potential to fully engage with the youth; Ibex Investments is here to be on that journey with you. Our focus is on renewable energy, healthcare and education. We are not a charity but profit orientated. We give investors a decent return… though the businesses we work with must help Afronians in their daily lives.'

'Let me put you in touch with our Minister of Trade and Investment. He'll introduce you to a business incubator program,' Blaise warmly smiled.

Müller and Watson were just two of an increasing number of international businessmen and women, diplomats and consultants in Afronia's sprawling political and commercial capital, and where an increasing array of hip new bars and nightclubs were springing up to allow the increasing number of the well-heeled to chase the night away.

Hillview was the epicentre of the renaissance, a hub of creativity and cool. Previously, it had been infamous for bohemians and squalor in equal measure, but since the peace accord it had gone through a radical transformation. A few entrepreneurs had struck gold in the property boom by turning whole city blocks from slum dwellings into expensive flats and art galleries. However, most Umoja City's residents were still on the outside of society: poor, living in burned out and bullet scarred, windowless, derelict buildings with no electricity or piped water. It was these citizens who would habitually clean up the detritus of the revellers who inhabited the newly constructed plush houses, hotels and flats; it was a two-speed revitalization.

'Nothing has really changed,' Charles Ontago, the former second-hand clothes seller, complained to Innocent Shembles, the journalist one evening after both had finished their work. 'I was unemployed and living off scraps before the war… and I still am. My old neighbourhood is being turned into a fancy marina and yet I'm forced to live in a squat; regeneration should be for everyone. We are suffering capitalist genocide as there is no safety net for the poor; this is what Altimus Solomon had wet dreams about. There is nothing wrong with prime land being sold by the city for high prices, if A) it creates jobs and, B) money is pumped into low-cost housing developments the poor can afford.'

'That sounds great, Charles, but what about those wanting to move? For instance, Mauritius Avenue. That neighbourhood has rubbish strewn streets with many living illegally in residences. There are massage parlours, pawnshops and bottlestores; prostitution and crime are rife.'

'They are mainly rural villagers who moved to Hill-view over the last fifteen years. They think they live the good life and are not willing to give up what they have despite the appalling conditions. Unless the city council can provide them with alternative accommodation they will remain; they will not move from one indignity to another without a fight; they would rather be imprisoned or die.'

'Death is not something to talk lightly about—'

'And neither is eviction, Innocent. Besides, it is the underclass, the guards, domestic workers and day-labour-ers who serve the rich. If they are moved to the edge of Umoja City their commute would become prohibitively long and expensive. This another set of daily problems they would have to face. Decisions shouldn't be based on some corrupt British developer who has greased the right city official's hands to get a plot of land they want. Forced relocation entrenches inequality. If it's only the rich who live on the prime plots and, the poor are forced to the outskirts of the city and fringes of society, it will cause long-term problems.'

'But staying in such squalor is also not an option; it's an abuse of human rights. The city needs to find the funds and have the political will and administrative ca-pacity to adequately rehouse those rendered homeless by development.'

The lively discussion on the future direction of the capital continued late into the night. Across town in the poorer neighbourhood of Little Wahili, on this hot and humid night, was another type of entrepreneur. Down a potholed—but surprisingly busy road—a young crowd had packed into the tight bottlestore, Friends In Beer, and were listening to a comedian who gave a voice to the masses who called this suburb of Umoja City their home. The Phenomenon of New Afronia, was the self-titled billing.

'No one dared to run a joke under the Great Redeemer, the former Life President, Altimus, but now we are free to call him what he was: a corrupt, pompous ass. We are recovering from civil war and skyscrapers are going up faster than Solomon's hands up a young girl's skirt. His manhood, so he claimed, bigger than Umoja Tower.' This got a round of applause, but not the reaction the comedian was hoping for. 'If the president really wanted to show that he was a man of the people, he should have drunk AfroJaeger rather than BritBeer... then he would know how hard it is for a poor man to get a girl...' this got a louder laugh, 'and while we might be poor and drink moonshine, we at least know how to laugh and not get assassinated.' Such a brazen statement, whether in jest or not, was a sign of the times; it would have been an unthinkable utterance a few short years earlier.

Chapter 4

TWENTY KILOMETRES NORTH of Umoja City, a pitted dirt track linked the village of Zarusha where there was intermittent electricity and haphazard municipal services, to the main northern highway. While some villagers got sun scorched working in the fields the majority plied the sea for their living, but either way, they were not thinking about hipster coffee houses or art exhibitions, rather the very real and current problem of climate change and which over the last decade had seen neighbouring villages consumed by rising tides. The only sign there had once been life where the sea now moved unabated, was that at low tide a row of mangrove trees could be seen sticking their branches out of the mud. The sight was a warning for those living on the coast of what was in store.

'Five generations of my family were born here,' Desmond Baganda, who languidly sat on a skiff and looked out to sea, said to Innocent Shembles in a resigned voice, 'but now our land is for sale to any foreigner with money.'

The selling of our seas—Afronian fishermen facing the dual challenge of globalisation and climate change.

With soaring global meat consumption food companies are increasingly looking towards protein rich African seas to feed their factory-farmed animals; it's the humble fisherman who is caught in the vortex of globalization and cross-continental supply chains.

In the bustling market in the coastal village of Zarusha, the fug of rotting fish guts is thick in the air. I observe traders busy on their phones calling in the daily prices of the morning catch. There is a long row of tables where women are smoking fish. "These are for the new hotels," Violet, head of Zarusha Women's Smoked Fish Association, says referring to the building of a luxury resort nearby. "It's fish that sends my kids to school."

However, local fishermen are being squeezed as their catch gets smaller. They now need to go further offshore which increases both their costs and level of danger. "I don't mine gold or diamonds like the Southis. I don't have forests for logging like the Wahilis and, I'm not a pastoralist like my brothers in Harari region; my income comes from the sea. It's the only resource my family has known for generations," this from Desmond, a local fisherman who had yet another disappointing voyage. "Some now rely on explosives to fill their boats," this in reference to the increasingly common practice of dynamite fishing which has a catastrophic impact on the coral reefs, a main draw for the emerging tourist sector. "We used to catch barracuda and red snapper. Crabs, lobsters, prawn, tuna, and squid were all sold in great abundance and at low prices, but now it's the opposite as no matter how many times we venture out we never catch much. The engine on my trawler has not been properly maintained for many a month as there is no spare cash. Neighbours who do blast fishing are the only ones who make a decent living. It's easy to bribe poorly paid construction workers or soldiers for dynamite or grenades."

Part of the reason for the decline of Desmond's catch is that three kilometres up the coast a British fishmeal plant has been under construction for the last six months, this just one of five being built. Fish are turned into farm animal feed as the fishmeal powder is nutrient rich in oil and Omega 3 and which are vital to grow factory farmed chicken and pigs in the shortest possible time.

The foundation stone for the first factory was planted with much fanfare by the Minister of Trade and Industry, and who enthusiastically declared: "Fish will bring jobs to Zarusha and tax to the country. Afronian entrepreneurs will have the opportunity to bring prosperity to their families through harvesting the riches from the seas." With the completion of the first factory a little over a year ago, the negative impact on the local economy can already be felt. The fish, which are caught are smaller as they don't have time to reproduce, and yet are sold for a premium, the price overtaking that of chicken and soon beef. With a growing population that need to be fed, and dwindling shallow water fish stock, local fishermen are rapidly seeing their way of life nearing extinction.

"We are worried," Violet expresses her fears. "The price is increasing little by little every week. We normally only eat fish in this village as meat is too expensive; we only eat beef and chicken at festivals and weddings. When the other British plants are finished, who knows if we will still be able to afford to eat fish or whether we will starve."

"Soon the British businesses will bring their own fleets of commercial trawlers and no longer buy from us," this from Desmond, who has a different set of worries. "They are destroying the shallow beds through using massive nets. There are no more fish and so we travel far out to sea; it's more dangerous and still we come back with a smaller catch. If we can't fish, our village will be nothing. Without fish, there will be revolution," Desmond angrily says as he walks discontentedly towards the market.

Down the coast, the outskirts of Umoja City have been transformed by Chinese investment into Afronia's first deep-water port. Where not so long ago the wharf processed thirty skiffs there is now a lavishly decorated casino and betting dens that cater to mainly Chinese workers, $100 bills slammed down as quickly as Tsingtao beer is thrown back. Construction is 24/7 and land is being bought at triple the value it was last year. The speed of development is dividing locals between those who have employment or business opportunities and those who are worried their traditional way of life fast fading away.

The processing plants and hotel in Zarusha and the capital's port and casino are just a few examples of vast construction projects that have started in the last twelve-months, others include: a new airport, power plants, a national stadium and a ring road. There is even talk of an AfroDisney with Mickey Mouse, water parks, hotels, shopping malls and an artificial snow run; there is growing expectation that Umoja City will become the Dubai of East Africa. And while some Afronians have undoubtedly benefited many are struggling with the rapid transformation as the speed which money is pouring into Afronia is leading to increased rents, and the price of land skyrocketing so much so that many Afronians are being forced out of the housing market by both foreign manual labour and business executives. The divide between the Afronian rich and poor is widening on a seemingly daily basis. The questions politicians need to consider are, for how much longer will the average fisherman accept the change and, what will happen if they don't feel they are included in the new Afronia?

Desmond hadn't read Innocent Shembles' article, he had other challenges on his mind. 'The sea will get her revenge,' this as he looked at a newly built tourist resort. 'That's fool's gold,' he despairingly mocked, even though the development was a potential employment salvation if he was forced to give up fishing. 'I once had five canoes until they were all lost in a terrible storm...' he looked wistfully out to the great blue yonder. 'Now my sons have no choice but to help build that horror.'

'Even with all their concrete and fancy designs, no one and nothing can stop water,' agreed the smoking seventy-year-old village headman of Zarusha. 'Already, the tide seeps under their concrete fence at high tide; it's just a matter of time before that monstrosity, a blight on our ancestral land, goes the way of other villages.'

'The climate is changing too fast. Every year the rains are getting heavier or there are none. Gales are more vicious and beaches are washed away. We will be forced to live in city slums when our homesteads have been devoured by the God of the Seas or bought by foreigners.'

Chapter 5

A S MUCH AS DESMOND worried about the disappear-ance of his way of life there were Afronians who had fled during the reign of Altimus Solomon or during the civil war, and who, with the economy rapidly growing were returning.

Yohanis, a Southi, immigrated to London at the out-break of the Northern War against Taberia in the late 90s. Growing up in Croydon, he had struggled with the academic demands of school. In 2005, aged sixteen, he left full-time education and started an apprenticeship as a kitchenhand. Ten years later and having gone through the gamete of culinary jobs, from pub dishwasher to Sous Chef at an internationally renowned Mayfair eatery, he was now widely lauded for his Afro-European fusion cui-sine. Yohanis had found his vocation in life but it was not until his thirtieth year that he knew his purpose: to preserve the richness of Afronian culinary traditions by bringing the glories of our cuisine to the wealthiest and humblest in my motherland.

Afrusion was located in a newly opened development on the Hillview promenade. Smoke from sumptuous slabs of steak could be seen rising from the restaurant—and when mixed with that of rotisserie chickens—gave a magnificent aroma. Carried on the sea breeze anyone downwind would need much self-control to pass the newly opened eatery and not enter.

The meat, prepared on a low flame, was sold to both passers-by from the outdoor stand and to those with deeper wallets in the lush surrounds of the tastefully decorated interior where a bottle of house Afronian red wine went for $25. Customers were served in the restaurant till midnight, though the street stand operated twenty-four-seven and thus Afrusion quickly became the de-rigour after (night) club location of choice for the wealthier of Umoja's residents and who wanted to listen to chillout music while relaxing on the beach and seeing the sun rise over the Indian Ocean.

Yohanis was Afronia's first celebrity chef and became a well-known food blogger, this all part of his marketing ploy to build his personal brand. 'We are in a new Afronia and people want to experiment with innovative takes on traditional Afronian dishes,' he was regularly quoted. 'Food is to be enjoyed, savoured; it's sexy eroticism for the senses. We as a country can for the first time freely express ourselves. Adding flavour and texture to traditional dishes is no longer taboo,' he would often end his blog, media interview or indeed discussion with a customer at his increasingly popular and profitable enterprise.

Yohanis' aspirations to delight the taste buds in a market that was economically booming and where labour and raw materials were relatively cheap was just one example of hundreds of talented young Afronians returning to their homeland as part of the Afronia Rising movement which President Blaise had so espoused to help transform the lives of millions through engineering an innovative and business friendly environment.

'Afronia is a vast commercial dam just waiting to explode,' Yohanis said one evening to Jacob at the business incubator, this after a networking event which aimed to match business mentors to a new generation of entrepreneurs. 'I know so many Afronians who want to return, so many who live in the UK and suffer under debt mountains and poorly paid jobs; they want to come home but are wary of what they'll find.'

'There are many opportunities for re-patriates,' Emmanuel, Jacob's co-director answered. 'In many industries there is very little competition for new entrants. We need textile designers, light industry processors, property developers, renewable energy service providers, financial services, artists… anyone with a skill and passion can make business here. There is more chance of success than failure in Afronia. For instance, there is a need to digitally map the streets. Giving each house an identifiable address would be a good start in helping both the city council and business alike. It's currently almost impossible for the postal system, businesses or city administrators to track down a person or place. Imagine a home delivery service dropping a book ordered on an Afronian e-commerce platform or the distribution of public information—'

'Not to mention voter registration,' Jacob cut in.

'There are many technology-based business opportunities,' Emmanuel summarized.

'Yohanis, you're a high-profile re-pat. You should tap into the growing tourist sector, specifically, experiential tourism. The Instagram generation want experiences rather than generic package holidays. You could also start a cook school for teenage novices or the urban middle-class.'

'Thanks for the suggestions, Jacob. I've been approached to front a primetime TV show,' this referring to one of the independent TV stations that had blossomed after years of media suppression.

'Many African economies are plateauing since the Chinese slowdown; countries focused on raw material exports are struggling. They must go through structural change and encourage light manufacturing and import substitution. Afronia, with such a low base, can only go upwards as the economy moves from extraction to service industries,' this from an enthused Emmanuel. 'The Afronia Rising narrative is very real if nuanced.'

'True, but there are many challenges with bureaucracy, expensive financial services and a lack of human resources,' Yohanis pointed out.

'That's why we established the incubator,' Jacob smiled, indicating his statement was in jest but also heartfelt. 'We are helping an entrepreneur acquire the appropriate licences for a private hospital that will be staffed by over 100 Afronian health professionals who are currently practicing overseas. It will have modern equipment and serve the growing upper class and expatriate market segments while having an outreach program in Umoja's slums as part of their corporate social responsibility strategy.'

Inside the presidential palace, the Minister of Economy, Professor Rashid was less bullish. 'As Afronia grows there will be winners and losers. We must be careful not to have a lost economic generation of entrepreneurs who once bitten are twice shy. We must spur growth while ensuring prosperity for all. We need a careful mix of fiscal and monetary policies to promote inclusive growth; we can't be beholden to foreign investors or debt.'

'I absolutely advocate free trade, but this will be at the expense of leaving some people behind... that is the nature of capitalism,' Blaise admitted. 'Russia of the early 1990s was an extreme example. I understand that as the economy grows we must redistribute wealth but not at the expense of incentives for entrepreneurs otherwise we will have no tax base for social services.'

'We have to be careful in following the globalization model. If we don't protect some industries they will be swallowed up by low wages and insecure employment. We must ensure that offshore corporations are not able to take billions in profit out of the economy.'

'It's a tight line to walk,' the president conceded.

'And this does not consider the national debt which stands at ninety-percent of Gross Domestic Product.'

'What?' a flabbergasted Walter uttered.

'Debt was accumulated by Altimus Solomon's profligate investments in white-elephant infrastructure projects and his nephew's civil war military spending binge. We have to be very careful that we don't get into a situation whereby families are starving to pay for a debt crisis they didn't create.'

'What can we do? Many are starving and critical infrastructure is crumbling; what should we prioritise?'

'The bulk of the debt is held by the Paris Club of creditors and who are imposing stringent penalty interest rates. Due to the time lapse between the end of the civil war and now, we aren't classified in the heavily Indebted Poor Countries Initiative and so can't receive funding from the World Bank's International Development Association. If we don't want to be under fiscal servitude to our debtors, we have little choice but to, A) ask for our arrears to be written off, or B) sell equity in state owed companies.'

'Is it not risky to sell our infrastructure to foreign investors?' a concerned president asked. 'Will that not be a form of economic colonization?'

'You are indeed correct, Sir, but we have little choice if we want to get the economy back on track; our debt will not be written off; they have us by the short and curlies! The term: failed state, was invented for Afronia and, I think that is what some of the vultures want.' There was no irony in the professor's voice, just sad realization. 'Our future remains at the whim of financial markets. We are but a pawn being moved around the chess board of international finance. The truth is, we may be sacrificed at any time Mr President. I can't reiterate how vulnerable our economic position is unless our national debt is cancelled.'

'And the recently signed trade agreements?'

'There is the duty-free access for Afronian goods into the EU but there are barriers around standards. There are quotas on some products before tariffs are introduced.'

'Such as?'

'Agriculture. The Europeans want to protect their farmers from world markets. Signing the European Partnership Agreement has no significant benefits other than highlighting the need to urgently reform our economy to do more processing… and for that, we need investors; we are in an economic catch 22… like much of Africa.'

Chapter 6

ROBERT YOHAN HAD NOT given up on his quest to be the head of state, indeed, his conversation with Ulrich Müller had given him much confidence. 'Blaise is as repressive as my incorrigible friend and your late father,' he complained one evening to Tamsin Solomon. 'He has no legitimacy and is leading the country into further debt and servitude to our European and American financial overlords.'

'What do you suggest?' Tamsin asked from the comfort of the jacuzzi on the Sun Deck of *The Lady Freedom*.

'Support the campaign by the Afronia Freedom League to remove the dictator and salvage the country.' Yohan gave out a great big belly laugh, knowing full well that his proposal had nothing to do with emancipation of Afronians, but rather the disaffected elements in the diaspora was a vehicle Yohan thought he could manipulate.

Tamsin had heard of the Afronia Freedom League from the lips of her lover, Hamza Leso. *The expression on his face and tone of voice suggesting they were a potential threat to the Blaise presidency.*

The leader of the Afronia Freedom League, Jay Peters, could be found in a bright yellow building on a tumble-down street in Little Harari, a suburb of the Afronian capital. The house in question had been nicknamed: The Second Embassy. There was a portrait of Queen Elizabeth II hanging over the reception desk and a Union Jack proudly dangling at the foot of the stairs leading onto the first floor; it could easily deceive the unaccustomed that it was indeed a genuine embassy. However, that was the only similarity to a consular... there was a garage selling spare parts to one-side of the gaudy building and the bottlestore on the other blasted loud music out of the cracked windows all-hours of the day and night.

MH-16, the criminal gang controlled by the merciless former Royal Marine Commando and mercenary, Mike Henshaw, had been going from desperate village to famine devastated town over the past twelve-months selling counterfeit Afronian passports and visas to the UK for the extortionate sum of $5,000, this being the price to get around the laborious process to gain a valid travel permit. For this fee, the undocumented Afronian would also be given certificates declaring them: a teacher, dentist, or businessperson (as requested) and a printout of the appropriate bank, school and professional records. Another common ruse for those wanting to leave Afronia, was pretending to be a musician, the desperate migrant lip-syncing to a music video in-case they were stopped by the UK Border Force. Once the Afronian arrived in the British Isles they would often vanish upon reaching Hazelstone, Hull, Halifax, Huddersfield or one of the many other hundreds of towns and cities as they tried to make a new life.

Jay was mid-conversation with the owner of the counterfeit enterprise. 'Blaise is nothing but a fraud,' he started to complain. 'He promised the people roads, schools and hospitals, but nothing has changed for the peasant who scrapes together a living. Torture and state killings are sanctioned everyday of those who are disobedient. Walter Blaise is a hypocrite, incompetent and is selling the Afronian soul and resources to corrupt western governments and businesses. He must resign immediately or face the consequences. Afronia needs a responsible, disciplined and transparent leader who will defend the weak with compassion from those who economically, politically and militarily abuse them. I will gladly lay down my life so that the children of this fine country enjoy the freedoms and civil liberties that is their birth-right,' he pompously continued on.

Jay had lived and become wealthy in the UK, and it was from there where he'd established the anti-Altimus Solomon, Afronia Freedom League a decade earlier. He had returned to Afronia before the presidential election and given his wholehearted support to Blaise, but when Walter became president and hadn't given Jay any of the contracts that he expected, he'd decided, *That I should be the rightful leader. I will free the Afronian man and woman from the yoke of injustices.* 'A successful endeavour, whether revolution or business is not about highfalutin words, hard-hitting ideas and fiery passion, but money and planning.'

'And how will you start your war Jay?' Henshaw asked, and only just about managing to keep a smirk from his face.

'I have cash,' this from his investment in the Church of Heavenly Bodies that he ha'd established with his friend Pastor Frederick Gondwe. 'I have supporters here and in the UK.'

'What don't you have?' Henshaw didn't want to beat around the bush. 'You found me, that is the only reason why I'm giving you five minutes to make a proposal; don't waste my time.'

'Weapons.'

'Let's talk numbers,' came a most business-like response.

There were many who were making their financial mark in Afronia, some like Jay through property development and religious duping, while others were underhandedly winning government contracts as although the civil service was going through a process of transformative consolidation there were still many corrupt officials in the procurement departments of government ministries. 'Root and branch cleansing of the curse of corruption is no overnight thing,' the president had said to his trusted confidente Hamza Leso on more than one occasion.

There were, however, increasing numbers who were making an honest living like Yohanis. One such entrepreneur was Aya, an artisanal miner from the Southiland Mountains. While many of his rural contemporaries had moved to the city slums in hope of employment, Aya could be found waist deep in water, slamming a pickaxe or shovel into the muddy earth of a riverbed with such ferocity that his palms would blister or, sieving gravel until his fingers had lost all feeling and his nails broken, this in his pursuit of diamonds.

Aya's life for the last eight years—since his thirteenth birthday—had been absorbed in his quest to find a gemstone that would change his life, such as the 1,111 carats Lesedi La Rona found in Botswana in 2015 or, the Incomparable Diamond from the Democratic Republic of Congo in 1984.

Aya would report to his "master" and who for a percentage of any find, would provide one square meal a day, accommodation and dole out Panadol as the cure to any ailment. He'd never seen the person who provided the funds to his master, though it was rumoured that prior to the civil war it had been an army general. However, for the last three years, payments had variously come from ISiSS, rebel leaders who at least offered fairer terms, renegade army officers, and now one of Mike Henshaw's lieutenants, the Brit determined to diversify his criminal empire.

After a particularly heavy storm, Aya could once more be found knee deep in the dangerously fast river, the rainfall making rock and mud lose and thus making it easier to sieve for a small jewel. As the sun dipped behind the mountains, he was still shaking his pan, his fingers raw from the punishment. *Another thirty minutes,* Aya tried to motivate himself, when, in the middle of the sieve, he saw a sparkling object. *Is it a diamond?* he dared to dream, *or just a corundum?* the latter having little value. *A diamond,* he whispered, as he cautiously looked round to see if anyone had seen the wonder on his face. *It's a dia-*

mond! He was convinced, *Maybe four-carats? What should I do? I must keep my precious find out of sight of my master.*

With a look up and down the river and seeing the other miners collect tools for the end of the day walk back to their accommodation, Aya waded into the swampy grass and out-of-sight before anyone realized he was missing. It took him three days of walking on foot along mountain trails to reach Nyala, and which had, once again, become the centre of the diamond trade since its liberation from ISiSS. He exchanged his prized stone for the equivalent of $5,000, a fortune for one of such meagre origins. He didn't spend the money on booze, girls, and clothes, as many miners would customarily do with a fat wallet, but rather gave half the money to an aunt so they could start a business together. He used $500 to purchase a modest one-room house of sorts in the Nyala slum... but which he could call home. $250 was paid to a school so he could get a formal education as he hoped, one day, to become an inductee into the newly opened Nyala business incubator. The balance was put into a bank account for future business opportunities.

Unlike Aya, not all tried to earn an honest buck. Chief amongst those willing to take as many shortcuts as needed was Mike Henshaw, the tentacles of his criminal enterprise now spreading into neighbouring countries. MH-16 was considered one of the most brutal gangs in Africa, this on a continent that had more than its fair share of psychotic charlatans and power-hungry despots.

Two days before Aya had arrived in Nyala, the bodies of three teenage males who'd been distributing cocaine along the seafront for a rival gang, had been found on the capital's beaches; their heads on their chests, this MH-16s's gruesome signature and a method of punishment suggested by Mustafa. The heavily bearded former ISiSS commander of Nyala had recommended the decapitation technique to Henshaw during a drink and drug fuelled whoring session. 'We need a brutal initiation process... just like the good old days in Nyala,' had been his exact words.

'What do you have in mind?'

'We target poor, at-risk teenagers,' he unashamedly proposed. 'To join, they need to commit a crime, preferably a murder. Killing is control,' Mustafa casually continued as if he were talking about membership to a tennis club. 'The last rite of passage is a large tattoo. They are branded members for life, the only way to leave... in a coffin.'

Eavesdropping on the conversation was Abeker and Jamil, the two nomads who had run from ISiSS in Chad and Afronia, the rebels during the civil war and, who'd been hounded out of antiquity smuggling. Almost predictably they had become MH-16 gang members. Fortunately for them, considering their weak composition, they hadn't gone through the ritual Mustafa recommended, as while they were more than willing to exploit the disadvantaged—as had been Abeker's stock in trade as a people smuggler—neither had ended the life of another.

For the last twelve months they had been living close to the seashore. Their days, weeks, and months, revolving around hijacking cargo ships or demanding a ransom from private yacht owners; they had not been very successful.

'YOU TWO!' Mustafa thundered at the pair, 'come here.' They walked slowly fearing the former ISiSS commander would finally recognize them from the time when they had briefly met in Nyala, this when trying to sell Mustafa several crates of booze. 'Why can't you bring us money?' Mustafa rhetorically asked. Jamil kept tight lipped and stared at the floor. 'If you don't answer me, NOW… you'll both be the target of the next initiation.'

Mike Henshaw, sitting in the corner with a scantily glad girl no older than fifteen on his lap, looked on amused with a sardonic smile spreading across his face, Mustafa's rage a distraction from the ongoing problem of a vigilante systematically executing his gang members. *However, I can recruit faster than they can kill. How should I answer the offer of alliance?* He queried, as he thought about the anonymous letter he'd received the previous day. He looked at the handwritten note once again.

> Mr Henshaw,
> You have extensive operations in Afronia. You have a network of contacts and a variety of business lines that my associates would be interested to partner with you on.
> If you wish to parlay, be at the Golden Tulip Hotel tomorrow at 6 pm.
> Regards

Is this message genuine or a trap? Henshaw wondered.

Crossing the line between the illegal (MH-16) semi-legal (Aya's diamond mining) and legal (Yohanis restaurants)

was Imani, a goldsmith who'd learned about valuable metals in the Southi Mountains when as a young girl she'd watched her father doing the back-breaking work of prizing the valuable metal from the land.

Imani had been raped by her mathematics teacher and become pregnant at the age of thirteen. At the time, Altimus Solomon had a policy that any girl who gave birth should be expelled, "as they are finished; they can't be taught when they leave the classroom to breastfeed." The current Minister of Education, under specific guidance from Walter Blaise, was reversing the legislation, the president promising that schoolgirls should be readmitted and not denied an education. And that, all girls should be protected from predatory teachers; the vile men imprisoned for twenty years and forced to work the land to feed their new-born.

With twin sons, Imani had needed a way to pay for food and accommodation as she was damned if they were going to work in the gold mines like their grandfather, and so she had become an apprentice goldsmith to her uncle, this after seeing the potential escape from poverty though designing jewellery pieces. When her boys reached puberty, Imani enrolled in the Umoja City incubator that Jacob and Emmanuel had established.

'Goldsmithing is a tradition as old as time itself. It is simultaneously an art, a currency, and an investment,' Imani started her presentation to potential investors at the monthly Afronian Wolves Lair Pitch Night and which followed the format of the BBC's Dragons' Den. 'There is the Gold Standard, and when currencies are in trouble the global economy turns to gold. When times are good gold is a craft… but when economic times are harsh gold becomes currency. Goldsmithing is one of a few businesses that thrives whatever the economic outlook.' Imani took a nervous pause and a sip of water from the newly formed Afronia Spring Water bottling company, that business founded by a former incubatee and who was sponsoring the evening.

'Gold is part of Afronia culture. Most religions have references to the precious metal. Southis have crafted gold coins since the thirteenth century and was one of the regional currencies for more than five centuries until the Europeans came. The skylines of our cities are dominated by gold tipped domes, spires, crosses and moons. Hotels have the word gold, in their name… and yet ninety-five percent of all gold mined in Afronia is sold as nuggets on the international market. This means the artisanal miners remain poor, there is no job creation and, only exporter middlemen become rich. Afronia Gold Limited wants to create a golden future whereby all Afronians prosper from one of our most abundant natural resources. 'I'm looking for a $10,000 investment. I project revenue after six-months of $15,000. I'm offering twenty-percent equity.'

Imani took a lungful of air to calm her nerves. Looking around she saw two wolves taking copious notes. 'Do you supply machine-made jewellery?' one of them asked.

'Absolutely not. I truly believe in hand crafted pieces. Experience shows that technology can kill the economic stability of communities. Youth are forced to work in mines rather than fishing, farming, or becoming apprentices. I will use half the investment to set up an outreach program to guarantee my supply chain, the other fifty-percent will be used to establish a franchise business model.'

'Do you have any existing partners or investors?' another voice solicited.

'We have partnered with the Brits for Afronians Foundation, and who organized a collection of pieces in London; it was very successful.' There was a murmur of appreciation of what Imani had achieved. 'The founder, Mohammad Ahmed has established a profit share shop in Notting Hill where he exhibits and sales work from artisans. It is no secret, but most gold mines were previously controlled by the Solomons and so I guarantee ethical practices including not using poisonous mercury to isolate gold from rock and debris. My processes will not pollute streams nor cause serious health risks. Our workshops will maintain health and safety standards. I will ensure there is always benefit to the communities we buy raw gold from.'

'I'll give you all the money,' one potential investor said having come to a quick conclusion, 'but I want thirty-percent of your business.'

Chapter 7

Tom Finch—the former Regimental Sergeant Major of the SAS and mercenary in David Stephens' Clearwater Solutions private army for hire—had for the past two years been on the payroll of MI6. He had been seconded to the Afronian Army as the Commanding Officer of an elite unit tasked with hunting the remnants of ISiSS. He reported directly to Colonel Abel Hussein, the Head of the Afronian Ranger Special Forces Regiment and who was responsible for all the army's counterinsurgency efforts. Finch's second-in-command was Prince, the former unit commander of the Southi Republican Army and fiancé of Adela, the rebel leader and young sister of the deceased patriot Ali Lanya.

The unit's number one target was the former ISiSS commander Mustafa, but so far there had been no leads as to his whereabouts.

'I'm getting intelligence that ten women and three children have been abducted and taken into the Harari desert,' Prince informed Finch. 'They vanished after militants razed a rural village; there are twelve dead.'

'Assemble our team; we move in an hour.'

Ten hours after the attack had been reported, the hunter-team arrived at Nyala Air Force base. 'We move out in five minutes,' Tom told his motley platoon of thirty men and five women, the team made up of professional soldiers, former rebels, wildlife rangers and interpreters; they had specialists for all Afronia's regions and every environment.

After a chilly two-hour drive in the back of open-top trucks, the early morning sounds of the forest penetrating the thick fog, the attack team were dropped at the village of Modab. The man leading the pursuit was forty-three-year-old Maher, a poacher who used to hunt antelopes, wild pigs and baboons, but who after his family has been murdered by ISiSS had volunteered his expert tracking skills to find Jihadis. 'Firstly,' he insisted, 'we make offerings to the mountain spirits.' No one complained. Whether they believed in the rituals or not, each member of the team was acutely aware that their backgrounds meant they needed to accept everyone's diverse beliefs.

'Will we be protected from the vampires?' Sira, the newest female member asked.

'What?' Finch raised his eyebrows in surprise.

'Vigilantes have attacked villagers who've been identified as vampires,' Sira stated with deadly seriousness.

'Really?'

'Five people were killed last week by a mob in a village less than ten kilometres away. They were accused of sucking blood. Witchcraft is very common.'

'A French hiking couple were abducted and killed after being alleged to drink blood,' Maher, backed up Sira's assertion. 'It's dangerous. When foreign NGOs and the United Nations are withdrawing their staff, ISiSS stepped into the void.'

Huh, so that's the explanation, Finch considered, *I never would have guessed! And that's why local knowledge in my team is so important.* 'You sure it's not wealthy individuals who are targeted out of jealousy?' Modab district was one of the poorest areas of the country. 'Isn't it a metaphor for inequality... the economic elite sucking wealth from the poor? Is there hard evidence... or ISiSS mischief making?' Finch queried aloud.

'People have died,' came a universal response.

'My cousin had her blood sucked. She had two piercings on her right shoulder near her neck.' Sira pointed to her jugular.

'We are here to take the fight to ISiSS,' Finch brought the ghoulish discussion to an end as the sun shone through and evaporating the fog of the new day, the temperature and humidity once again suffocating. *If ISiSS are the source of the vampire rumours, all the better we kill them.*

In the quiet Maher doused his fellow hunters with a blessed potion. He made a small dot on their foreheads. 'You are now protected from evil spirits... and bullets.'

Spiritually satisfied and having assessed the intelligence, the team started to follow Maher who having looked at the tyre tracks in the sand started the twenty-three kilometre, five-hour hike to the village which was attacked and where there was an illegal gold mine. Since the fall of the caliphate in Nyala, precious metals and stones were once again taken to the Southi capital where they were mixed with legally mined gold and sold to foreign companies to export or process into luxury goods, the smelting process making it impossible to discern where the constituent parts of the bar had originated.

Walking through the steaming vegetation and following a footpath or animal tracks, bright sunlight occasionally pierced the jungle canopy, the hunters used sign language and bird sound to communicate. Three hours into the walk they came to a small but fast flowing river, the team wading through the chest deep mountain water. 'We'll have an early lunch,' Tom decided when seeing his team tired and soaking wet. *It's never good to walk in wet socks.*

Socks dried and a lunch of rice and beans eaten, Tom and his team moved back into the thick scrub, thorns scratching exposed skin and ripping clothes. Four hours later, the going much tougher than anticipated, Maher crouched down. 'There, by the mine,' he whispered to his commanding officer. 'They are heavily armed. Women and children are held in a hut near the well,' this being on the western side of the village and which contained a raucous bar, two shops and a guesthouse cum brothel.

'Call in support,' Finch whispered to Prince. 'We need more Rangers and heavier weapons if we are to attack.'

'We don't have time… and they will hear the helicopters coming; its better we get close and hit hard and fast.'

Finch looked at Prince for a full thirty seconds to size the man up. *He is no coward, but can I put my life in this man's hands?* This being the first mission they had been on together.

As Prince looked at the SAS veteran, he saw a smile appear through the camouflaged face. 'Let's go,' Tom instinctively decided. 'Prince, take ten men up the left flank. Maher, ten on the right; I'll come with the rest straight up the middle.'

Tom stayed crouched as tense minute followed tense minute. 'In position,' finally came the whispered confirmation from Prince through the radio static, shortly followed by the same words from Maher.

'Good luck. ISiSS will come to know and fear us,' Finch said to his band of Jihadi hunters. 'In five, four, three, two, one,' Tom counted down before gunfire shattered the humdrum everyday noises of the village. Grenades exploded and mortar rounds landed on the roof of the building which had been the Jihadists' temporary barracks. Prince charged from his position before taking cover behind one mound of mining mud, his team following closely behind. Maher closed in on the mine from the opposite direction, dashing behind bushes or huts while firing from the hip. The surprise attack caught the Jihadis unaware, their voices to flee drowned out by the rat-a-tat-tat of machine-gun fire and booms of exploding grenades.

After five violent minutes peace once again ruled the village, the bodies of fifteen Jihadis lying in the dust, flies already converging on spilled guts. Blood trails led into the forest of the escaping wounded, but Maher and two four-man teams were already in pursuit. Entering the hut where the hostages had been held, Tom saw three dead bodies. *Stray bullets or executions?* He wondered as he looked at the relieved faces of the rescued.

The mission completed, Finch went back to headquarters in Umoja City, and it was from here that he was conducting his private mission against Mike Henshaw. He was in the information gathering stage of his one-man operation, though, when and if the opportunity arose, he did not hesitate to take out an MH-16 gang member.

Chapter 8

Two weeks after Mike Henshaw had received his mysterious letter, Walter Blaise was touring the stalls in Presidential Square and sampling a variety of delicacies. It was an event to promote Afronian cuisine and had been organized between Yohanis and Jacob.

'Yummy,' the president complimented with his usual enthusiasm as he put a small slice of toast liberally spread with locally produced raspberry jam into his mouth. He licked his lips. 'My wife worries about my waistline rather than enjoying wonderful tastes,' he joked before moving to the next stall, a pop-up business which sold three varieties of Cashew Nuts: chili and honey, salted and, glazed coconut.

Next stop was The Soup Butterfly. 'I've only had cow hooves soup the traditional way,' Blaise smiled at the chef who was gently coaxing passion fruit seeds out of their peels. 'My mama would not be happy if I told her how delicious that was; some dishes are sacred to her.'

'Mr President,' Yohanis tried to steer the delighted man to the next stall.

The sign identified the business as: Challenge. 'We want to challenge the concept of what it means to be Afronian, both in terms of food... and the ongoing stigma of having HIV.'

'Excellent.' This was the stall that Walter Blaise had been looking forward to visiting the most. 'I was informed by Mr Yohanis, that all who work at this kitchen have tested positive.'

'Yes, Sir. We want the joy that food can bring to challenge the preconceptions some citizens have about people who live with HIV.'

'A wonderful idea for an inclusive Afronia. My family, like so many, have lost loved ones from suicide; some can't handle the stigma and rejection,' the president revealed his family secret. 'What are you cooking?' he added in a cheery voice after a moment of reflection.

'We have butterscotch with cinnamon and maple syrup.'

'Delicious.'

The head chef cut a small slice of the vegetable and in doing so accidently cut his little finger. 'Damn it,' he swore as he pulled his pinkie back in pain. He looked at Yohanis with a face which can be best be classed as a mix of shame, annoyance and guilt.

'Take your time,' came the president's calming voice.

Three minutes later, a new butterscotch was taken from the oven and sliced, the chef's finger with a plaster on it, passing the plate to Walter. The cook saw the bodyguards anxiously look on, not sure if the president would take the food after blood had been spilt. 'There's absolutely no risk of infection—'

'Scrumptious,' Blaise congratulated the nervous entrepreneur as he pulled the now empty fork from his mouth.

'Thank you, Sir,' the relieved chef bowed.

After half-an-hour of further sampling and now with a very full belly (chili cashew nuts, cow hooves soup, butterscotch, cream cheese dates, prawns and avocado salad) the president was sampling the last of the tasters, Afronian Smoked Salmon. A salmon farm, in part funded by the Scottish Government, had recently been opened in the Southi Mountains, the business supported by a Scottish NGO who understood the difficulty of reproducing spawning grounds when breeding in captivity.

'Mouth-watering,' the president complemented as he took a small mouthful of the pink gold before proceeding to the lectern where he was to give an address to the crowd and present a prize to the winner of the inaugural Afronian Taste Bonanza.

An hour later and back at the presidential palace, Walter Blaise started to feel his stomach rumbling and rushed to the toilet. As minutes turned into hours and his illness got steadily worse, he was admitted to Umoja City Hospital and was attended to by the Chief Gastro Doctor and his Minister of Health, Dr Ralph Lisoyga.

Two days later, the Head of the Afronian Internal Security Services gave a press statement.

A foreign power has tried to assassinate His Excellency, President Walter Blaise through the poisoning of food at the Afronia Taste Bonanza. One of the dishes was tainted with an unspecified radioactive substance which the president ingested as he toured.

While the culprit country has not been identified, we know some states wish the worse for Afronia and have a long history of state sponsored assassinations. This is a terrorist act against the Afronian people and will not be forgiven or forgotten. We will find those responsible and bring them to the court of the Afronian and global public.

The president will resume duties as soon as he has recovered, provisionally at the laying of the foundation stone for the Central Umoja City Train Station and which will link freight and passenger trains from Umoja City to the new capital in Mapulwe and onto the regional cities. The president has made it clear, that anyone found vandalising the track, rolling stock or guardrails, will face two decades in prison. Afronia is on a journey to becoming a regional powerhouse. Under the unifying leadership of President Blaise, he will not tolerate delinquents and hooligans who commit economic treason.

'What's the word from inside the presidential palace?' Charlie Daniels asked Hamza Leso.

'We know which food stalls he ate from and we're working to the assumption that's where he was poisoned—'

'Don't tell me the obvious,' Charlie interrupted, keen to be on his way to meet his barely legally aged girlfriend.

'Steady on, old chap,' Hamza mimicked Charlie. 'At the moment, the Russians are the key suspects.'

'Because Blaise kicked them out? For supporting Isaiah George and then Sheila Solomon?'

'Igor Victov would certainly like regime change.'

'Assassination of a serving president is a bit steep, even for him, isn't it?'

'It's not subtle,' Hamza agreed.

'Anything the British government can do?'

'Keep the money rolling in,' Hamza advised. 'Afronia is starting to transform the economy and needs all the help it can get.'

Thus, with Hamza's word in mind, Charlie went to his next meeting at the British Embassy to meet Terry who worked with UKAID, the British International Development Agency. 'We need more private sector corporations to invest in Afronia.'

'I thought you were a spook?' Terry said with half-a-smile.

Charlie publicly declared he was a private security consultant, though amongst the British diplomatic community it was an open secret he moved in more mysterious ways. 'Like you, I'm just trying to help UK PLC,' he replied deadpan. 'I can help channel extra money where its most needed.'

'How about a challenge fund?' Terry suggested. 'Business is not going to invest in risky ideas in a high-risk country unless they're given de-risking grants.'

'What do you have in mind?'

'Building capacity of the financial sector through advocating for digital financial services; that would tick many developmental goals.'

'Go on.'

'In Kenya, and noticing mobile customers were transferring prepaid mobile airtime to friends and family as a quasi-currency, we gave Vodafone £1million to develop a digital payment solution that would increase financial inclusion while helping to tackle corruption in the public sector. M-Pesa really took off after the 2007 election violence. It's been a resounding success for both the Kenyan Government and a British company.'

'Mobile money has started here,' Charlie pointed out as he took a long gulp of Earl Grey tea, the idea of being directly involved in the financial services sector much to his Machiavellian liking.

'And that is why we put a twist on it. We already support British agricultural businesses, mining companies and those building health facilities, schools and water utilities. For instance, HydroDevelop recently won the national water project and they could use mobile money to pay their staff. Everyone wins. The businesses become more operationally transparent while reducing operating costs. The tax authority gets greater insight from a digital, rather than cash economy. And, AfroTel—which is now forty-nine percent British owned—achieves a volume of payments which they can use as a starting point to go on to dominate the market just as Safaricom has done in Kenya.'

'I'll see what I can do.'

Chapter 9

Eric found-out about the success of HydroDevelop's proposal twenty-four hours before Charlie. The win in no small part thanks to Prince James who'd wined and dined the Afronian Minister of Water and Irrigation at Buckingham Palace... this being on recommendation from Daniels.

'Exciting news,' Eric declared to Sylvia and their two teenage children.

'What's that, dear?'

'We're moving to Umoja City,' this a fait accompli rather than topic for discussion as far as Eric was concerned.

'I'm not,' came the surely response from Peter, the elder of the two boys. 'My friends are here, and I've got my GCSE's next year.'

'There's a highly recommended international school.' This was a white lie. The school had been open for less than a year and was going through the learning process of what was required to meet the expectations of expats and wealthy locals who were able to pay the $15,000-a-year fees. 'It'll be better that you are outside rather than always on our computer.'

'This is not the Eighties, Dad… when you were at school.' Sarcasm dripped from every one of Peter's withering words.

'Not being on Snapchat and Instagram every waking second, might make you a more sociable being. The decision has been made; we leave in four weeks—'

'Four weeks! That's before the village fete; I'm part of the organizing committee.'

'I'm sure they will manage without you mum.' Sarcasm was Peter's flavour of the evening.

'Tomorrow evening, Mo has organized Afronian speed dating—'

'What, Dad?' Peter asked as David, the younger sibling, watched on amused at the family squabble. Unlike his brother, he was quite excited about imminently moving to a new country.

'With many Afronians now living on the Beaufort Estate, and with much mistrust and ill feeling in the village, Mo thought it would be good to have a question-and-answer session in a bid to build better relationships in the community one conversation at a time. He's called the evening: Ask an Afronian anything.'

'That sounds fun,' Sylvia said, though her voice implied it would be anything but, the shock of her husband's decision with little consultation had jarred her greatly. 'That country,' Sylvia continued once the boys were out of earshot, 'is full of AIDS riven savages fighting tribal conflicts; we daren't take the children.'

'Honestly? I'm surprised at your racist views, especially after your fundraising efforts.'

'It's because I've been there that I know what to expect. There was brutal human disfiguration in the civil war; it was especially vicious against whites—'

'Are you referring to the mercenaries?'

'No. Landowners who lived there for many generations; it's simply not safe for us to go.'

'That is colonial-era prejudice. I suppose you think the Queen only continues with the Commonwealth so she can see smiling white teeth from black African faces?'

'And you think, like Tony Blair, that Africa is a stain on the conscience of humanity.'

'There is so much in Afronia that's truly humbling. They are jumping generations in technology and bringing vast swathes of the population out of poverty at a time when the population is doubling every three or four decades. Africa is on the cusp of a business and economic revolution.'

'Nonsense.'

'I'm going whether you and the children come with me... or not.'

And thus, despite her reservations, Sylvia found herself sitting opposite Sara in the George and Dragon the following evening. 'I was in a cycle of poverty and domestic violence; I had to leave Afronia,' Sara explained. 'Ask me absolutely anything; I will be candid in my replies.'

Over the course of the next two hours, and with Ben Shields laying on free food, many of the villagers heard first-hand about the women who'd been forced to marry their rapist, abductor husbands and/or, men who had worked in appalling conditions in mines from a tender age. Others explained about friends and family who had served in the militia, died in the Denga Chemical massacre, or the many atrocities propagated by the state including extrajudicial executions.

It was Sara's last conversation of the night. She was sitting opposite David Howells and who had originally come with the sole purpose of disrupting the meeting… but in the hours of listening to the personal stories of those whom he had been taking advantage of, he finally felt an ounce of sympathy. 'I know many don't want us in Hazelstone,' Sara, unaware of Howells' reputation or racist disposition, started their conversation. 'Many fought and died for freedom during the civil war. You can't imagine what life was like under Altimus Solomon. Many, just like me, felt we had no choice but to trust people smugglers and pimps to get us out of that country.'

Howells had fallen into a contemplative silence, the number and variety of harrowing stories he'd heard having overwhelmed him.

'Afronians are loyal, generous and hard-working. We also want the same opportunities and rights that many in this beautiful village take for granted. I might struggle to change the hearts of those who hurl abuse as we walk the streets, but compared to what we have endured, we are happy to find people like you who want to understand what drove us to leave our motherland.'

I will never look at Afronians in the same light, Howells, much to his surprise, admitted as he left the George and Dragon and took the ten-minute walk back to his cottage. On his route, he was reminded of his sister, a Border Force Officer at the ferry port of Dover and whose explicit role was to stop illegal immigrants entering. He tried to remember their last conversation. *Having heard countless terrible stories, one day I took pity on a boy no older than five,* his sister has said. *The child jumped out the back of a moving lorry, fell on the road and then rushed to the treeline; that's when I knew something must be so desperate for one so young to be in such fear. Something clicked in me and I knew I had to do something to help.*

Not at Ask An Afronian Anything, despite being invited as guest of honour, was Jay Peters; he was in the slums of Umoja City. He was meeting the dandy Yaya and who was flamboyantly dressed in a pin-stripe Dolce & Gabbana suit and Versace shoes. 'Why should gays be allowed to roam free or breastfeeding girls return to school. Blaise is nothing but a puppet of the liberal west.'

Yaya's views were in dramatic contrast to the way he dressed and which in spite of the grinding poverty he lived in he was nevertheless one of a growing band of men and women who went without food so they could spend hundreds, often thousands-of-dollars on designer suits. Yaya and contemporaries had been inspired by the Sapeurs in Kinshasa and who followed the fashion trends of their hero, the deceased Congolese Rumba king, Papa Wemba.

'Why always a peaceful approach?' Jay rounded on Yaya. 'Do you think Blaise really pays heed to your protests? Do you think your clothes we sway those dressed… normally?' Jay, finally finding a suitable adjective to describe the man opposite him.

Also, at this eclectic get-together was Robert Yohan. 'We have to find a different way.'

'Was it your friends who poisoned the president?' Yaya asked Jay.

'Don't be silly,' was the dismissive put-down. 'When the time is right, everyone will know who Jay Peters is. I'll make no bones about restoring democracy and being a true African leader.'

Idiots! Yohan thought. *Pliable fools.* 'You have the right ideas,' this while patting Jay on the back. *He just needs enough rope to hang himself… but not until he has built popular support.*

'The people want change,' Jay stated. 'I can feel the pulse of revolution. Blaise has been making big promises which he fails to implement. The people are tired of his continuing support for the Somalitreans and not taking to task the previous regime. Afronia needs a real leader. As Thomas Jefferson once said: the tree of liberty must be refreshed from time to time with the blood of patriots and tyrants. That time is now.'

'What do you propose?' Yohan wanted to know.

'Before independence, the regions used to have strong cooperatives, whether savings cooperatives, farming co-operatives or housing cooperatives.'

'That's true. Altimus Solomon, inspired by Idi Amin, did away with them as he also saw them as a potential threat,' Yohan concurred.

'We start by building support with the Hararis. Their region is still suffering from drought despite the recent rains, and in Little Harari, the low-lying districts over-flow after the rains. Children play in sludge and stagnant water carries a host of diseases when overflowing sewers seep into houses.'

'They want land to build settlements that will last for generations,' Yaya stated. 'The government refuses to give them money to move from their appalling conditions and so they are setting up housing cooperatives. Ten families combine to buy a plot. They save costs through economies of scale when buying concrete and iron sheets.'

'I know of other cooperatives,' Jay confirmed.

'Working as a group for mutual benefit can be a force for social cohesion and prosperity,' Yohan acknowledged. 'If we want to lead the cooperative movement we have to move quickly.' For the rest of the evening the trio discussed how to reinvigorate cooperatives before strategizing how and when to start a revolution.

Chapter 10

Eric, having a beer in the George and Dragon, knew nothing about Sapeurs or cooperatives, and nor did Steven who'd been appointed as his right-hand-man. 'Are you ready for the challenge of your life?'

'I was praying we'd win,' Steven confirmed.

'How much do you know about Afronia?'

'Only what I read when preparing our proposal, plus what I've seen on the TV down the years.'

'Afronia has gone through enormous economic and political flux in the last few years,' Eric said as he finished his first pint of the afternoon.

'Our project will have a very positive impact,' Steven concurred as he quickly finished his pint when he saw his boss' glass empty. He indicated to Jeffrey Shields to pour another round.

'Are you ready for the move?' Eric asked while thinking of his clan's own misgivings.

'I think so. It's too good a professional and financial opportunity to turn down.'

'We had to really push the boat out to secure your services,' Eric joked about the contract to lure his deputy. It included a housing allowance, flights and a tax-free salary of $12,000 a month.

'How politically stable is Afronia?' Steven, acutely aware of former colleagues who'd been airlifted out of hotspots when on assignment asked.

'We were supported in our proposal by the British Embassy... who confirmed the environment is steady... though having just come out the other side of a brutal civil war you must manage your expectations. There will be power cuts, terrible bureaucratic snarl ups, problems with logistics and the moving of equipment, challenges with local communities, potentially interference from activists against the project; you name it, anything could go tits up. We have a big budget for security operations but you will always need to be careful and never take personal security for granted. But it will also be a great adventure. You can go on safaris, camp on beaches, explore the mountains all while saving a good chunk of money; it really is a once in a lifetime opportunity—'

'And that's why I applied,' Steven interrupted with a smile. He'd calculated when applying for the role, that if he stayed for the five-year length of the contract then he should be able to finish paying off his mortgage plus gain the experience needed to apply for a project director's job for his next role; the rewards more than outweighed any potential risks as far as he was concerned.

If a crow flew thirty miles north-by-north-west from Hazelstone it would be over Westminster, specifically, the boardroom of 11 Downing Street, the residence of the Chancellor of the Exchequer, Andrew Sinclair, and who was hosting the first meeting of the African Enterprise and Investment Council. Around the table were Chairmen and CEOs of some of the UKs most prominent business- es and who had commercial interests on the continent, including in the mining, agricultural science, retail, heavy industry and tourism sectors. The guest of honour was Sir Hillary Chapman, the Chairman of HydroDevelop.

'We must deepen our corporate interests in Africa,' the Chancellor started the get together.

'Including a shift in aid spending?' Chapman wanted clarifying.

'Yes,' came the unequivocal response. 'Aid must work in the UK's interest. Going forward, the budget will focus on private sector long-term economic capacity building rather than short-term poverty reduction—'

'Whatever the social cost?' Sir Hillary queried against protocol.

'Whatever the cost,' Sinclair re-iterated. 'Let's not kid ourselves… the UK spends twice as much on overseas fos- sil fuels as it does on renewable energy; we have to be prag- matic and do what is in the national interest. Gentlemen, the next global financial crisis is just round the corner and we need to be prepared. We must have an economic miti- gation strategy as there are many existential threats to the world economy. The Pound is steadily declining against a resurgent Dollar. The North Korea and Iran nuclear deals are shambolic and the minute hand is moving inextricably closer to the midnight-hour of nuclear war as China, the USA and Russia show-off their military muscle. Personal debt is out of control due to credit cards and car loans. Mortgages have reached the same level of toxicity as the

2008 financial crisis. Sovereign debt is as unsustainable in many developing countries as it was prior to Gleneagles. Climate change and global migration do not have consensus solutions. Trade wars are increasingly aggressive in nature. Greater automation in the workplace is leading to a surge in global unemployment. Bond yields in several European and Asian markets are dropping. Inflation is running rampant in many middle-income countries.' Sinclair took a breather. 'Any one of these could trigger the next financial crisis. Leading academics, politicians and captains of industry predict global economic disaster and is a matter of when rather than if. Gentlemen, we will soon be fighting for the economic survival of our island nation; the gloves are coming off. Rest assured, whatever your actions you will at all times have the full backing of the British Government.'

'Empire part two?' one wag suggested.

'If you like,' the Chancellor responded, the implication of what the companies could get away with now unmistakable. 'We must consider how best to support the British private sector and have been assured by the Foreign Office that all efforts will be aligned. If you are in the health, finance, telecommunications or retail sectors, know that you have a helping hand to meet the priorities of your shareholders.'

'There is much risk but also potentially huge rewards for investors in Africa,' Sir Hillary chimed in. 'You can dictate the terms of contract as we did for the national water project; now is the time to strike. Countries are borrowing at an alarming rate from both the private and public sector to kick start their economies and are willing

to offer large incentives for high-risk high-reward investments.'

'Won't unquenchable thirst for sovereign debt put
African economies in long-term risk?' a voice from the
back of the room wanted to know.

'Potentially, yes,' the Chancellor admitted. 'But if
they can't pay you will own the asset.'

He wasn't joking about Empire part two, the questioner
thought on hearing this reply.

'Such is Afronia's current level of debt, Walter Blaise
has no option but to liberalize and de-regulate the economy… and that gives you, gentlemen, a great deal of lee-
way to do what you do best… make money.'

'How will the British government support us?' another voice in the room wanted to know.

'We'll push the continent towards becoming a free-trade
zone and establish a number of challenge funds to de-risk
your more creative ideas. It's not a blank cheque, but all
ideas will be met with an open ear.'

'The UK needs to ensure long-term food security,' the
Chancellor's Chief Economic Advisor entered the conversation. 'Climate change is putting the world's food
supplies in jeopardy.' There was a sober silence in the
room. 'The term, Black Swan Event refers to major unexpected challenges which can lead to systemic disruption
in emergency food stocks. For example, it's well known
that in major crop-producing regions, such as the US and
Russia, aging infrastructure is being tested by more frequent and increasingly violent storms. Additionally, there
are some key chokepoints such as the Panama and Suez
canals which are vital to global food trade. If a devastat-

ing climatic event destroyed this infrastructure it would have dramatic consequences for the global food supply chain. For instance, the ban on wheat imports from Black Sea countries—when the region was drought stricken—contributed greatly to the Arab Spring.'

'Gentlemen, we must protect and grow the British economy,' Andrew Sinclair started to bring the meeting to a conclusion. 'When climate change impacts global trade we must have access to appropriate levels of natural resources to ensure political stability in the British Isles. Any questions?'

Chapter 11

'A FRONIA IS ROOTED in corruption, nepotism and tribalism,' Jay stated at his third meeting with Robert Yohan and the ever extravagantly dressed Yaya. 'I might do things that bend the law, but I don't break it. I don't fear the authorities. I'm respected everywhere I go,' he asserted as he pulled his shirt up to reveal a handgun tucked into his trousers.

He's a delusional lunatic, the two men opposite Jay simultaneously inwardly laughed.

'Afronia needs new leadership,' Jay continued his favourite topic and one on which he could wax lyrically for hours. 'Blaise shows no direction. Economic planning is myopic and development uses an apartheid methodology that favours the regions over Somalitreans, who lest we forget, are the majority. Roads are impassable, hospitals not available and, there has been no technological revolution as promised. Corrupt businessmen and politicians are vampires sucking money from peasants. Blaise has not been prosecuted but left to roam the corridors of power. Afronia is a republic of cronyism and the country is being destroyed more every day. We must stand up, now, and give our nation a new destiny.'

Is he ever going to shut up and do something? Yohan considered, *or just talk, talk, talk?* 'What are your plans?'

'I have funds to buy weapons; revolutions aren't free,' Jay cryptically replied having spent many hundreds-of-thousands of pounds on airfares and smuggling weapons into Afronia through the ports with the support of MH-16, the money coming from his investment in the Church of Heavenly Bodies. 'As John F Kennedy once said: when you make peaceful revolution impossible you make violent revolution inevitable.'

With Jay's war-mongering revelation at the forefront of his mind, Robert Yohan set up an emergency rendezvous with Tamsin Solomon. 'I want to come out of the political wilderness,' was his first full sentence after kissing Tamsin fully on the lips while his hands pulled and pinched her supple body. 'I'm a political animal and I miss the day-to-day sparring in parliament and managing a ministry.'

'Blaise would never agree to it—'

'I'm certain he would have his reservations, but you and he have an understanding; you can put in a good word for me.'

'Why?' Tamsin retorted, as she pushed his groping hands away and moved towards the lounge while pulling her skirt down. *The pig.*

'I love you,' he lied as he looked her square in the eye.

'Robert... this is a relationship of convenience... for both of us.'

What has she been getting from me? I know what I've got from her, he thought lecherously. *Has she been fooling me, and if so, for what purpose? Is she in league with someone?* 'Have you been playing me?' he decided to ask outright.

'No more than you me,' Tamsin countered with a smile. Her cards now on the table she felt liberated that the Septuagint would never get in her pants again.

'Ok, ok. I presume it's someone in Blaise's inner circle that's been dipping your honeypot.' Solomon's lack of response gave its own answer. 'I have information which suggests there'll be a coup attempt in the coming months.' *An exaggerated timeline, but whoever Tamsin passes this information onto will urgently want to know exactly what I know; this will be my bargaining chip.*

'Interesting.'

'If you can get me a seat at the table, I'll share the details.'

'And if this gets passed onto the security services… you'll be arrested for treason.' Tamsin enjoyed playing hardball.

'That's a chance I'm willing to take.' *I'll call her bluff.*

As the conversation carried on, Hamza Leso in the security room of *The Lady Freedom* listened in with great interest. *Do I make myself known now, later or not at all?*

'You?!?' The former vice-president spluttered when Leso sauntered into the stateroom two minutes later. With Hamza's outsized ego there was only ever going to be one outcome to his own question.

'Hello, Robert,' Hamza replied with a twinkle in his eye. 'It's been some time.'

'Houdini,' was the only word Yohan could utter.

'Some prefer, Casanova or Machiavelli,' Hamza joked, though in truth he was proud of all his nicknames.

'You are the other man?' Robert queried, his eyes flickering between Hamza and Tamsin.

Hamza let the suspense build in the extravagantly decorated and furnished room. 'No,' finally came the lie. 'You have been under surveillance for some time and Tamsin has been working with the National Security Agency to uncover what you know; she has been commended by the president for putting her country first.' This was also a lie; no one other than Charlie Daniels knew that Hamza had been working Tamsin for information.

'Selling her pussy, you mean?' This earned Yohan a sharp slap from the woman but which brought him a few seconds to plan his next move while he exaggeratedly rubbed his face. 'There's something about you, Hamza, I don't know what, but as the Brits like to say, you never play with a straight bat.'

Does he know more about me than he is letting on? Hamza considered the British reference.

'Birds of a feather flock together,' Tamsin sarcastically interjected.

'If you like… and you, also, my dear.' Walking over to the drinks cabinet Yohan poured himself a single malt. 'Another saying,' this after taking a swig, 'it takes a crook to catch a crook, and that is why, my friend, Hamza, I think we have more in common than either of us might want to acknowledge.' Yohan took a gulp from the tumbler. 'I have decades of political experience. I know what the Taberians are thinking. I know all the tricks the foreigners play in winning mining concessions. I could be a considerable asset to Blaise with all the dirt I have at my fingertips—'

'Including a coup?'

'It's something I've heard through my network. I have information that could build or destroy Blaise's Second Republic.'

'Are you trying to reinvent yourself, Robert? Expunge the past?' Tamsin asked.

'Yes, just like Hamza somehow managed to white-wash his indiscretions.'

'Cutting to the chase,' Hamza wanted to move the conversation on now all knew where the others stood; he had a briefing with the president in two-hours time, 'what do you have?'

'There is a certain gentleman who is well connected to civil servants in Whitehall and who has greased many hands to win building contracts. He's a well-known busi-nessman and political activist in the Afronian diaspora; he has quite the international following. He's a megalo-maniac and not afraid to use criminal means to reach his goal; he has his sights on becoming president.'

'Jay Peters is quite the character.' Hamza instant-ly knew who Yohan was referring to. 'What of his coup planning?'

'Quid pro quo, Hamza,' you need to give me some-thing.

'I'm meeting the president shortly.'

'Then I wait with baited-breath for feedback to my proposal.' Yohan walked towards the door that led onto the main deck of the super yacht and thus ensuring the conversation finished on his terms.

Chapter 12

As Jay's watch struck 00:45 am three days after his meeting with Robert Yohan, he could be found cruising Hillview Promenade in a Land Rover Discovery. In the vehicle were three junior Afronian army officers who Jay had befriended several years earlier when they had all been at Sandhurst, the British Army's Officer Cadet Academy. They had all secretly joined the Afronia Freedom League while in the UK. Since returning home, two had been in the Army Intelligence Unit, their prime responsibility to crush gangs that had sprung up since Blaise had dramatically cut back the role of the secret police, the upshot of which was a power vacuum on the streets and into which Mike Henshaw's MH-16—and similarly minded violent individuals—had ruthlessly exploited. It had been the army officers who had made the introduction between Henshaw and Jay.

There were four cars in the convoy with a total of eighteen men and one woman. All were heavily armed with assault rifles, pistols and grenades. There was a palpable tension for those involved in Operation Afronia Reawakening.

At 1 am, and when Jay considered it safe, the convoy drove towards Presidential Square. After driving downside streets and circling the palace twice, he parked in the shadow of a line of Royal Poinciana flame trees. Peering through the darkness towards the president's residence, Jay said to those he shared the car with and into his walk-ie-talkie, 'When there is no respect for the state by the people and the government doesn't allow citizens their rights, you have a failed state. Tonight, we bring respect back to Afronia.'

'Ready,' Mr White replied. 'When the state and army are weak, criminality becomes a way of life. ISiSS will reappear and rip the country apart.'

'Ok,' this from Mr Blue. 'Umoja City is run by ma-fias; tonight, we will write a new chapter in our country's history.'

'Waiting to start a new future,' Mr Green concurred. The code names for the leaders in each of the vehicles were inspired by Quintin Tarrentino's film, Reservoir Dogs, and which Jay had watched for the first time the previous week this as he finalised plans for regime change.

'First,' Jay had explained two days earlier, 'we use these,' he held up a pair of night-vision goggles, 'to count the guards. We then taser the sentries on duty outside the palace. Once in, we chain the doors shut on the barracks and swiftly move through the building using minimum force until we get to the president's bedroom. We get him to renounce his leadership on live television.'

'Let's go,' Jay gave the order as he stepped out of his car and donned his NVGs. 'Fuck!' he swore. There was no green glow when he turned his goggles on, this he'd hoped would give his group a decisive advantage.

'Mr White, is your gear working?'

'No. the batteries must be dead. Are we aborting?'

'Shit. No. We go ahead tonight. Mr Blue, what about your goggles? Mr Green?'

'Negative,' they replied in unison.

'Fuck! Wait in the cars while I check out the guards.' Jay removed his weapon and other incriminating paraphernalia and put them in the boot of the Discovery before donning an overcoat to cover his urban camouflage uniform. Looking up and down the street and seeing no one approaching, he casually sauntered towards Presidential Square. Nearing his target, he sat down on a low wall and started counting the number of guards wearing ceremonial uniform; it was the same as he'd seen the previous three evenings when reconnoitring his objective. Satisfied, he returned to his followers and with no misgivings or thought of safety, Jay gave the hugely risky order. 'We go now.'

Jay and his group of loyal liberators crept in the shadows towards the palace gates when, suddenly, they were mown down in an ambush, a volley of silenced bullets by army snipers—wearing (working) night-vision goggles—slamming into the approaching rebels. Three were killed instantly and five mortally wounded, the rest, including Jay swiftly rounded up by the Presidential Guard, a force ten-times as large as Jay's and which had been stationed in nearby buildings surrounding the square. As a wounded Jay was led away from the slaughter, he wondered, *Who betrayed me?*

Chapter 13

'I DON'T KNOW HOW Peters thought he could over-throw the government with such an amateurish plan,' Walter Blaise mused. He picked up his cup of tea and finished it in one go as he looked round the room. 'But,' the president slamming his hand on a table and rocking nearby coffee cups, 'who was the power behind the attempted coup?'

The politburo looked at each other with blank looks. 'As far as my sources know,' Yohan spoke up after thirty-seconds of silence, 'he was a lone wolf. A charismatic fantasist with a fat wallet.'

'How sure are you?' Hamza asked, not trusting Robert and seeing a possible challenger to his undisputed position as key advisor to the president.

'I can't be 100-percent sure, and have no evidence, but my intuition tells me Victov somehow has his fingers in this particular pie.'

'I've heard similar whisperings,' Hamza confirmed. He had been told by Charlie Daniels that there were unsubstantiated reports that Russia was indeed involved, though exactly how, no one knew.

'Do we believe this?' The president rhetorically queried. 'If, yes, what's our response?'

'We need to investigate further before rash decisions are made,' Yohan said, his generic words adding nothing to the discussion.

'I'm in agreement,' Hamza concurred. 'Victov has motive and opportunity to cause Afronia problems. If a link is found, or not, we must step carefully.'

'Very well,' Blaise concluded. 'Hamza you will lead the investigation and have the full support of our Foreign Office and Internal Security Services.'

Hamza nodded and then looked across the table at Yohan who was taking a sip from his water. *What game is he playing?*

'To the next order of business,' the president continued. 'Minister of Education, how is the school refurbishment program advancing?'

'The plot would have been years in the making,' Charlie Daniels voiced to Hamza that evening in the President Obama Hotel. 'I doubt the inspiration was Jay Peters alone as he's no mastermind; I expect there was expertise and funding from a foreign state.'

'Which one?' Hamza asked. 'The Taberians? Victov? And if there was support, why did it go so spectacularly wrong?'

'We think Peters had the backing of the Kremlin.'

'How sure are you? This is not a conclusion Afronia can afford to get wrong,' the implication being that deliberately misleading information would not be tolerated.

'We are friends of Walter,' Charlie, using the royal, we, to indicate he was speaking on behalf of the British government. 'We want Afronia to be stable and grow. What is good for Afronia is good for British companies who invest here.'

Even after all this time, I still find him hard to read, Hamza considered as he looked at the man opposite and who was tucking into a crab salad that had been liberally covered in an Italian sour cream dressing.

'Do you have any proof?' Hamza probed as he dipped the prawn at the end of his fork into the homemade 1,001 Island Sauce.

'Peters received a transfer of half-a-million pounds six-months ago from an offshore bank which has links to the Kremlin.'

'Is that it? That payment could have been from anyone and routed via such a bank to act as a red herring.'

'Quite possibly, but that's all we have… for now.'

'What are the possible politics of the coup attempt?'

'Undoubtedly, Victov has no love for Blaise, but whether he would so blatantly interfere… is a known unknown.'

After the dinner meeting with Charlie, Hamza next met Yohan and who he trusted even less than Daniels, *When a snake sheds its skin… it's still a snake.* 'What do you know?' Hamza asked.

Robert felt equally weary of Leso. 'Sometimes things fall into your lap. I followed the plot for some time; I was intrigued. Why would Jay Peters, a successful entrepreneur, risk spreading his wings? He was very vocal on social media and so it would be no surprise if Russian analysts picked up on it. Sending half-a-million dollars to sow confusion, anonymously, is no big deal for the Kremlin.'

'How sure are you it was Victov?'

'Gut feeling... but when you consider Victov's animosity towards Blaise... and that Igor is ruthless and very strong willed, as the Brits like to say when playing snooker, it was a shot to nothing.'

There he goes again mentioning the British; what does he know about them, or me, that I don't?

'If it wasn't the Russians, who?' Yohan angrily demanded. 'Victov has always followed a strategy of bluff, money and international espionage; that's business as usual to him.'

'Very true,' Hamza agreed. 'Do you have any hard evidence?'

'Proof beyond all reasonable doubt is always a challenge.'

Hamza saw a smile creeping onto Yohan's face, *Professional admiration for Victov or something more?*

I'm still the king of misdirection; Hamza is but a young pretender, Yohan congratulated himself as he saw Leso's mind whirr.

Chapter 14

FOR THIRTY KILOMETRES after leaving Lake Wahili, the River Wahili gathered strength and swelled from tributaries running of the Southi Highlands before cascading 1,000 metres through a web of cliff-lined gorges and plunging over the majestic Grand Afronia Falls. The river then plateaued on the semi-arid plains that formed the border with Taberia, this where alligators sun-bathed on the banks before the waterway meandered towards Rapoli, the Taberian Capital on the coast.

'Mr President,' Greg Maduhu, the President of Taberia started, 'Afronia's national water project will be an ecological disaster for my country. Waters from the River Wahili, floods the Taberian water basin once a year. The Southiland Renaissance Dam will restrict the flow to our irrigation projects; this is nothing but economic terrorism by other means.'

The geography of the River Wahili was of little concern to Igor Victov and who kept the phone five inches from his ear not wanting to hear the rant, besides, *I know the gist of what was going to be asked*, his Ambassador in Rapoli having been summoned two days earlier at the personal request of Maduhu. 'We will second your motion at the next meeting of the General Assembly at the

United Nations,' Victov assured his counterpart. *But I won't antagonise Blaise, its Afronia and not Taberia after all which has all the riches.*

'The rainy season arrives later and are shorter than in years gone by. No longer do fat droplets pour from heavens until roads become impassable and inland seas emerge overnight.' Maduhu paused. 'We have started our green belt strategy, but we must have waters from the Wahili River.'

While the international diplomacy was pure posturing, the Afronian dam and waterways project did pose a significant threat to water security for Taberia. The Russian Embassy had hired environmental consultants to conduct an impact assessment and it didn't make for pleasant reading. 'The dams will slow the flow of water and thus stop the annual floods and therefore deprive Taberian farmers of the nutrient rich silt they need for the soil; crops will die in the fields and prices soar—'

'My Ambassador has already started discussions with your Ministry of Food Security to export maize,' Victov reassured the Taberian.

'Many farmers are leaving the countryside and moving to towns and cities which further adds to the urban challenge of overcrowding and underemployment; the Afronian dams are an existential threat to Taberia.'

'All options are on the table in how we can support you,' Victov reassured his regional ally. 'We are no friends of Blaise; he treated Russia with disrespect even when our soldiers and airmen gave their lives to end their civil war. We never stand idly by when friends are in danger.'

'Thank you, that river is life to Taberia.'

The main discussion over, Igor Victov had a question of his own, 'What do you know of the Blaise assassination and coup attempt?'

There was twenty seconds of silence, Maduhu contemplating his answer. 'We have no love for Blaise... but they are our neighbour. Without reassurance from friends we would not jeopardise peace.'

Perfect ambiguity! If Taberia had a reason to start a war, and I gave Maduhu my reassurance and armaments, he could be talked into a pre-emptive strike. However, it sounds as if he was not culpable for the attempted regime change, therefore, who was responsible for the mischief making?

Blaise downplayed the coup attempt as that of a fantasist not worthy of his time and that he had more important matters of state to contend with. As for the potential involvement of the Russians, 'Without a smoking gun, we have zilch,' he started the discussion with Hamza. 'There is nothing to be gained by pointing accusatory fingers at Victov if we don't have evidence; we will seem desperate rather than dignified. By doing nothing, we gain extra support from our friends in the west who are very aware of Russia's interest in the region.'

'What about Yohan?' Hamza asked, having been convinced by the president's argument on Russia.

'It is good to keep your friends close but your enemies closer; he can be an advisor to the president... but no more than that.'

'Won't that be dangerous? What if he turns against you?'

'Then he will be signing his political suicide note. Every Afronian knows his past; they see him for what he is... an opportunist.'

'We will have to pick his portfolio very carefully.'

'I was thinking, tourism. It's economically important but a politically weak ministry; he won't have a seat on the politburo. Yohan has a wide network of international contacts and can encourage investment and which can only be good for the country.' Hamza nodded at this sage calculation. 'Of greater importance is the water problems we have in the regions, and this despite the recent heavy rainfall which has topped up our rivers and reservoirs. I'm looking forward to the HydroDevelop presentation,' the president concluded the quick get-together as both went to the adjoining conference hall where ambassadors, members of the media, cabinet ministers and selected invitees were waiting patiently.

'Your Excellency,' Sir Hillary Chapman started his address from the podium, 'guests of honour, ladies and gentlemen. Afronia was at a crossroads when the decision was taken that the citizens of this beautiful country deserve to have safe, secure, reliable and affordable water supplies that can power electricity, move cargo and provide safe water for consumption. HydroDevelop is honoured and determined to see the president's vision for Afronia become reality on time and under budget.' A round of applause rang out giving Chapman enough time to have a sip from the bottle by the lectern, and which all in the audience assumed was water but was actually vodka.

'That's what they all say about these type of big projects,' Blaise whispered into Hamza's ear and which brought a smile to his advisor's face.

'Why, despite usually abundant rainfall does Afronia not have access to fresh drinking water nor have the electricity or supplies of aqua that is needed in the quantities and regularity that will help make Afronia a middle-income country on the back of a light-industry renaissance?' Sir Hilary paused and let the congregation contemplate this fundamental question. 'I take the example of the Harari regional capital, Darsburg, and where micro-processing businesses need a relatively large volume of water. BritBrew has built a brewery there which is producing a fine ale,' he said, a photo of him holding a bottle of beer appearing on the presentation screen behind him; there was lite laughter. 'Most of the residents are forced to walk long distances to hand-dug wells with yellow jerry cans to get their water needs, this despite many houses having water pipes. Investment has been made by the private sector in bore holes and pumps, but significant challenges remain: 1) planning, 2) environmental sustainability and 3) collection and delivery. HydroDevelop will address the last of these issues as part of the National Water Integrated Plan and build the hydroelectric dams and water highways to transport water and goods from the mountains in Southiland to the regional cities and the new capital, Mapulwe. There will be sufficient supply for both consumer and business use, even for water intensive industries involved in processing and refining. The reservoir and waterways will supply water for irrigation to the ten districts in Harari region which regularly suffer drought.

We will be advising government and business in regards industrial waste and water pollution more generally so that pollutants and other waste materials don't get into the rivers and deplete soil fertility, kill livestock and ultimately enter the food chain.' As Chapman came to the end of his presentation he received a standing ovation.

Next was the Minister of Water and Irrigation. 'At the village level we will be following a community water service model that has been hugely successful in Paraguay and is now being rolled out across South America. Many areas in Afronia suffer from water shortages in the dry season, and yet schools, clinics and residents need access to clean drinking water every day. President Blaise has instructed my department to report directly to the Minister of Health as clean water is a basic human right and the treatment of water a public health priority.

'Secondly, responsibility for water and sanitation will be given to boards of volunteers at the village administrative level. They will maintain the infrastructure, set tariffs and repay government for the initial costs. For an average of $3 a month, every Afronian family will have access to clean water; the incapacitated will have their share paid by the community.'

'What do you think, Hamza?' the president queried once they'd left the auditorium.

'Ambitious,' came the answer. 'A massive undertaking that will take many years if not decades to complete and at a cost we can only start to imagine.'

'What you say is true. It will be time consuming and expensive but that is what implementing a vision, rather than playing politics for short-term gain, is all about. Believe it or not, the national water strategy is not much removed from that drafted by Altimus who was clever, a genius, a born leader, but who was corrupted by self-importance and greed. Technology has improved and we have a better understanding of environmental sustainability, but if the former Life President had followed his convictions rather than be swayed by the power of office, Afronia would have been a vastly different country than it is today... and dare I say it, Solomon might still be president.'

'I serve at your pleasure.' Humility was not Hamza's natural way, but with Blaise he felt humbled.

The pair entered their next meeting. 'Where are we on our green revolution?' Blaise asked his Minister of Agriculture, and who'd been an agribusiness owner all his life and was also one of the few from the Altimus Solomon regime to be retained. 'It matters not a jot how the rest of the economy performs if our citizens are not fed and can't make a livelihood from the land.'

The Minister of Economy, Professor Rashid, had reminded his boss at a breakfast briefing, 'If Afronia can't harvest enough crop, our foreign exchange earnings from mining, tourism and the like, will be spent on food imports. This, to an extent, is what did for Altimus Solomon... there wasn't enough money to be both stolen for his family and to feed the country.'

'Better farming requires better inputs,' the minister started to reply, 'whether improved seed, fertilizer, pesticides, access to the latest extension knowledge or appropriate financial services... better inputs lead to better outputs. We need the efficiencies agricultural science and technology can bring if we are to feed all Afronians and become the regional breadbasket,' this the president's stated aim. 'Using the correct amount of fertilizer, with improved or hybrid seed, can double or triple yields.'

'You are talking about genetically modified crops? Industrialized agricultural systems?'

'Yes, Sir. Agriculture is critical for a unified, progressive Afronia. Sir, if the people go hungry they will revolt. We must have a sober debate and not let mischief making organisations spread false lies; farmers who eat genetically modified maize won't become sterile. Activists proposing traditional methods have fat bellies. We can't keep subsidising subsistence farmers; it's not a sustainable way of life or how the nation will feed itself. We must break from the agricultural norms Altimus Solomon promoted, and who knew, that by reducing crop yields he would keep the regions economically subservient to Somalitrea, the only region that started an agri-tech revolution. Solomon's commercial farms are a blueprint the whole country should follow.'

That explains a lot, Hamza realized, *about how Altimus Solomon managed to keep a grip on this country for so long; he really was a cunning bastard!*

'Farmers need to make money,' The Minister of Economy, and who'd been sitting quietly, suddenly interjected. 'They need to either have their own sustainable plot or be employed by commercial farms. Without privately held funds education, health and all other rural services, will have to be state provided. The rural population must make contributions, directly or through taxation, if we are going to make proper investments in national infrastructure and not be beholden too foreign investors who are only looking for a financial return. The current practice of growing only enough to feed a family… is not economically or politically sustainable.'

'Agriculture as enterprise, has to be our new motto,' the Minister of Agriculture concurred. 'We should work with foreign corporates to provide better inputs and educate farmers with appropriate technical advice.'

'How do we regulate foreigners so they aren't exploitative?' this from Hamza.

'Farmers understand, that if their inputs cost more yields will be higher. We must help farmers weigh up the pros and cons of buying more expensive farm inputs,' Professor Rashid reiterated. 'We should regulate the multi-nationals so that they meet all ethical and environmental standards, but we must also give farmers the tools to lift themselves out of poverty.'

'What is our annual agricultural budget?' the president asked his Minister of Agriculture.

'Afronia committed ten-percent of her national budget at the African Heads of State meeting in Maputo in 2003. Altimus Solomon reconfirmed this at the Malabo Declaration ten years later—'

'That's pie in the sky,' the Minister of Economy interrupted his erstwhile colleague. 'In reality not more than five-percent of our budget goes to agriculture. It's no surprise that we need to import food and export wealth and jobs through this lack of investment.'

'Thank you, professor,' the peeved Minister of Agriculture responded.

'Can we increase the budget, Rashid?' the president interrupted the spat.

'It is not just a matter of more money but knowing where to spend it. Colleagues in other countries increased funds but didn't see an increase in productivity... civil servant allowances and corrupt officials are often the main beneficiaries of any budgetary increase—'

'Due to poor public financial management,' a sarcastic Minister of Agriculture testily interrupted.

'The question we need to answer, Mr President,' Professor Rashid continued, 'is whether we want the agriculture sector to be state-led and subsidized... for political reasons... or create a business-friendly environment which encourages local and foreign direct investment and use the national budget on other sectors.'

'Work together and send me a budget and roadmap by the end of the month,' the president had the final word.

'Do you know what the scariest thing for a gay man is?' the Minister of Health invited Walter Blaise to guess during the president's last meeting of the day.

'No,' this after pondering, *What indeed could be the most terrifying thing for a member of the LGBTQ community?*

'It's entering the doctor's examination room and being instructed to lower your trousers. In a sanctum where one should feel absolutely free with a medical professional, many gay men are forcibly held down as a doctor inserts a tube or his fingers in a person's anus.'

'What's that got to do with being gay?' the perplexed president asked; he was genuinely baffled at what such an examination might reveal.

'To see if the man has semen there!'

'Surely not! That's absurd! Is the practice widespread?'

'Yes, and not just in medical clinics but also police stations, military barracks and anywhere the state can inflict humiliation. You are gay, is the easiest accusation an official can make to project power. It's difficult to disprove a negative for those who aren't gay or bi-sexual. Its repellent bigotry and standard procedure for any man or woman arrested on non-heterosexual related charges. These are surviving laws from 19th century pseudo-science that started during the scramble for Africa. It is on a par with the gross violation of human rights for women who enter the army or police and endure virginity tests.'

'This torture, for there is no other word, must be stopped immediately.'

'It happened to me,' Ralph told the president in a quiet voice, this partly out of embarrassment, though primarily because of the mental scares. 'I was arrested at the age of twenty-two for no good reason. In the police station I had to push my trousers down; I didn't know what to expect. I cried hysterically when I felt the doctor insert a cold metal tube, the man scolding and laughingly telling me to stop crying like a baby. After he removed the tube, he inserted first one, then two and finally three fingers. At this stage, four other doctors entered the room. Each had their go pulling apart my buttocks and feeling me up; I could smell the alcohol and shisha on their breath. It took me over a week to be able to sit comfortably, but it was that horrific experience that encouraged me to study harder, to be the best doctor I could be so that I can make changes from within the circles of power.'

'I'm so sorry.' The president hugged Ralph. 'You are a courageous man and a great Afronian. I will gladly let you bring a change in legislation to parliament; you will get my full backing for a complete outlawing of this medieval abomination.'

After two weeks of going forward and backwards with the medical council, and an all-night drafting of legislation following discussions in parliament, much to his delight the president was able to declare, 'Afronia has become a more inclusive society and one where our friends, colleagues and family members in the LGBTQ community will be treated equally. Gay men will no longer be subjected to anal examinations. Virginity tests for females entering our armed forces and security services have been banned. Young women will not be subjected to sexual initiation. Male adults who take advantage of the vulnerable and expose them to sexually transmitted diseases, such as HIV/AIDS will be imprisoned. A girl child will no longer be subjected to Female Genital Mutilation. All these corrosive practices leave the innocent mentally and physically scarred for life.

'I have instructed our traditional leaders to ensure that all these despicable acts are outlawed and will hold them personally responsible for any future crimes. On behalf of the government of Afronia, I offer a profuse apology to all who have been subjected to such demeaning acts. My government is committed to an equal society which respects everyone's human rights.

'The legislation that my government has passed, enshrines in law the basic right for all women to have the right to choose if and when they have children, whatever their circumstances in becoming pregnant. I believe in sexual education, family planning, sexual health, and post-abortion care. Afronia will be an inclusive society and I am determined to have a fair and humane culture where every colour, creed, religion, gender, age and sexual orientation, can contribute to the Second Republic as we move Afronia from poverty to prosperity through development for all.'

Chapter 15

THE GENTLEMAN'S CLUB, Number Thirty-Three, was nestled along the leafy Grosvenor Street, Mayfair, and was among the most expensive properties in the land. The cost of the 25-year lease on the five-storey building, while undisclosed, was however known to run into many tens of millions of pounds… though this was thought a price worth paying if the right people were appropriately looked after.

A sharply uniformed serving staff approached a table on the left-hand side of the dining-room. On the right was a roof terrace and cocktail bar, both stocked with the finest complimentary wines and aperitifs. Gazing around at the great and good of the political, business and hereditary elite, was Andrew Sinclair. 'With increasing sovereign, corporate and consumer debt, we expect a financial crisis will soon be unleashed. The British Government has a strong mandate to use any means available, including the use of the aid budget to support British businesses.'

'We are against a globalist agenda,' a voice with a French accent said. 'How is the plan going to help us transcend national borders and sovereignty?'

'By taking positions in gold and Bitcoin,' the Chancellor responded confidently as he looked around the room. 'We expect that during a financial chaos markets will move into these alternate commodities. Individually, your wealth will grow exponentially and from which your contributions will help to bankroll revolutions in strategically important countries through the support of opposition political parties and the purchase of media houses. At the same time, creditors should demand repayment of loans so that African governments will be forced into more liberal regulation and give greater incentives for foreign direct investment.'

'We expect to get ownership of large parts of Afronia's water infrastructure if the government defaults,' the ruddy face of Sir Hillary Chapman guffawed with a big grin. 'They are a historically divided people wanting strong leadership; how else do you think Altimus Solomon remained president for so long. The average Afronian is weak and malleable; only a few dare to stand up against their oppressors; they have no collective warrior tradition, like for instance, the Kenyan Masai. It's only the Southis who are willing to die for principles. Afronia is the perfect country to start implementing our strategy.'

'Our respective governments are strategically supporting African governments through building capacity in their Public Private Partnership units.' Sinclair paused, as he searched for a bearded face. 'Many of you already know the philanthropist, Mr George Smithe, but I would like to formerly introduce him to the Jobuja Group.'

'Africa is uniting,' Smithe started to address the assembled guests. 'This is good for the continent and good for business. What is missing is leadership. I believe the Jobuja Group can provide the unified vision that is needed.

'With half-a-billion Africans entering the workforce in the next 20 years, Africa will either be the centre of global economic growth or unprecedented migration, war and suffering. The choices are stark as population growth, urbanization, technological advances and climate change will not stop accelerating. The world has left it late to act… but there is still time to change from unmitigated disaster to a wonderful future as the biggest threats can also be a catalyst for the greatest opportunities.

'The African Union has adopted the free movement protocol and the Continental Free Trade Area. Governments are working closer than ever, but the change must be private sector led otherwise there will not be enough jobs from which to realise social cohesion and economic gain. The business community must either hold governments accountable for acting on the accords… or be the government; there is no third option as the time for procrastination has passed.

'For there to be appropriate political will and international finance to work on continental infrastructure and climate change mitigation activities, business must lead and not just be a voice at the table. With the demise of the nation state gathering pace through decades of globalisation, autonomous technology, rampant corruption, growing inequality, deregulated finance, information overload, big data analytics, dark money and religious militancy, compounded by a democratic deficit, the current African political systems are obsolete; they are authoritarian kleptocracies that are increasingly seen for what they are. So now is the time to implement a new vision. One in which government runs to the tune of demand, where authority is centralized, decisions are made on a continental basis and, where there is global cooperation, peace and justice. The nation state model is no longer able to attain this vision and is no longer fit for purpose. The United Nations and other such illegitimate bodies are rooted in national self-interest and have no political authority. Democracy is broken and no longer brings meaningful solutions to the cacophony of existential threats the human species faces.

'I believe in an open society where anyone can be anything. Africa has been held back through individuals not being able to be all that they can be because governments haven't invested in primary social services, especially education. Many countries rely on protectionist policies that restricts competition and enables an environment for corrupt businessmen and politicians. Billions go into their greedy pockets rather than invested in future generations. Of course, there are rich Africans, but much of that wealth is offshore in tax havens rather than being re-invested in their brethren.

'With the tidal wave of humanity coming to Europe's shores through the twin challenges of climate change and unrestricted population growth, it is imperative that the world take action so that Africa can become a leading light in finding solutions rather than a potentially fatal obstacle. There is abundant mineral wealth on the continent, but poor democracy, weak governance and, a lack of transparency stymies economic growth. By working together there are opportunities for all in this room and on the African continent. And so, Africa needs to privatise her economies, open her markets to competition and welcome foreign investment. The less government interference and regulation the better the market will work, and if prosperity for the masses can be achieved, democratic institutions will quickly be forgotten. The transformation we all envisage however requires uncompromising leadership.'

Chapter 16

'FANCY A BEER?' Emmanuel asked Jacob after a long, hot but fruitful day in the business incubator.

'Why not,' came the typically English acceptance to the idea. Fifteen minutes later they were at their usual watering-hole AfroBeat, Tigist's lounge cum bar. The lady in question was not around, Jacob quite happy as it meant he could have a discussion without being side-tracked. 'A contentious question for you... and which I quote one of my good meaning if misguided friends, hundreds-of-thousands live in slums due to globalisation and free market policies.'

'What tosh,' Emmanuel spluttered into his brew. 'They live in slum conditions as it's better than the alternative. This, by the way, just one reason the president advocating for a green revolution—to reduce the pull of cities and towns.'

'I didn't say, I agree with my friend, I was just articulating his point of view.'

'Jacob, opinions are like arseholes... everyone has one. I bet he's also of the school of opinion that much of Africa's woes can be traced to colonialism,'

'Well, yes, he does actually—'

'Is that what you believe?'

'No. I think it has been poor policy, predatory presidents and the move towards socialist rather than free market ideals at independence. At the time, when the newly independent countries needed to be at their most entrepreneurial all the factors one could imagine impinged that spirit.'

'Some would argue, that in the 1950s and 60s following the Soviet model was the wise path. During the 1930s the USSR had undergone industrialization and transformed a nation of peasants into a super-power.' Emmanuel had decided to be the Devil's advocate. 'In the 60s the Soviet Union looked like it was going to win the scientific battle with the West and represented a future that was the absolute opposite to colonisation.'

'I know why Africa followed the route it did,' Jacob conceded, 'and why limited protectionism was important while the economy found its feet and a civil service was established... it was an understandable if not sustainable strategy. My point is that since the 1990s and the dying of the strong men of Africa and one-party states, the continent has liberalised and it's been in the last two decades that the most progress has been made.'

'Afronia was in a prime position to learn the lessons from the African independence movement, but unfortunately Altimus Solomon was the ultimate example of commercializing a country for selfish reasons.'

Meanwhile, in the centre of Umoja City, 'First,' the British Ambassador said to Charlie Daniels as he started huffing, puffing and walking round the elegantly furnished study at the embassy, 'there's no point giving free drugs to Afronians, whenever Blaise requests.' The appeal having been made earlier in the week. 'On a restricted budget, many life-saving drugs are simply too expensive for a country like Afronia to subsidize those with no insurance. British pharmaceutical companies get a bad rap for over-priced medicine… but the truth is, aid should be targeted to improve medical infrastructure and training doctors… and the British have the technical expertise and the private sector companies to provide it!'

'It's a judgment call on how best to keep on the right side of Walter Blaise. I agree, big pharma can't give products away as they'll have no funds for research & development.' Charlie paused dramatically; deep in thought, he began plotting. 'We must support the Afronian government to go in a different strategic direction… and one which is more commercially sustainable for UK PLC.'

Charlie's second evening meeting was with Jake, the special advisor without portfolio. 'We must prioritise British supermarkets and agribusiness to expand their supply chains in Afronia. Big-up to Blaise's green revolution… but if we use every trick in the book and don't worry about negative publicity around the idea of the British taxpayer giving money to corporate behemoths then we can have a winner on our hands. Besides, the average tabloid reader has no idea of the game we play nor how the economic future of the UK is at stake.'

'Any specifics?' Jake asked as he stifled a yawn; he was now used to Charlie's grand schemes.

'Training for farmers and exposure visits are an easy

sell… even if the effectiveness is hard to monetise.'

'Cutting to the chase Charlie, are you suggesting that we bribe British businesses to invest in Afronia using a slush fund?'

'The correct parlance is de-risk. We de-risk companies to invest in Afronia.'

Bloody spooks. If he knows how to do my job, why doesn't he apply for it. 'Any other advice?' Jake's voice full of sarcasm.

'There are opportunities for British transportation companies.'

'That's a bit left field, even for you.'

'Exactly! Currently, there's not much donor or commercial activity in the sector.'

'But what about the big infrastructure projects like the HydroDevelop dams, the train network, the port etc? What do you have in mind?' came the weary voice of the embassy man.

'I was thinking… road safety. It could be a great corporate social responsibility project for a company like HydroDevelop.'

The man opposite Charlie continued to look pensive. *What crap is going to next spew from our resident MI6 officer?*

'Did you hear about the minibus crash near Lirobi?' this being the capital of Wahilistan.

'No.'

'School children on their way to take exams… their minibus went over a pothole, crashed and burst into flames; all the students died.'

'Afronian drivers and roads are simply terrible. And the police asking for bribes rather than removing licences from dangerous drivers doesn't help,' Jake contemplated. 'What's your suggestion?'

'A dual strategy. First, grants should be given for road safety campaigns. Secondly, we do capacity building projects for the police and Road Traffic Administration. We advise on the tendering process and so ensure a British company wins the contract.'

'You mean, re-route the aid budget into the private sector?'

'Quite ingenious, isn't it?' Charlie was incredibly pleased with himself for coming up with such a ruse. 'Building the private sector overseas is one of the government's priorities. This way we can still legitimately claim to be keeping to our zero-point-seven percent of Gross Domestic Product commitment.'

'That's duplicitous. It's deceiving the British taxpayer and denying an Afronian entrepreneur who could provide the service at a fraction of the cost.'

'What's your point? What good would an Afronian winning do for the British economy?' Charlie was annoyed at the impertinence.

'Thanks for your suggestions, Charlie, but we're already inundated with similar requests from Whitehall. We're in the early stages of implementing an e-learning program for hard-to-reach secondary schools. We are giving tablets, laptops and the requisite solar equipment to schools who are off-grid. Digital learning will revolutionize education in the next few years.'

'Are British companies the suppliers?' Charlie wanted to confirm.

'Yes,' Jake laughed as he saw the irony of what he'd

previously been dismissive about, 'but such capacity building for distance learning is what the Minister of Education asked for; the days of bricks and mortar teaching are coming to an end... even in Africa.'

Charlie's third and final meeting was at the annual embassy garden party. The get-together between the two gentlemen had been facilitated by the British Chancellor, his order having wound its slippery way through the various levels of bureaucracy and diplomatic channels so that an introduction would be made.

'Afronia is growing,' Ulrich said with his usual understated pizzazz before taking a sip of Armand de Brignac Ace of Spades Champagne, and which sold for $300 and came in a gold bottle with a massive, embossed ace in a black lacquer. 'Where others see risk, I find opportunities. I represent individuals, corporates and sovereign wealth funds who want to make money.'

'Who are your investors?' a clearly intrigued Charlie wanted to know; he had a limited grasp on the finer intricacies of hedge fund management... or so he pretended.

'I can't go into details, Mr. Jones,' Ulrich replied to Charlie's alias for the evening.

'What type of projects do you invest in and what sort of return are you looking for?'

'Afronia is a high-risk high-reward country... but we are not afraid to invest in dangerous places. We find success in unstable regions; people can't fight forever. Besides, Standard and Poor's gives Afronia a BBB+ rating and Moody's a Baa3, both of which are investment grade.' Ulrich paused after painting a far from encouraging picture. 'We will be investing in Public Private Partnerships in the areas of infrastructure, agribusiness, mining and financial services. We expect an annual average rate of return of nineteen-percent based on the PPP lasting not less than ten-years.'

'I'll be in touch in due course.' Charlie raised his glass of champagne and clinked it with Ulrich's before moving in the direction of a waitress who had caught his eye. On his leisurely way, he considered, *How can I ensure his hedge fund invests in British companies?*

Ulrich for his part had another meeting. He first went to meet his guest. 'Mike, I'd like you to meet a friend of mine.'

The person in question was of wiry build and indeterminate nationality. It was Julius Stewart, and whose stepfather had been in the French Foreign Legion and mother a Parisian cabaret dancer. Julius had first come to Afronia when he'd rigged the ferry bomb shortly before the presidential elections where Altimus Solomon had squeezed out a victory. As the Life President refused to disappear into the political sunset he'd paid with his life, this when Julius had assassinated him on *The Lady Freedom.* Julius had weaved his own brand of black magic of political interference on his second visit through rigging the explosion in the King of the Mountain Hotel and the elimination of Khalid Omar. His third trip had been at the end of the civil war, this when he'd been contracted to murder Jessica Webb, her investigation into the origins of the Afronian civil war leading her to Switzerland and which was too close to comfort for his client.

'Nice to meet the urban legend,' Julius said as he stepped forward and shook Henshaw's outstretched hand.

Chapter 17

ERIC'S FAMILY HAD ARRIVED three weeks earlier and were getting used to life in Afronia. They lived in a four-bedroom house, one of twenty houses in the very desirable Ocean View Residence in Hillview, each property had a private quarter-acre garden with a small orchard of lemon, mango and apple trees, and a swimming pool.

Two years earlier, the plot of land that Eric and family now called home, had been a slum that housed fifteen families and close on 100 people. The combined monthly rent of the previous occupiers was less than half the $8,500 that HydroDevelop paid the landlord, an Afronian who lived in Manchester and who had bought the entire plot for a relatively paltry $250,000. While the total development had cost $10million, the combined rent of the twenty houses would guarantee a profit within five years and see the asset value double; it was a shrewd investment.

'I never pictured coming to the other side of the world,' Eric stated to Sylvia as they started to prepare the braai. That evening Steven and some of Eric's other colleagues, plus their families, were coming around for a pool party. 'I truly love this place,' he said looking over the large garden which was sumptuously filled with flora and fauna, *The financial and professional rewards of the contract are bloody marvellous as well.*

'I don't like it,' Sylvia retorted without a second of hesitation. 'The children are disturbed and neither they nor I have friends.'

'It will take time to adjust,' Eric acknowledged. 'That's the reason why we are having the BBQ, or braai as they like to call it in this part of the world.'

'There is so much to organise,' Sylvia complained, this even though she was one of life's great home entertainers.

'There's Mercy and Audrey,' Eric replied, referring to their newly employed cook and house helper. He didn't add, Mr. Bombay the gardener, Henry the driver nor the three security guards, all of whom were setting up the outdoor table, chairs and whatever other jobs needed doing. Eric was responsible for the full-time employment of seven, and in the case of Audrey, provided servant quarters where she lived with her two young daughters and husband, one of the guards.

Being directly responsible for the well-being of so many at home was a new experience for Eric even though he was used to managing large teams in the office. Currently, he managed 237 on the various water projects, the number set to multiply many times when construction started; home economics raised up a different set of challenges for him.

'Henry is a thick African,' Sylvia contemptuously spat. 'I honestly don't know why we pay him.' The Afronian in question was within earshot but stayed utterly silent despite the insult; he was fearful his Madam would fire him from his highly desired job.

'Sylvia, how can you talk like that?' Eric admonished. 'Control yourself; we are guests in this wonderful country.'

Managing a staff of seven wasn't the only adjustment Sylvia had to make. 'The cost and palaver of maintaining the swimming pool is more hassle than its worth.'

'Can nothing make you happy? You craved a pool when we were in Hazelstone; the boys love it.'

'And now I don't have my own car.'

'We agreed we would buy a Land Rover Discovery for you,' this in addition to Eric's office car, a Toyota Prado.

'Supermarket prices are astronomical.'

'Well, if you refuse to go to the local markets and insist on expensive imported goods…' there was now exasperation to Eric's voice.

'And the school run is horrendous.'

'To the very good international school, I might add, and which by the way HydroDevelop pay the full $5,500 per term fees… for both boys.'

'We deserve the help for all the extra stress I have to put up with,' Sylvia said to end the conversation as she skulked towards the kitchen. 'The weather though is marvellous,' came Sylvia's voice from between the sound of a heavy knife rapidly crashing into a wooden cutting block. 'But it's too hot.'

Give me strength. Eric wisely kept his own counsel rather than starting a new argument. With the welcoming sea breeze and watching his sons horsing around with inflated toys in the gleaming twenty-metre swimming pool, Eric's mind moved from domestic issues to the weekly meeting two days earlier.

'When we diverted the Wahilistan River in preparation for the first phase of the dam, it seems to have unleashed a localized outbreak of a particularly virulent strain of Malaria,' Steven had informed the Executive Committee.

'We'll need a dual strategy of containment and eradication,' HydroDevelop's consultant doctor recommended.

Eric stood up and walked over to the whiteboard, marker pen at the ready. 'Let's brainstorm. We don't want this to become an elephant in the corner of the room. We have a clean sheet of paper and should think outside of the box to see if we can turn this to our advantage.' *What business bullshit,* he laughed to himself when he sat down and looked expectantly at his senior management team. *My dad,* a miner in the South Wales Valleys, *would be turning in his grave if he heard me.*

'We should advocate all locals to do extreme gardening,' the Environmental Impact Assessor suggested.

'Continue.'

'To prevent malaria, we must cull the mosquito population. This can be achieved by cutting their food supply. By removing flowers from common shrubs, depriving the older, adult female insects of nectar, and they are the ones that transmit malaria, research indicates this strategy will eradicate many through starvation.'

'There's certainly a logic.' *Thank God we are fully medically insured,* this being one further perk to Eric's compensation package, together with thirty days of paid holidays and three flights for the whole family back to the UK.

'There is no need for insecticides or drugs in this method; it's very cost efficient.'

'Any other suggestions? We also have to think of the bigger picture, have a strategy that benefits HydroDevelop; we have dues to pay.' *Am I a heartless bastard for posing such a demand?* Eric questioned, before remembering, *Charlie Bloody Daniels is the real heartless bastard; he didn't stop reminding me how HydroDevelop owes the British Government big time.*

'Malaria is a country wide problem, everybody acknowledges the challenge,' the Chief Financial Officer, a minority shareholder in HydroDevelop pointed out, and who had also been in the meeting with Charlie. 'Health services are only one human or natural disaster away to being overwhelmed. The Ministry of Health is woefully underfunded and understaffed. They have a wish list of capital projects and technical assistance requests as long as your arm,' he continued confidently as he caught the eye of Eric. 'Malaria can never be attributed to HydroDevelop, but we could use some of our CSR budget to build medical clinics, do medical outreach, support the extreme gardening and... bring in British teams who have expertise in Malaria eradication through trialling genetically modified mosquitoes which can't reproduce; a single breeding female could cause havoc.

'Do you have a British company in mind?' Eric asked as he teed up the CFO.

'Why a British company?' a voice innocently enquired.

'Don't be naïve,' an irritated Eric rebutted. 'Who do you think helped HydroDevelop win the contract; this is payback.' He paused and pondered. 'It would not be the worse outcome if the outbreak continued a little longer than necessary with the objective to help establish the British company into the Afronian health sector—'

'And the government would be ever more grateful to the British for helping to control the outbreak—a win-win for HydroDevelop and the Westminster mandarins.' *And Charlie Daniels*, the CFO didn't add. 'Aid and development is a, you scratch my back I'll scratch yours, business,' he clarified, when he saw the expression of shock at the real politick on the faces of some of those round the table.

'And the villagers that die of Malaria?' a lone voice questioned.

'Collateral damage,' Eric mumbled as he stood up, the meeting ending abruptly.

I have reached the pinnacle of my profession, but did I sign a deal with the devil when signing my contract? Eric, for the first time queried the ethics of being the senior engineer and de-facto Afronian CEO of HydroDevelop.

Steven hadn't been present at the meeting with Charlie Daniels. While his boss was discussing the intricacies of British soft power, he was in an off-licence buying a bottle of Afronia white wine to take to a new friend's birthday party.

Nice garden, Steve thought to himself, this after he was let through by the guard and drove into a $3,500 rent per month property, *That's presumably paid by the NGO that Josh works for.*

Parking the car to the sound of loud music, he looked on covetously while he considered his two-bedroom apartment on the twelfth floor of a newly opened block of flats. His jealousy was suspended when two teenage bikini wearing girls ran past him with Super-Soaker water pistols; they were being chased by the host, 59-year-old Joshua Scott, the Chief of Party of Brits for Afronians. *It's going to be that sort of party; what fun!*

'Welcome to my villa; come on in,' the host invited his guest. 'Thanks for the wine. Come in, feel free. There's plenty of drinks... and girls to go around. And don't worry if you didn't bring swimming trunks... skinny dipping is very much encouraged.'

'Are the girls old enough?' Steven was a little concerned.

'You clearly haven't worked in a developing country before?' Joshua belly laughed.

'No.'

'Stop worrying. They all said... they're over 18. Worse-case scenario, I give the Police Commissioner a bottle of vodka, some beers and $30 to make any mischief go away. Don't worry, this is not puritanical United Kingdom. Besides, John Banwell, the British embassy spokesman is here. These girls will be glad to get paid and have free drinks, and maybe they will hook themselves a boyfriend? Stop worrying, enjoy yourself. Beautiful young girls are a perk of the job for working in countries such as Afronia.'

Chapter 18

'MO, CAN WE HAVE A CHAT?' This polite request with the ever-popular Geordie, Muslim fisherman, had much to the surprise of the charity founder originated from David Howells.

'Sure.'

The unlikely pair were in the George and Dragon, a pub that up until two-months earlier David had been loath to enter due to his racist views, and the embarrassment from his last visit, this being when steaming drunk and he'd threatened Dr. Ralph Lisoyga, Innocent Shembles and Charles Ontago—the latter two at the time were working on his trawler—with a shotgun. 'Is it right that taxpayer money should pay for international development and support British supermarkets who are already making billions in profits? That money should be spent on the NHS or our armed forces,' his voice rising in pitch from one of pleasant conversation to mild outrage.

'By promoting economic inclusiveness, health and security, we stabilize vulnerable parts of the world,' Mo serenely replied. 'If our tax didn't go on these efforts there would be more not less migrants arriving on these shores. There would also be more and not less terrorists.'

'That's utter nonsense. Liberal gobbledygook.'

'Is it?' Mo questioned in a hard voice. He looked David square in the eye. 'Do you remember the 2013/14 Ebola outbreak in West Africa that killed more than 11,000 people? What do you think would have happened if it had been left unchecked to the country's crumbling health infrastructure?' Mo paused to see if David would come up with a response—he didn't. 'It was fortuitous that health workers on an anti-polio campaign in the region bravely volunteered for reassignment. The epidemic would have been much worse if it had not been contained with taxpayer money from rich countries, including the UK.'

'Ok, what else?'

'In the West, the HIV /AIDS epidemic is predominantly limited to sexual minority groupings and drug users, whereas in much of Sub-Saharan Africa and where a good deal of refugees come from, it's within the heterosexual population. What do you think would happen if those countries didn't have donor money to help prop up their health systems?' Mo paused again to see if David would make a suggestion; again he kept quiet. 'First of all, their working age population would be decimated. governments would be overthrown and countries would become failed states due to a falling tax base and faltering economy. And then refugees in even greater numbers would come to Europe. Do not think British taxes are just for do-gooder projects that have not relevance. Of course, if there were fairer trading agreements, the global financial system was more even and the use of offshore tax heavens was restricted, then the need for aid would be replaced through tax revenue generating activities.'

'Hmmn.' David was flummoxed.

'Investing in avocados, macadamias and other food stuffs in developing economies helps increase supply to meet western demand and keep prices in our supermarkets reasonable while building viable business opportunities for African farmers and increasing tax income so that their governments can invest in social services and their citizens don't become refugees in the first place!'

'But what about—'

'The stories you read in the papers?' Mo interrupted. 'Red-top fodder. Yes, there are some bad projects and, yes, money isn't always spent wisely or goes missing through corruption, but that's a minority of cases. All in all, aid money is socially good and an economic necessity. Don't let the right-wing media dissuade you from what is morally correct and a social and economic imperative; a more equal and just world is better for everyone.'

'And if we stop giving aid?' David asked, his views starting to waiver.

'Great question,' Mo, congratulated without a hint of sarcasm. 'This is what we must ask our politicians. Just think of Syria. The rural masses were faced with their worst ever drought and which drove them into the cities and where they started to question why their government didn't do more for them. With limited foreign support, and admittedly with many other factors at play... the revolution started and refugees poured into Europe.'

'I read the underlying problems of Syria started in 2008.'

'Correct, around the time of the financial crisis. Western democracies claimed they had no money to spare... but consider how much the consequences of the Syrian civil war has cost western taxpayers.'

'Oh.'

'Why do you think American generals and admirals wrote a letter to their president and argued that USAID programs should continue… they understand the impact soft power has in preventing chaos and conflicts. Less than a penny in every tax pound goes to aid projects; it's a great investment.'

'Is it right that so many Afronians live in Hazelstone?' that number now exceeding 500.

'Yes, though the conditions they live in are a disgrace. As a community, Hazelstonians must take responsibility; that's why I started Ask An Afronian Anything,' this being the forum for where the conversation was taking place.

Just under a mile from the George and Dragon, on the Beaufort Estate, Sara was in her boxroom where the wallpaper was peeling from damp, mould was growing on every surface, the windows were cracked, the heating didn't work and, there were loose wires protruding everywhere she looked. 'I worry about my health,' she complained to Grace and who was similarly wrapped in layers of donated clothes to keep out the biting cold. 'I constantly get a fever or cough. My eczema is a real problem.' Sara peered disdainfully round the room the UK Home Office had described as habitable. 'My furniture is broken, appliances faulty and rodents come through the skirting boards or holes in the walls. I wish I had the chance to go back to the new Afronia I read about on Facebook.' A smile spread across her face at the thought of seeing friends and family again.

'There is too much death and fear for me to ever go back. I saw people being cut to pieces in front of my eyes. I was raped many times. I will never willingly go back; my family sacrificed so much to raise the money to get me here, it would be an insult to return.'

Outside the dilapidated block of flats there was a group of teenage Afronian boys and girls, alliances made solely on where one was from or which migratory route had been taken. All were restless as no education was offered and there was little to keep their inquisitive minds at bay; the unaccustomed cold and damp kept them indoors in unstructured idleness.

A group of thirteen boys walked into the village. They were led by the eldest and tallest, sixteen-year-old Abdullah. He had collected what little money the gang had. 'Three bottles of Cider K,' he ordered the two-litre, cheap, super-strength white cider.

'Are you old enough? Are you from the estate?' the newsagent asked with a look of undisguised mistrust.

'I'm buying,' Abdullah responded slapping a fist full of coins on the counter and daring the proprietor not to take it. The store owner grudgingly took the cash, the financial reality of running a small business meaning he turned a blindeye to underage drinking. It was a scenario played out by teenagers and liquor store staff up and down the land, the entrepreneur trying to keep their enterprise afloat, the teenager wanting to drink away their sorrows while talking wildly of their hope and dreams for a better tomorrow.

'Fuck, them!' Farouk, an agitated fifteen-year-old who had seen his father obliterated in a Death Eagle drone strike, said when looking in the direction of a group of local kids, this while taking a long swig from the industrial strength wine he'd stolen while Abdullah had blocked the entrepreneur's view.

'Anger will get you nowhere, brother,' Abdullah tried to reason.

'White kids our age look, point, laugh and taunt us; they have no idea of the life we left behind.'

'That's the point, brother, they don't know their luck in being born in this peaceful country.'

'They mock our accents, our poverty,' Farouk continued as he looked appreciatively at an approaching group of Afronian girls, 'our culture and our ethnicity.'

'They are ignorant. Like us, they are also trying to find their way in the world.'

'But they must have been taught to hate otherwise, why would they insult us so? We are just poor niggers to them.'

'They are patronising,' Sharon from Lirobi complained. 'They say we should be grateful for the shitholes we live in.'

'My father was a surgeon at Umoja City Hospital,' another girl informed the now enlarged group. 'These people mock him as a witchdoctor if he so much as administers a plaster or prescribes Penicillin.'

'Soon we will be part of their community. Adults will teach us and we will play football with their kids; we must have patience.'

'And how long will that take?' Farouk wanted to know before taking another long swig. 'Afronia had its problems, but it' just as beautiful, fun, romantic and energetic as here. It was our dreams which were squeezed by fear.'

'I laughed when I saw a sign on the gate to the horse farm, saying: don't feed the animals. It was in English and Arabic, as if these are the only languages we know—'

'Or that we had food to spare,' Abdullah added. 'It is us who live like animals. We should have signs around our necks, saying, approach with caution.' This brought out a loud round of drunken laughter.

'I will open a shisha bar on the estate,' the entrepreneurially minded Farouk informed his new friends. 'There is no prohibition against smoking strawberry or melon.'

'And I'll have a hair salon,' this from Sharon. 'Back home I helped my sisters when I wanted pocket money.'

Before long, the alcohol was finished and the teenagers departed in ones and twos, carelessly leaving behind broken bottles, puke and cigarette butts... just as the British youths did, but it would be the Afronians who would inevitably be blamed by the majority of villagers.

Chapter 19

AFTER A LONG DAY, Eric and Steven were taken from their HydroDevelop office to Lesotho Street, the capital's party area and where once again foreigners mingled with locals in the shopping malls, at the cinema or in the numerous bars and restaurants. The drive was slow, the Ford Explorer edging through the traffic-choked city, the lanes crammed with white NGO Land Cruisers, ancient Toyotas, overflowing minibuses and green tuk-tuks which buzzed between the mayhem like angry gnats.

As part of his role, Eric was the chairman of Hydro-Develop's Corporate Social Responsibility committee. 'We have a large budget and we need to use it,' this said while supping from a cold bottle of BirtBeer as the pair waited in the congestion.

'Do you have something in mind?'

'I have lots of ideas, but it's not my job to come up with them, it's yours!'

'There's a budget of $50,000?' Steven wanted to confirm. 'We could use it on one event that will capture the public's imagination.' He paused to take a drag of beer and started to hum-and-har in deep concentration. 'An annual showcase that we sponsor and become eponymous with. How about a multi-stage bike event?'

Eric, a keen cyclist, was thrilled by the idea. 'Make it happen,' he summarily decided. 'Ensure the route goes past some of the sites we're working at. Also…' Eric thought back to his meeting at the Yacht Club the night before with Charlie Daniels, 'make sure there are messages around road safety for cyclists.'

Cycling through the scenic wilderness of Afronia was of no concern to Professor Rashid and who was attending a politburo meeting. 'We have to be careful of not fostering a two-speed economy. We can't have industrialists, privatizations and foreign direct investment with favourable tax incentives on the one hand and, not supporting micro-entrepreneurs in the informal economy on the other; we will be storing up trouble. Already there are symptoms of economic discontent.' He nodded to his personal assistant to hand out an article to all attendees.

Afronians dying for a drink
No one knows exactly how large the Afronian slum of Little Wahili is nor the number of inhabitants and which is guesstimated at anywhere between two and four hundred thousand. Located on the northern shore of the Umoja City River, as one walks through the litter strewn backstreets and alleyways, one passes timber sellers, bicycle repairers, bottlestores, massage parlours, second-hand clothes shops, coffin carpenters, fish mongers, Halal butchers… and every other con-

ceivable type of informal and untaxed business, the adventurer never sure what they will find round the next corner.

The residents are proud, hardworking and loyal, many going on a daily exodus to lowly paid jobs, whether as a nanny, garden-boy or guard. Those with vocational skills: plumbers, builders, mechanics and electricians, carry the tools of their trade under their arms as they either take a mini-bus to work or walk to save the fee. Many live in deplorable conditions. Children play in open sewers and handicap beggars in torn clothes are a common sight, but the residents of Little Wahili are more than slum dwellers, they are humans who like nothing more than to share joys and sorrows, chat politics over a coffee, have a beer or cup of tea and, smoke cigarettes, joints or pass a shisha pipe around. In the words of Walter Blaise, Little Wahili is a God-fearing community and the moral compass of the nation; they can either be your friends or foes... but they are never ambivalent.

Like Hillview before it was developed into an upmarket area, Little Wahili is the undeniable heartbeat and soul of Afronia, but it has an increasingly worrisome problem with alcohol consumption as seen in the rise in the number of booze dens where 24/7 imbibers can be found.

It's 7 AM when I enter Beethoven's, the ironically named drinking establishment which blasts reggae music round the clock and is located in the centre of the huge cornucopia of stalls and shops from where an estimated 50,000 people earn their daily living selling everything from fruit and dried fish to cheap sex and car parts.

On a broken plastic chair in the corner are N'gaa and Michael, two plumbers in their late twenties and whose voices have slowed to a slur from a night of consumption.

"Solomon Brew costs 90 Shillings," N'gaa informs me, the draught beer coming from the re-nationalised brewery that was once the pride and joy of the former Life President. "A shot of AfroJaeger is only 10 Shillings and it's just as effective," he adds with a glint from his bloodshot eyes, this in reference to the fifty-five percent proof illegal spirit whose slang name is "Quick Times", the tipple being the most sought after of the highly lucrative and often deadly moonshine trade that's sweeping the country.

While the newly affluent in the redeveloped areas of Hillview drink highly taxed imported beers and spirits, the urban poor have no choice but abstinence or cheap and potent illegal brews whose content has been known to include a noxious concoction of river water, stolen industrial cleaning agents and even diesel fuel. The only time this illicit trade is acknowledged is when a particularly poisonous batch ends in drinkers going blind before fatal liver and kidney failure. "What else can we afford that will get us through the day and allow us to forget?" Michael sums up the predicament of many.

Foreign investors in the brewing sector have asked for tax breaks so they can produce commercially viable, cheap and safer alternatives. However, providing affordable alcohol in large quantities brings its own set of problems: low economic output, an increase in the number of Sexually Transmitted Diseases, fights, murders, domestic abuse and road deaths. In the last festive season alone, close to 5,000 motorists were arrested for driving under the influence of alcohol, this in a national carpool of little more than 100,000 vehicles.

It's now 8 AM and N'gaa tries to get up from his plastic chair, "Now I have courage to find work," he unsteadily informs me. "I have a lorry driving license," he starts to say when suddenly the chair he's been holding onto flies backwards and he falls to the ground in a heap, this much to the merriment of Beethoven's regulars.

'We can't abandon the people living in the slums,' the president said in a voice that betrayed his inner worries. 'We must improve all aspects of life for every single Afronian. No one can be left behind in the Second Republic. What suggestions do you have?'

'We have to acknowledge that alcohol is a big part of socializing, whether in well to-do neighbourhoods or booze dens,' the Minister for Health stated. 'If you walk the squalid streets of Little Wahili you'll find many more watering holes than health clinics, libraries or schools; some claim to the magnitude of ten. Getting excessively drunk is part of our culture.'

'What about community efforts in educating how to drink safely,' the Transport Minister—and who had been specifically invited to the politburo meeting by Professor Rashid—suggested. 'We must treat those drunk behind the wheel more harshly than just detaining them a short while to sober up before then appearing in court to receive a paltry fine, or worse, bribe a traffic police officer to evade charges.'

'This is a public health issue,' Dr Ralph Lisoyga started to argue. 'We should raise the age limit to buy alcohol from eighteen to twenty-one.'

'If someone is old enough to vote and serve in the armed forces, then they're old enough to decide how to spend their money,' Professor Rashid countered.

'We could make vendors liable,' the Minister of Trade and Industry suggested. 'If they sell alcohol to someone who's already drunk, their license should be confiscated.'

'We would risk a host of challenges, namely, what is drunkenness?' The female Justice Minister replied.

'These are all worthwhile suggestions which need to be investigated,' the president agreed as he stood up. 'But is excessive alcohol consumption a symptom or a cause of social disharmony? In the case of deadly moonshine, part of the cause is poverty. For the more well-heeled,' Blaise paused and looked round the room catching the eye of a few who liked more than the occasional glass of Afronian red, 'we have to educate about the dangers of drink driving and drunken fornication.'

'Drinking is partly an economic problem. We need more tax to invest in schools, hospitals, social services and development of the regional capitals,' Professor

Rashid spoke up. 'We must create the environment for competition and make it easier to, A) start and grow a business and, B) make paying tax an honourable endeavour rather than a game of cat-and-mouse.' With no dissenting voices, he continued. 'We have opened our doors to foreign investors, but with the economy forecast to grow at fifteen-percent this year, now is the time to examine our cocktail of incentives for investors, especially in the extractive industries.'

'We must renegotiate our mining and logging agreements with multinational companies,' the Minister of Natural Resources said, this after taking a sip of water to wet his parched lips, 'We should raise the threshold of Afronian ownership or we will not have the tax base to fund our social development programs. I propose that all extractive companies pay two-percent of their annual turnover direct to the treasury. Prospecting rights must be sixty-percent Afronian owned mining rights can be thirty-five percent. Procurement of mining products and services from Afronian companies should be raised to eighty-percent. We must reverse all current exploitative contracts or Afronians will never enjoy the fruits of our natural resources as the current laws and investment incentives are effectively a means for mining companies to not pay tax.'

'Really?' the president queried not realizing the size of the task at hand.

'The current Mining and Logging Act allows for 100-percent ownership by foreign corporations. They enjoy five-year tax-free holidays, can repatriate 100-percent of their profits and, have VAT exemptions on imports of capital goods. It's common practice that when the tax holiday ends, the contract is sold by the parent company to a subsidiary and thus they enjoy another five years of extraordinary profits.'

'Will your proposed changes limit investment?' the Minister for Industry and Trade asked.

'I don't think so and not if we introduce competitive corporate tax rates based on a tariff structure, for instance, fifteen-percent for the first five years and twenty-percent for the next ten. Importantly, we must ensure transparency between the government and investors so there are no corrupt deals; audit trails must be open to independent scrutiny.'

'We must also stop companies benefiting from double taxation treaties that were signed under the Solomon regime. It is reprehensible that foreign companies can decide where to pay tax. This is tax avoidance,' Professor Rashid clarified, 'and we lose an estimated $500 million every year.'

'That is untenable,' Walter slammed his fist onto the boardroom table in a fit of rage. 'We can't fritter money away and which should be used to build schools and pay doctors. We must maximise our natural resources. A commission into multi-lateral economic agreements must be set up. Immediately! And this brings me to the last part of the meeting.' The president stood up and started walking round the table and handing out a sheaf of papers. 'Twenty kilometres up the coast is the fishing village of Zarusha. The once sleepy fishing village is being turned into an industrial zone with towering, foreign owned trawlers. Processing plants are appearing in great numbers. The rickety shacks that once lined the shore and canoes which harvested the fish for generations are being forced out of business. While we must encourage foreign investment, profits must be re-invested in these communities and the villagers employed. Otherwise, first, they will sabotage foreign owned businesses and scare them away and, after that, they will hold the government liable. If we are not careful, we will create an environment ripe for revolution.'

Chapter 20

KAMDONYO WANJUBI, A twenty-three-year-old mecha-nical and electrical engineering graduate from Umoja City University, was a serial entrepreneur. An orphan from humble beginnings, he'd earned his way through school and university through numerous money-making schemes. He got his big break when his anti-piracy drone was selected by Jacob and Emmanuel to be in the first round of business incubatees. He had recently gone back to the incubator to ask for seed-funding for his second prototype, an agricultural drone that could spray crops that tractors and traditional farm machinery couldn't reach. These drones were powerful enough to carry 20-litres of fertiliser or pesticides and could follow pre-mapped GPS routes; in some mountainous regions it was the first time they had ever been farmed.

Amina, Kamdonyo's girlfriend, was forced into mar-riage at the age of thirteen to a man fifty years her senior and who had grandchildren older than her. When her husband suddenly died of a heart attack, she refused to go back to her parent's village and instead went to the Second Chance Orphanage claiming her parents had died. Returning to school aged seventeen, Amina entered primary year five. She was the eldest in her class of seventy-two and was ashamed of this fact but happy she could study once more. The teachers and Kamdonyo supported Amina throughout, and for three consecutive years of hard study she completed two academic years inside twelve months.

Completing secondary school as the Umoja City Peace Accord was being drafted, Kamdonyo and his beau decided that nothing would stop them building a new Afronia. Amina entered a teacher training college to give back to other orphans and her boyfriend became a businessman.

Kamdonyo newest project was very close to his heart. 'I need to do something that gives back to the teachers that help so many,' he said to Amina as they started to brainstorm.

'What are teachers' biggest challenges?'

'Apart from a lack of materials, poor training and not getting a sufficient salary... basic communications. I remember a rural teacher complaining that she missed an important meeting, by a week, as the get-together was organised on WhatsApp and she didn't have a signal.'

Kamdonyo's brain switched into business gear. 'Phones are cheap. Basic feature phones are only $10 and even smartphones can be bought for $50, but that doesn't matter if there is no network coverage, and which understandably follows the major trade routes rather than sparsely populated rural areas.'

'We need a low-cost base station specifically designed for rural areas,' Amina summarised. 'But how? Solar would seem the logical solution for energy. We need a business model that the mobile operators can buy into.'

The pair started to research online what the costs of a basic base station would be, how big an area it could provide a signal to, what were the solar energy requirements and, where were suitable rural communities that had a dense enough population that such a service would be financially sustainable.

Developing social businesses was what the two lived for. At college, Amina had recently established an environmental group of fellow student teachers, deciding, *In villages and towns throughout Afronia, teachers have the potential to be transformational, not just for students but for the respect they are afforded by the community at large.*

'We must address climate change,' Amina had implored at her first meeting of: Teachers for the Environment, 'otherwise there will be no biodiversity for future generations. Our rural brethren will flock to our already overcrowded cities seeking jobs as the farming life becomes increasingly impossible.'

'What suggestions do you have?' Kamdonyo, who was attending as Amina's guest, had asked.

'Rapid deforestation for charcoal burning, firewood and timber, will end in desertification; look at Harari Region. We must start reforestation.'

'To be sustainable it has to be commercially viable,' Kamdonyo advised. 'Orchards are good as they can be part of the supply chain for local fruit processors rather than importing juices.' This idea got him a round of applause. 'I will talk to some programmer friends at the incubator to see if they can develop an application to map where deforestation is a problem and where tree planting projects are already taking place,' he offered.

'That would be great,' Amina enthused. 'If we can get every Afronian to plant just one tree, once a year, we would start to turn back the clock.'

'Why so conservative?' Kamdonyo dismissed. 'We can take inspiration from other African countries. In Zambia, they have launched a campaign—Plant a Million Trees.'

'That's not a lot,' Amina pointed out.

'I don't get the name as their target is 2 BILLION trees by 2021! This will also help to diversify the economy away from their overdependence on copper mining. They want to literally grow money through carbon capture and various fruit and wood-based livelihoods while supporting the environment. It's part of their commitment to the 2015 Paris Agreement.'

'In Walter Blaise I'm sure we would have a willing supporter. Reforestation will contribute to Afronia's attainment of the United Nations seventeen Sustainable Development Goals.'

'We must use social media to raise awareness and get people involved, especially the youth,' Kamdonyo recommended.

'We can educate the multi-nationals who do so much of the damage and use some of their Corporate Social Responsibility money to pay for community projects,' another voice suggested.

'We must reach out to those who are project managing Africa's Great Green Wall,' someone else proposed.

'What's that?' Amina asked with a tinge of excitement. She'd not heard of the project but the mere mentioning of a Pan-African ecological venture exhilarated her.

'It's a 4,000-mile task along the southern edge of the Saharan Desert. It has the triple aim of stopping desertification, restoring degraded land and promoting green business for income generation and food security. There is hope that it will also stem the flow of migrants to Europe and which has profound as impact on where the refugees leave as to where they go. There are estimates that 60 million refugees will leave Africa and go to Europe by 2030 due to desertification alone. That's why projects such as the Green Wall are financially backed by the World Bank, European Union and others.'

'Is it realistic?' a dissenting voice tested.

'While it was originally conceived as a literal physical barrier of trees against the desert, in reality it's a range of projects with common aims, after all, it is not just those from war or famine hit countries that migrate.'

'It sounds like a pipe dream of well-meaning whites, who while having a sundowner and enjoying their fat expat salaries think they can save the world. It has no chance,' this from Muhammad and whose father had recently been made redundant from a British NGO, this two days after the compensation packages of senior foreign management had been leaked to the national press. The scandal had caused opprobrium in the Afronian parliament and naval gazing by the international aid community.

'Ethiopia has already reclaimed 15 million hectares and Nigeria 5; Afronia has to do its bit,' Amina replied, as she saw tears come to the eyes of Muhammad.

Leaving the student teacher meeting with a long to-do list, Amina and Kamdonyo went to the newly established

Village Water Scheme in their sector of Little Wahili; they had volunteered to be board members. The water supply and management problems had been brought into sharp focus earlier in the week when incessant rains had turned the slum into an open sewer, refuse and sewage flowing freely down the small alleyways as gutters and rain trenches were blocked and became breeding grounds for mosquitoes and Cholera.

'We have three significant problems which need to be solved if we want consistent water supply,' the chairwoman started the meeting. 'Water supply, water wastage from cracked pipes and, removal and treatment of wastewater and sewage.'

'The government will be investing in all appropriate infrastructure,' the city council representative informed the gathering.

'Is there sufficient budget?' the dubious chairwoman examined.

'Yes,' came the quick-fire reply. 'The investment will be in phases,' he qualified. 'First, we will work on supply; anything the community can do in restricting wastage the better.'

'What are the main sources of water loss?' Kamdonyo probed.

'Burst pipes, unregulated meters and… home consumption in the bathroom.'

'Flushing the toilet?' Kamdonyo wanted to clarify.

'Yes,' the councillor confirmed, 'and that's why there are so many latrine pits as it's simply too expensive for many to build, maintain and fund the cost of water for flushing toilets. It's a social and public health imperative that restroom facilities in Little Wahili are improved; a contagious disease could emerge any time.

Another entrepreneurship challenge, Kamdonyo considered as the meeting concluded and he walked home hand-in-hand with Amina to their humble abode after an exhausting day. *Where and how do I start to find possible solutions?*

The next morning, Kamdonyo went to the outdoor privy in their backyard, and which measured fifteen square meters, this a relative ocean compared to virtually all their neighbours. Three chickens flanked by their fluffy chicks wandered around the yard pecking at anything remotely resembling food. The selling of eggs from the barred windows in a small shack built into their brick fence was yet one more source of income for the entrepreneurial duo.

I need to design something cleaner than this, Kamdonyo thought as he looked at the roofless structure which contained their private pit latrine, this privacy a comparative luxury compared to the majority of Little Wahili's residents who were forced to use communal toilets. *It needs to be economically affordable, hygienic and safe,* he added to his list of requirements. Safety had been bought into sharp relief the previous week when a neighbour's child had fallen into the shit pit and literally drowned in excrement. *Something which can be indoors,* yet another consideration, *as women and children are often attacked at night while relieving themselves in public spaces. But this will bring up the challenge of smell,* he realized.

So, the solution must have an easy way to take-away human waste quickly but without the cost as plumbing and water or it will be prohibitively expensive for most.

Having noted the key necessities for his indoor, water-less, hygienic and safe toilet, he went for a walk through the neighbourhood to embrace the challenge and the potentially huge benefit he could bring to his community if he could find a workable design. *Can my mind work through the juxtaposition of the obstacles this task has set me?*

Without being conscious of where he was walking, after an hour of aimless ambling he found himself outside Geronimo's tea shop on the Hillview promenade, a ramshackle building which through popular demand had been saved from the developer's diggers, cranes and bulldozers. *If I can't use water, how else can waste be removed? Some sort of bagging system? How would the bags be collected, as bags of poo can't be held for a long time in a house? If it is removed, to where and for what purpose? Can it be used for manure, biogas or something else? Questions, but nothing which sounds impossible. As Plato would remind me: necessity, is the mother of invention.*

Chapter 21

As much as a culture of innovation and entrepre-neurship was being fostered in Afronia, so too was big business making its impact felt. Nationally, the big-gest maize crop since independence had been harvested and this after the devastating drought and the civil war had largely decimated the agriculture sector for the previ-ous five years; it was quite the endorsement for the presi-dent and his minister of agriculture.

'The bumper harvest was the result of finally having good rains and improved inputs. The extra produce will push food prices down; it's a welcome relief for many households,' the minister exalted in the quiet adulation of the press conference he'd organised. 'With the forthcom-ing launch of a micro-insurance product for crops, the launch of an Agricultural Transformation Agency and, a Crop Marketing Exchange, two quasi-government or-ganisations that follows Ethiopia's success, and the build-ing of the port, railway, road and waterway systems, Pres-ident Blaise expects Afronia to become the breadbasket for the region within the coming three years.'

There was good news on many fronts for Walter Blaise and his economic revolution, however, there was one fly in the ointment, a report had circulated in rural areas and which had been placed anonymously by MH-16. Henshaw, he of the utmost dubious morality, had been contacted by persons unknown to carry out this task and to place articles in national newspapers that disparaged President Blaise by questioning his self-promoted economic miracle. The first article—Mike had one of his minions bribe a newspaper editor to place—concerned the rise in shebeens and the drinking of moonshine.

GMO conspiracy or Afronian reality?

President Blaise is heading the Green Revolution in an effort to make Afronia food secure and replace poverty with prosperity, but at what cost?

There is no doubting that Afronia is making the financial and technological commitments needed to increase crop production, and hats must be taken off as production figures indicate that 2021 will be a bumper crop. But talked about less is the use of genetically modified crops, better known as Genetically Modified Organisms (GMOs). Independent researchers state, "The government is suppressing data that shows certain seed varieties, chemicals and pesticides that they are promoting cause long-term harm to health, including male infertility. They may also end up causing food shortages through crops becoming more vulnerable."

It is a certifiable fact that Walter Blaise personally pushed through the re-nationalisation of Solomon Agri Company which sells both seed and pesticide products. The business is still part-owned by foreign shareholders and who provide the raw materials for both the chemicals and pesticides as well as conduct research on seed multiplication; this is a distinct conflict of interest. A Commission of Enquiry must be set up to investigate the president's involvement into these troubling revelations.

'It's hocus-pocus. Absolutely no truth to the insinuations let alone facts! Nevertheless, what should our response be?' the president queried his minister of agriculture.

'GMO's are safe and can help prevent certain malnutrition related diseases. Draught resistant crops can improve food security and will become increasingly important due to the impact of climate change. The arguments to use them are overwhelming when you stick to the science.'

'And what about the claim on connivance between seed and pesticide companies?'

'They are hollow words of conspiracy. We don't need to respond much less set up a probe. The re-nationalisation was done in a very transparent manner.'

'Very well,' the president agreed not wanting anything to distract from the significant progress being made. 'What about the Harari Region? Why is food still not getting to the neediest?'

'We are doing everything that we can, Sir.'

'That's not good enough,' Blaise thundered as he walked over to the window and looked out on Presidential Square. 'We are making progress in developing the country. Both tourists and investors see Afronia as an attractive country to spend their money, but if our people are suffering and the levels of inequality get too large, we could head straight back to civil war. We have to act quickly to resolve the issue of hunger in Harari region.'

'Yes, Sir. We know the importance of getting food to the neediest; many people are getting aid.'

'How many?'

'Approximately half the rural population still faces starvation. There is mass movement into the towns and Darsburg's public services are being overwhelmed. Food prices are increasing every day and there have been riots outside government buildings.' The minister paused as he took a sip of ice-cold water; he was not sure how to continue. 'I have to report... some local administrators are deliberately withholding aid from opposition supporters—'

'That is unacceptable, we are a democracy,' Walter boomed. 'Who is ordering them to withhold food?'

'No one knows, Sir. We have investigated... but there are no leads as to where the orders are coming from.'

'This is a criminal matter; we dare not politicise food. The implications are too grave if we don't get a handle on this and quickly. Whoever is behind this outrage I will order the Police Commissioner to charge with treason.'

There was one last issue that Walter Blaise considered especially pressing, 'What is the state of the landfill site?' The eyesore that gave of a pungent smell was located on the north edge of the capital, when the wind blew south the noxious gases would spread across the city. However, the health hazard was also a necessity for the quickly developing city.

'There have been proposals to move the refuse ten kilometres beyond the city boundaries, but moving the dump means re-housing those at the new site as well as this who call the landfill home and from where they scavenge a livelihood.'

'Moving it must be prioritised before there is a catastrophe.'

'The city mayor has an insufficient budget for such a large project.'

'Talk to the Minister of the Economy and find the money. Moving the city to being more energy efficient and less polluting must be a civic priority. We want an inclusive Afronia and that means we can't let our citizens live on landfill sites; it's a national disgrace. What options are there?'

'I have seen a proposal for a thermal power plant that can daily combust 1,000 tonnes of waste into energy through boiling water, the steam driving a turbine generator and producing 80 megawatts, about sixty-percent of the city's current energy needs—'

'Perfect,' the president interrupted. 'When can the project be commissioned?'

'The City Council is in discussion with the Ministry of Private-Public Partnerships—'

'If there are any challenges that slow this project down, inform me and I will personally make sure it moves forward. Just a thought, can the British help fund this?'

For three days rain fell in the capital and caused untold misery and illness in Little Wahili, though that was as nothing compared to the outrage when the landfill under the weight of the sodden refuse, buckled and then bowed, squatters and their meagre belongings buried alive as the enormous heap of detritus collapsed.

'There was an almighty bang,' fourteen-year-old Musa told the Umoja City News as he recounted the seconds before his wooden shack topped with plastic sheeting disappeared with his teenage brother and little sister inside. 'A wall of debris rushed towards us like the sound of a train, nothing could stop it. When the thunder stopped, I desperately searched for my siblings but nothing and no one could be found; they were eaten alive by the mountain we called home.'

Chapter 22

A S MUCH AS AFRONIA was making impressive economic, environmental and social welfare progress, there were many who were not included in the Afronian Miracle. Included in this list were Abeker and Jamil and who were now embedded in the increasingly notorious MH-16.

Jamil was wandering the streets of Little Wahili and on the lookout for victims or willing accomplices—depending on your definition—for a new service that Henshaw had instigated. Jamil passed a number of beggars, *Who are desperate and thus good candidates... especially the children. Pre-pubescent shoeshine boys have so little they are easy to convince... but today, I need an adult.* He continued walking and passed teenage girls standing on street corners selling their bodies. There were also youngsters hawking chewing gum and packs of tissues through car windows at traffic lights. He saw one waif thin girl, *Who can't be older than eight,* suddenly get into a vehicle. *So fresh!* He lecherously licked his lips as he imagined what she was about to do with the motorist, *but I need a middle-aged man,* this as Jamil remembered the picture of his client.

Finally! Jamil had spotted a forlorn looking security guard outside a recently opened bank branch. 'Hello, friend, I'm Jameson,' he introduced himself to the shabbily dressed man in a torn and patched grey uniform and black beret.

'Can I help?' Fletcher replied, and who was grateful for any work he could find after living on the streets for the past six months after being forced to flee his draught hit village in Harari Region.

'I've not seen you before.'

'I started last week.'

'You must be very proud to be working here?'

'It's a job. It puts food on the table,' came the stoical, emotionless reply.

'Why so sad?' Jamil, picking up on the lack of spark in Fletcher's eyes and his despondent body language.

'This is so poorly paid, I have a second and third job,' Fletcher answered to Jamil's delight.

'Maybe I can help?' the former Jihadi smiled.

'How, brother?' the voice of Fletcher pleaded, his two daughters in an orphanage such was his lack of funds.

'I search for exceptional people,' Jamil started his pre-rehearsed speech, 'who are willing to help others live fulfilling lives.' This translated to: I need desperate people who will sell their organs as a last resort. With the enthusiastic encouragement of both Mustafa and Henshaw, Jamil and Abeker had become highly lucrative organ traders.

'What's the job? I will do anything.'

'How much for your kidney or eye?' Jamil asked after a long pause, all the while thinking of a Kuwaiti client and another based in London.

'What? You want—'

'Lucky for you, I'm paying top dollar for an eye and/ or kidney… and not your ears,' he joked. 'I'll pay $5,000 cash after the operation for your eye and $6,500 for your kidney; it's quick, easy money.'

How has it come to this? Do I look so pitiful that a stranger has the courage to offer to buy my body parts? Then again, what do I have to lose? Fletcher considered as he thought back to his sons being massacred by ISiSS.

'I'll pick you up tomorrow,' a smiling Jamil proposed when he saw Fletcher's head drop in resignation.

The next day Fletcher was outside the bank branch in the same tatty uniform. Jamil came as promised, but this time not alone, he had two beefy men accompanying him.

A look of shock crossed Fletcher's face. 'I've changed my—'

'Too late, my friend.' Jamil motioned for his two companions to accost Fletcher and put him into the back of the van where they blindfold him.

The vehicle drove the unwilling passenger for ten minutes arriving at a small, non-descript, dilapidated two-storey shack in the crowded back streets of Little Wahili. Jamil came to a halt, switched off the engine and turned in his seat. 'Give him the anaesthetic,' he commanded.

Two minutes later, Fletcher's unconscious body was lifted out of the van and taken through the front door of the building, under a blue tarpaulin and into a back room full of broken furniture and discarded electric fans with loose wires. There was a noisy small fridge humming in the corner and which Jamil proceeded to stock with water and various food stuffs. There was also an office desk which had seen better days, the drawers broken and spilling out faded and stained papers. In one corner of the room was a mattress with stains on it. *Its dried blood,* this as best as Jamil could tell, *though I can't rule out urine or excrement.*

The small party went under a clear plastic sheet into a temporary clinic where a doctor in full surgery garb was waiting for the unwilling, unconscious kidney donor. The operation to remove Fletcher's kidney took a mere forty-five minutes, after which he was patched up and placed on the skanky mattress, Jamil popping in to see him once a day for a week to both ensure the wound had not become infected and to top up the fridge.

'Why don't we kill him and keep the money?' Jamil complained to Mustafa on the fourth day after Fletcher's operation.

'We wouldn't get donors,' was the simple answer. 'This is an easy way for the desperate to make money; soon others will be coming to us rather than us having to search for them.'

While Jamil went searching for his next organ donor, Abeker was on an altogether different sort of hunt. In the vernacular, they were known as Afronian Ghosts. The individuals being referenced were albinos, that is to say, those with a congenital disorder which affected the production of melanin, the pigment which colours skin, hair and eyes. It was claimed by witch doctors, in myths, rituals, and superstitions purveyed over generations, that an albino's leg could detect gold and diamonds, a hand was good luck for fishing... genitals would increase fertility.

All body parts had some benefit to the end consumer and a whole body could fetch up to $50,000 on the grizzliest of black markets.

'What about that one?' Abeker pointed at a female child with albinism.

'She is too young; they must have breasts,' Abeker's criminal comrade reminded him.

'Surely, children have some worth; they must be good for some traditional medicine?'

'Of course, but that is not what we have been tasked to find.' And so they continued to drive on the still a widely held belief, despite recent public awareness campaigns to the contrary, that if you raped a woman with albinism you would be healed of any illness, including HIV / AIDS.

'Her?' Abeker inquired twenty minutes later as they drove past a trading centre on the outskirts of the capital.

'She will do,' came the heartless reply. 'We still need one more.'

Two days later, the pair of albino ladies were handcuffed and blindfolded, this as Abeker drove down the same street in Little Wahili where Fletcher's kidney had been cut out. The protesting women were taken into a building and lead down a flight of stairs to a basement where they would live out their days being sexually abused in the most horrific ways until their murder, suicide or escape would end their misery.

Chapter 23

NOT HAVING TO CONTEMPLATE the awfulness of organ donation or the kidnap and rape of albinos, were the members of the Jobuja Group and who were in a heavily guarded and secluded schloss in Alpine Bavaria, Germany. The billionaires, technology giants, aristocrats and political elite were attending a secretive two-day conclave to discuss the fate of nations.

'What do we think of Blaise?' came the ominous words of the chairman.

'He's pro-business,' a Hungarian politician pronounced.

'He isn't afraid of privatizations as shown by his water policy,' Sir Hilary Chapman of HydroDevelop gleefully commented.

'He is causing us problems,' Ulrich spoke up, the eyes of all conference attendees moving in the Swiss' direction. 'He's taken out a private lawsuit against UK Fuels and is in the process of altering regulation which would be detrimental to mining businesses. The worry is that if he is successful, and quite frankly there's little reason to expect he won't be, then other African countries may follow suit; the most we can do is to delay the inevitable.'

'What are our options for Afronia?' the chairman posed to the gathering.

'He has a reform agenda,' Chapman spoke up. 'You are taking one for the team, Ulrich,' he joked at Müller's expense.

The Swiss didn't find this at all funny, his face glowing red with anger. 'We need regime change. We bring back Isaiah George as he will do whatever we require him to do.'

'Afronians will never stand for that,' the chairman said dismissively. 'If there was a viable alternative that was sympathetic to our goals that would be a different matter. We must identify someone who is acceptable as president to the majority and who can then pursue our agenda.'

For the next two hours there were many suggestions as to how the Jobuja Group should move forward with Afronia, even from those who had no specific interest in the country but had influence and/or investments in other African countries.

'We'll have a secret ballot,' the chairman concluded, suggestions having been whittled down to five scenarios.

As discussions were happening in the German Alps, an article by Innocent Shembles caught the eye of President Blaise.

Solomon dictatorship denialism.
President Blaise's comments doubting the number of deaths during Altimus Solomon's dictatorship is a worrying sign. The question that needs

to be asked, is, whether denialist rhetoric in mainstream political discourse is a pre-emptor to Blaise becoming Afronia's next dictator?

Afronians suffered terribly under the brutal dictatorship of Altimus Solomon. For twenty-five years many were imprisoned or disappeared. Unknown numbers were killed by Death Eagles and village reprisals in the mountains of Southiland. The rebels claimed it was genocide, a view re-enforced by the Denga Chemical Massacre carried out by Isaiah George. There is no logical, ethical or moral justification to question the number of deaths by the state, unless there is a conspiracy the president is preparing the country for.

Earlier this week, Blaise was probed, "How many Southis were murdered during the Solomon era?" he replied, much to the consternation of the human rights community, "No one can be sure, but estimates range between 50,000 and 100,000." However, The Truth and Reconciliation Commission placed the minimum at 250,000. Sympathizers of the former regime claim this number is greatly exaggerated and that many of the deaths should be attributed to rebel terrorists, nevertheless, this estimate has been independently verified as the official number, and as president, Walter Blaise should honour the dead and missing.

While important work of identifying the human remains in unmarked graves continues, the political ramifications of the president's denialism are yet unknown.

In the same paper that Mike Henshaw had paid the editor $5,000 to ensure that the denial story appeared on the front page (falsely under Innocent Shembles name) there was also an article in the business section.

Blaise's toxic legacy.
"I want to be a doctor when I'm big," says thirteen-year-old Joseph. "All my family are ill," he clarifies. His family lives on the edge of Umoja City's Industrial Zone, and where, since Walter Blaise came to power, many of the environmental safety restrictions that were in place since independence were removed in the president's strategy to encourage foreign investors. However, economic growth seems to be at the expense of the next generation. "Kids playing here is unbelievable," said a local clergyman. "Blaise must be held responsible," so demanded a businessman and father.

According to pollution experts, there is unprecedented lead, mercury and chromium poisoning in the soil and water and from which many of the poor residents have no choice but to use for washing hands and clothes. Drinking water comes from nearby contaminated wells. Everyday infants and children—and who are particularly susceptible due to their underdeveloped organs—play in the poisonous area and become increasingly affected with brain damage, paralysis, blindness, and ultimately fatality. The signs are there, the children's performance at school comparing very badly to the national average. And yet, while the dangers are known, the president refuses to acknowledge the problem. No new restrictive or preventative measures have been enacted unlike the oil clean-up Altimus Solomon instigated when leaks were found in pipelines, the far-sighted vision of the former Life President ensuring long lasting and sustained economic development for the country.

'Where are these stories coming from?' Walter Blaise asked aloud, even though there was no one in the room. He was generally baffled. *This is a concerted attack against me, but why? And who? Hamza? Has that cheetah changed back to his old spots? No, I don't think so. Yohan then?*

Determined to see if there were any more stories which portrayed him in a bad light he went through the rest of the paper; another headline caught his eye.

Afronia's mobile money revolution gathers pace. Since the relaxation of financial regulations, combined with the issuing of three mobile network operator licences, Afronia has been on a whirlwind implementation of mobile money services and which has seen levels of financial inclusion go from a paltry twenty-two percent to over sixty. With business old and new wanting to be part of the technological revolution, and while there is still much work to be done to ensure mobile money agents earn enough commission to make a financially viable income, Afronia is set to become the second truly digital African economy after Kenya.

A study commissioned by the Central Bank of Afronia highlights the financial sector revolution. "Digital payments in Afronia have reached a critical point," the Governor declared on the public release of the report. "Banks and the retail sector must adapt or be declared dinosaurs," he said with his customary belly laugh. "In just two years, six-percent of Afronian consumers are making digital payments and which compares favourably across the continent considering the short time span. Going cashless is good for business transparency, good for collecting tax and great for the consumer. The Central Bank wholeheartedly supports these initiatives."

Finally, some good news, the still bemused president considered. *Digital financial services can be the tip of the spear for making the whole payments and tax ecosystem transparent. But who's planting the derogatory stories?*

With no answer, he started to get ready for a politburo meeting and thus missed the third article placed by Henshaw's man.

Walter Blaise's anti-corruption crusade.

A flamboyant businessman known for his association with President Isaiah George, and their joint love of supermodels and supercars, has been arrested. He claims, "I'm the victim of a political witch hunt. I threatened to lift the lid on corruption within the Presidential Palace and this is what happens. Walter Blaise is trying to silence me. Don't be surprised to find me dead."

The President's Press Secretary released a statement, which stated. "No stone will be left unturned as we go back through the books of all dubious contracts that were handed out under previous regimes. We must move forward with a graft free society whatever the cost that may inflict in the short term. No one is immune from prosecution."

In a related development, the Afronian Courts have found ten employees of the Afronian Social Security Pension Fund guilty of corruption. They embezzled billions of Afronian Shillings through by-passing regulations on land purchase. The list of those found guilty, includes: Director of Investments, the Finance Director and, the Director of Human Resources and Administration. The removal of the top officers is a further sign that President Blaise will not let anyone stand in his way as he continues at pace to implement his reform agenda.

The President's personal intervention follows fresh details emerging from the Maize-gate saga which uncovered officials in the National Food Security Agency conniving to purchase only a few thousand tons of Maize from neighbouring Taberia but paying for the whole order of 100,000 tons, the profit being split between all members of the syndicate on both sides of the border. The question that needs to be urgently raised, is, why did this contract get signed by the Presidential Palace as it's well known that Taberia has neither the maize nor capacity to supply such quantities to Afronia. This worrying macro-economic challenge comes at a time of crises when the country has run out of forex, prices at the petrol pump increase every day and state employees—from teachers to soldiers—have gone months without a salary.

Chapter 24

NAMED, SPIRIT OF AFRONIA, many of Afronia's and some of the continent's cycling talent was at the start line of the inaugural three-day, 435-kilometre cycling event that would see competitors go through the mountains of Southiland on the first day, the lowlands to Mapulwe on the second, before a mammoth 180-kilometre third day which finished at Presidential Square in Umoja City.

This was Afronia's first national sport-tourist event. It had been organized by Robert Yohan and was part of his portfolio to promote Afronia as the destination of choice for tourists and sports enthusiasts alike. It was part of a broader strategy that focused on travellers with an active lifestyle rather than going head-to-head with the likes of Kenya and Tanzania for wildlife. Thus, he'd been very enthusiastic when approached by HydroDevelop who put up the money to sponsor the race and had even gone so far as to propose that the company could fund a four-day ocean race. Eric was seriously considering the request, not least, in his last meeting with Charlie Daniels, he'd been told, that money could be made available for such purposes from a slush fund with the specific objective to promote British interests.

As the thirty-five-degree heat beat down and Afroni-an pop music was blasting from a solitary speaker, in the middle of the melee of cycle helmets being strapped on and brakes being tested, was Eric on his prized possession, a $4,000 racing bike. With his belly hanging over cycling shorts he was the very epitome of a white middle-aged man in lycra, the visage in stark contrast to the lithe Afro-nians on their battered Chinese bikes who made up most of the field and who used their bikes as their primary form of transport whether as a security guard cycling to work or firewood seller transporting his cargo.

Next to Eric and looking a fish-out-of-water though thoroughly enjoying the hullabaloo, was the guest of honour, Walter Blaise. He had been in training for the last three weeks and was going to compete in the second-ary event, a twenty-five-kilometre loop; his bodyguard attachment was not enthused by either the forthcoming physical exertions or security complications this would cause.

At 10 AM, one hour later than planned, there was a noticeable rise of tension in the air as Robert Yohan marched towards the start line. 'Your Excellency, distin-guished guests, riders… thank you for cycling in the in-augural Spirit of Afronia race. We hope you enjoy the beauty of Afronia and will by the end of the tour consider our great country a leader in the sports tourism market as you cycle past all this wonderful country has to offer. Good luck,' Robert Yohan finished his short speech by sounding the klaxon, the train of riders speeding down the gentle slope and quickly spacing out as the few pro-fessionals quickly raced out of sight.

After twenty minutes the first moderate hill came into view. Leaning forward, Eric's worst fears were coming true as he sweated terribly, his body not fully acclimatized to the mixture of tropical heat, breathlessness from the altitude and exertion. *At least in the mountains the humidity is not so bad; God only knows how I will suffer near the coast.*

Eight hours and 123 kilometres later, Eric sped down the last decline of the day hoping to gather as much pace as possible before the final climb, the steep ascent chosen specifically to identify who would be crowned The King of the Mountains. Eric knew what lay ahead having driven up the slope twice during site visits when doing ground preparation for the hydroelectric dam. *This is going to be brutal, but I refuse to walk.*

As he neared the bottom of the decisive climb at full gas, he pushed his bike and body to the limit, *One false move and I could die,* this as he dodged an errant rock. The momentum of the downhill speed thrill left the tyres within fifty metres as the ascent started in earnest. Eric had visions of being cheered on as he rode… but in rural Afronia there were no spectators apart from a few children and some errant goats, both of which looked on at his pink, puffing face curiously.

Suffering in the saddle, he poured what little water he had left over his head as he reached the halfway stage of the climb, the water evaporating almost immediately. *It's me against myself,* he kept repeating as he pushed one foot down on the pedal and then the other as he slowly moved forward by willpower alone, all energy having left his limbs many kilometres earlier as one muscle group started to turn to mush and others tried to compensate… before they too started to shut down. The pain was unbearable, and not just in Eric's legs, but also his arms, back and shoulders from his hunched position. *I'm running on empty, but my soul will keep pushing me forward; it's purely a mind game now,* Eric chanted to himself. *I can't stop or my muscles will turn to cement and I'll never start again.* There was no hiding place, just the endless potholed tarmac reaching into the sky.

Finally, Eric rounded a familiar bend, 'ONE KILOMETRE TO GO, MOTHERFUCKER!' he shouted aloud for motivation. *One final push to the finish line,* this as the heavenly smell of braai started to reach his nostrils. *100 metres at a time; I'll not be broken.*

The last 500 metres were the hardest of Eric's cycling life, and took close to six painstaking minutes, but as the finish line came into sight he knew he would have that overwhelming emotional sensation when putting his feet onto stationary ground and endorphins flooded his body. The combined sense of accomplishment and natural high was a sensation like no other and was worth the proverbial blood, sweat and tears as Eric got off his bike and collapsed to the ground, his spent legs like jelly though his heart elated at the enormous relief of conquering his personal Everest. 'Have one of these, mate,' a grinning Steven thrust an ice-cold beer into his boss' outstretched hand.

Reaching a guesthouse two hours later and hydrated from the copious bottles of water consumed between beers, Eric had to be helped up the flight of steps by Steve. Collapsing on the bed, Steven undid the laces on his superior's trainers. 'Ready for tomorrow?' he mischievously enquired.

'As I will ever be,' Eric replied, though couldn't really be sure if he would even be able to get out of bed in the morning.

Eric didn't make it into the shower for another four hours, falling instantly asleep as his weary body touched the bed sheets, but after a good night's sleep and a huge breakfast of potato, rice, and all the carbohydrates that he could stuff into his suffering body, he could once again be found on the start line, something which twenty-seven of those who had started the day before weren't. *You can do it; you're a tough bastard,* Eric gave himself a quick pep talk as he saw Robert Yohan raise the klaxon.

Two gruelling days later Eric was in site of this finish line… though this was not the end of his ride. In discussion with Charlie Daniels, Eric had organised for Hydro-Develop to sponsor Afronia's first critical mass cycle ride. Where there was usually a sea of taxis, minibuses, motorbike taxis and tuk-tuks on the main road from the airport to Presidential Square, today it was peddle powered only, the British taxpayer sponsored event organised to spread an environmental message.

Chapter 25

As sweat was pouring profusely in Afronia, in the Square Mile of the City of London, Stacy Adams—a prematurely grey-haired lady in her mid-thirties who'd fallen on hard times after being made redundant six years earlier—was making her way to work.

Stacy had been a high-flying internal auditor specialising in corporate governance of financial services providers, though after a messy divorce brought on by her downward spiral into binge drinking, she now found herself working on a zero-hours contract for EazyClean, an office-cleaning company.

Alighting at London Bridge, Stacy walked until she came to the reception of The Shard. 'Walterson and Partners,' she said while digging in her handbag for the letter from EazyClean and her driving licence, the latter as proof of identification. She passed the two documents to the guard cum receptionist. 'Finance department.'

Walterson and Partners has a staff of over 450 in London, the firm specialising in supporting over 2,500 corporations and financial institutions that had interests in Africa. They had a global register of over 13,000 high-net-worth individuals who they'd helped register offshore companies to minimise or in many cases totally evade paying tax.

'The office is on the twenty-second floor, love,' the broad-shouldered and slightly plump Daryl replied as he gave her a once over with lustful eyes. With a charming smile he handed Stacy a visitor's badge.

Stepping out of the elevator, Stacy looked first to the left and saw a row of empty glass divided offices before turning to her right where she saw a receptionist desk behind which sat a pretty young woman with a beehive hairdo. 'Is finance here?'

'Yeah,' came an Essex drawl from pouting lips which moved rhythmically up and down as it chewed mint flavoured gum.

'Where is everyone?'

'Team building exercise in Windsor this week.'

'Oh,' a deflated Stacy mumbled. *I'll only be cleaning one day here then.* 'Where's the janitor's closet?'

'That way,' the strawberry blonde pointed down the corridor after pressing the door release button. 'It's the third door,' she added while looking over the top of her glossy fashion magazine.

Henry Walterson, the Managing Partner was not on the strategy retreat but in his office and in conversation with Russell Jackson, the imposing six-feet-four-inch tall, founder and CEO of Ibex Investments. 'Ibex's objective is to pull millions of lives out of poverty through equity investments into Sub-Saharan indigenous businesses. Our focus is on renewable energy, healthcare and education, three of the biggest challenges the continent faces,' Russell explained to his host. 'With growing populations and the ever more frequent challenges imposed by climate change business opportunities abound.'

Russell had no formal business qualifications, but since teenage years he'd invested cash from paper rounds and holidays jobs on the stock market. With clever investments during the 2008 financial collapse, he'd accrued a personal investment portfolio of £20 million. Reaching his twenty-seventh birthday he decided to take a sabbatical, during which he spent a summer working for an Afronian NGO that helped Southi farmers harvest water and use irrigation techniques to build an income stream while slowing the spread of desertification. In his own words, it was a life defining six-months. It was during the nights in a small mud brick, one room house, that gave him the genesis for establishing a social impact investment fund. When he returned to London, Ibex was born.

'My fund believes globalization can address some of the world's biggest problems. We are not a charity but profit orientated; we offer investors a decent return. The businesses I invest in are those that help Afronians in their everyday lives. As President Blaise's reforms take shape, I expect business to be very good.' Russell paused. 'What are the next moves?'

These were the five words that Henry Walterson had been waiting to be uttered. 'What do you know about war Russell?'

'It is not about spreading democracy, patriotism or any of that gumph,' Russell replied with a sneer, 'it's about money, whether that's supplying weapons, oil, mercenaries, jet fighters… or providing debt.'

Due south of the City of London, in the picturesque fishing village of Beachcroft, David Howells was preparing *The Eternal Hope*. Onboard the trawler were five illegal immigrants, who, much like Innocent Shembles and Charles Ontago some years earlier, were little more than slave labour to the captain. However, in recent months the crew had noticed a marked change to the normally spiteful behaviour of their taskmaster. 'He's mellowed,' Rafelo, a Senegalese, remarked one frigid evening as he tied a knot in a fishing line. 'His remarks are not quite so withering. The amount and variety of food he provides for the kitchen has noticeably improved. And he allows breaks during the brutally long hours.'

'Why the change?' a new member of the crew from Chad questioned as he held firmly to his mug of tea to get warmth back into his ice blasted fingers.

'Don't know, just be thankful,' an Ivorian advised.

At the luxurious 5-star Hôtel Métropole Genève, built in 1854 on the city's ancient fortifications, an emergency meeting was being held between three gentlemen of renown. 'Blaise is no longer acceptable,' this stated by Ulrich Müller. 'General Mutoni, you must show the army's displeasure at how Blaise is ripping the country apart.'

'He is a threat to national sovereignty and leading the country towards a second civil war,' Mutoni, still enraged at his vilification from the Truth and Reconciliation Commission, started to outline his strategy with a broad grin.

'Don't underestimate Walter. He might seem a naïve libertarian but he's actually a wily old fox that the majority of Afronians backs.' Robert Yohan was the third man.

'If he refuses to step down the army will step in after the recent allegations of state capture.'

'Those are rumours, nothing substantive, toxic, fatal,' Yohan pointed out to the erstwhile army man.

'But has enough cow shit been thrown for some of it to stick to the Teflon President?' Ulrich wanted to know.

'The economy is booming and every day new businesses, schools and hospitals are opening, he's done an admirable job.' Yohan sipped the imported Colombian coffee. 'Credit has to be given where it's due. Unless something unexpected happens, he's bound to win the next election.'

'His days are numbered,' Ulrich said with finality.

'He will never stand down; he has limpet like qualities.'

Mutoni, nodded his head to Yohan's assertion.

'If he won't jump… we push!' These last words coming from the Swiss entrepreneur.

Chapter 26

DIANA, AN AFRONIAN who'd been camped in a refugee centre on the French coast for the last seven months, knew nothing of the fierce reputation that proceeded David Howells, she only knew him as one of many volunteers in the soup kitchen, Howells' change of disposition coming from his regular attendance of Mo's community meetings. She had a small rucksack which contained all her worldly goods, that being a toothbrush, towel and a spare pair of panties and socks. She was wearing jeans that were several sizes too large for her now wiry frame—though which had fitted snuggly when she'd left Afronia—and a green hoodie to keep as best as it could the cold from her bones. She had given her sleeping bag and tent, her home, to a newly arrived couple from Algeria and their twin five-year old daughters.

It had just passed 4 AM on a blustery night, when Diana, led by Simon from Yorkshire (a new friend of Howells) started their five-kilometre walk. Carefully and quietly they passed through dense woodland as they navigated by moonlight; they didn't dare use a torch for fear of alerting roving bands of armed police, immigration officers and vigilantes. Circumnavigating road junctions which had armoured personnel carriers manning roadblocks, they cut and then crawled under barbed wire fences, until exhausted, cold and wet, they finally made the sand dunes as the sun was starting to rise.

Donning angling clothes from Simon's holdall, the pair incongruously carried fishing rods as they pulled a rickety rowing boat towards the thunderous waves of the English Channel.

I only met David a few weeks ago, Diana considered as she looked out to the foreboding sea. *Maybe he won't come? How can he be in love with me? I only gave him my body once. We don't know each other. Maybe he needs to feel loved as much as I?* She put her hand to her brow again and scanned the choppy horizon.

'Over there,' Simon, with the aid of a powerful pair of binoculars gesticulated.

'I see him,' a super excited Diana squealed, her guide through the woods barely able to hear her enthusiasm over the din of the wind and crashing waves. With no time to spare if they were to evade the attention of the French Coastguard, the fragile craft was soon cresting a half-metre swell and in danger of being overcome by the choppy sea. With muscle draining effort from pulling on the oars, the waves doubling in height, Diana was quickly more than 100 metres from the safety of the shore and the warm smile of Simon. *If I'm to die, death will be my final chapter of life,* Diana ominously contemplated as bile rose up her throat as the rowing boat took on more water than the terrified woman cared to acknowledge.

David Howells looked through his binoculars from the forecastle of his trawler and saw the petite figure straining against the mighty depths. *Last year I was a*

card-carrying member of the English Defence League…
and now I'm helping my migrant lover sneak into England's
green and not so pleasant land. Diana will not survive long:
the swell will overwhelm her.

Howells pushed down on the throttle and the one-kilometre distance quickly closed. 'Save her,' he screeched at the crew and who looked at him gobsmacked, the last thing they countenanced was rescuing a refugee. 'Do it,' Howells this time implored rather than commanded as he looked each man in the eye and saw an emotion he'd never experienced before, that of wanting to help but not physically able due to an inner fear which made muscles go brittle. *They are scared to swim, but if they don't… maybe they think I'll kill them.*

Howells rushed into the storeroom and picked up a bright orange lifejacket which he threw to the petrified Diana, every wave now crashing over her half-sunken boat. Taking off his boots and heavy anorak, he dove overboard. Despite being a strong swimmer, with no life preserver the weight of his clothes and the cold immediately numbed his extremities as he started to be dragged under. See the impending dual disaster, the Chadian threw Howells his life jacket while the Senegalese took control of The Eternal Hope and manoeuvred the vessel towards Diana. *She is a pretty girl… but only skin and bones.*

It took five life-sapping minutes for first Diana and then Howells to be pulled from the unforgiving waters, both shaking like leaves as they were heaved on deck. Helped out of their frigid clothes, they were given survival blankets and cups of tea to raise their core body temperature and ward off hypothermia, this as the trawler was turned around and started steaming towards the English coast.

It took eight hours before Diana was able to sight a small alcove five kilometres north of Beachcroft, at which point, a rejuvenated Howells prepared the inflatable to take her ashore before he would return to the vessel and go to port to complete all the necessary paperwork as required after trawling. However, unbeknown to all, the British Coastguard—and who had been informed of the rescue by their French counterparts—had been tracking The Eternal Hope as it entered British territorial waters. 'Where have you been, sir?' Neil Hendrix, the Senior Maritime Operations Officer asked Howells, this after first stopping and then boarding The Eternal Hope five miles out to sea.

'Up and down the English Channel looking for cod and haddock,' Howells lied. 'These days, there's hardly any left; it's been a waste of time,' he doubled down.

'Can I see your crews' documents?'

'Here.' David confidently handed over forged immigration papers for three of his crew, this as Rafelo and Diana hid in the engine room and were being deafened by the cacophony.

'We had a report that you stopped near the French coast.'

'That's true; maintenance.' Howells lifted his eyebrows and shoulders, in a "what can you do?" expression. 'I thought we would have to port… but we got the old girl going again. I turned around so I could fix her up before setting sail again,' he casually added.

'We'll escort you to shore… in case you get into difficulties,' Hendrix informed the skipper.

Howells' face dropped, the coastguard's pause informing Howells that the game was up. 'My crew are good men, be kind to Diana,' Howells pleaded. 'She's the only thing I've done right in my godforsaken life.'

Neil didn't know the whole story but could guess. 'If you have undocumented aliens on this boat... you'll be arrested for people smuggling.'

'I owe Diana and my crew... they are my redemption,' a trembling Howells replied as he sunk to his haunches knowing he would most likely receive a custodial sentence and hefty fine. He looked into the forlorn eyes of his crew, *How ironic that my future is now as uncertain as theirs!*

Chapter 27

IN WHITEHALL. 'RUMOURS HAVE surfaced of sexual impropriety by a number of NGOs we are supporting in Afronia,' this from the Deputy Minister for International Development to his boss.

'What do we know?' *It'll be my head on the chopping block*!

'Not much… so far. We received an anonymous report that senior staff from the Brits for Afronians Foundation, a UK funded 3-year, £10 million project, misbehaved with underaged girls.'

'So?' came an audible sigh of relief. 'That's nothing new.'

'There has been an official complaint by a whistle-blower. Mohammed Ahmed has forwarded the allegations to the ministry as required by their contract. They have not yet taken action.'

'If they don't think anything needs to be done, who are we to interfere? I know Josh Scott, their Chief of Party; he's a good man,' the two last meeting three months earlier at a private soiree in Umoja City and where he'd been luxuriating with multiple girls in a jacuzzi.

'There are claims that underage girls were plied with booze at his house, and hence UK taxpayer money—'

'It sounds like a storm in a teacup,' the deputy minister tried to brush off. 'Have any of the girls been interviewed? If the girls are underage, have the police been informed? Are any of the teens beneficiaries of the project?' To each of the three questions the deputy shook his head in the negative. 'Then there's nothing to be done. Any scandal will soon blow over.'

Two days after the meeting an expose appeared in the British national press.

"The culture of bullying and sexual harassment is prevalent."

One of the UK's most-high profile charities, Brits for Afronians Foundation, has been caught in a devastating sex-scandal which could put the existence of the charity at risk. "There is a culture of bullying and sexual harassment," claimed a former volunteer. "Racism was very casual. Misogamy is a way of life; there is a big problem that needs fixing."

In Umoja City's fancier districts, bars are filled with upper-class Afronians, tourists, business executives and international NGO staff, and walking between these fun palaces are flip-flop wearing teenage prostitutes who eye potential older foreign clients. To those in the know, cheap sex is one of the so-called unspoken advantages of a development job in Afronia.

The scandal in the aid sector that has been circulating since the beginning of 2018 with the Oxfam Haiti revelations has found its way to Afronia and where there have been multiple reports of paid-for sex with underage girls.

"The stories are sickening," this the official communication from John Banwell, the spokesman for the British Embassy. "We did an audit of all NGOs who receive money; all had a clean bill of health. If true, these accusations are beyond the pale though I've never personally heard of such impropriety."

"Paying for sex is banned under the foundation's code of conduct," so says Mohammed Ahmed, the founder and chairman of Brits for Afronians Foundation. "I take full responsibility for the behaviour of our staff. We did not inform the police as we believe they are in a transitional phase and didn't think suitable action would be taken. However, we publicly announced an investigation through reporting the allegations of sexual misconduct to the UK charities regulator."

"I made an official complaint," the whistleblower confirms, "but I never got an acknowledgment. There is a revolving door policy in the development sector and most lifers are too scared to put their head above the parapet. Women fear career reprisals from senior white men who are often the main culprits and consider such ongoings as little more than, boys on tour."

Harry, a development worker, had a different opinion. "I'm a middle-aged white male and have been working in the aid sector for twelve years. I've lived in five countries and married a local girl—I've heard it all. The things said behind my back would turn your ears blue. "Prostitute" is the most common insult by women to other females."

Steve, a water engineering contractor with HydroDevelop argued, "Judge me on my work not what I do outside the office. We have incredibly stressful jobs, 24-hour days for weeks or months at a time and with limited options how to let off steam other than having a drink and going to nightclubs. You ask any aid worker, military personnel or business executive who has been to a developing country, and they will tell you that girls hang around the hotels, in bars and nightclubs, and are looking for paying customers. This is a fact of life and not something to hang people out to dry," he added. "Why should those in the aid sector be held to a higher moral standing? Unless you've worked in such countries you can't begin to understand the unique stresses and strains. There are constant power cuts and no running water... but this is not a reason to revolt as would be the case in many developed countries. Even in many capitals, there are no cinemas, racetracks or casinos, and recreational drug use can be harshly punished; alcohol and sex are two of the few leisure activities that are plentiful.

Paying for sex should not be treated harshly in a society where promiscuity and infidelity are social norms, no matter how pious or God-fearing a country professes to be. If the girls are underage that is a criminal matter. If they are beneficiaries of the charity, that raises ethical questions. If it is neither of these scenarios, then it's a moralistic question and there should be no difference between whether you are paying for prostitutes in Bangkok, Umoja City or Birmingham. The context should not be a reason for moral outrage, and especially not by those in ivory towers who don't know what the words, getting your hands dirty on the frontlines, actually mean."

No matter Steve's arguments, and which some in the press applaud, the Afronian scandal is far from over. The British Chancellor, and who ultimately decides how money is best spent to benefit the host country and the British taxpayer, said, "I will personally take action to find out what happened through interviewing the responsible people at the British Embassy in Umoja City. If appropriate, I will cut off funding to any organisations implicated."

Some politicians and media barons who have a particular hate for aid will no doubt use the recent controversy for their own agenda, but amongst the much good the money does, there is an undeniable rotten core of senior, largely white aid workers who partake in child abuse. They are not the same as sex tourists, but rather, they are paid and housed by British taxpayers and sully the name of the many well-meaning, hard-working people who donate their money and time to help those less fortunate.

If Brits for Afronians wants to be a moral standard bearer and continue the undoubted good work the majority of their staff do then they must be utterly transparent. As for many a liberal, myself included, we expect development workers to be morally upstanding. And so, while Steve and Harry make strong arguments as to the reality for many working in difficult circumstances, this does not absolve them of lowering their moral standards. They are engaged in a noble endeavour and doing something "good", but this is not a green light to do moral wrong even if it's not legally or socially prohibited. On the contrary, development workers and peacekeepers have a higher moral obligation to those most at risk as even in tremendously challenging situations they are recruited to lead by example.

Mo Ahmed read the newspaper for the third time. 'Joshua had a clean CV when we hired him… didn't he?' he wanted to double-check with his wife before contemplating how to curtail this unmitigated public relations disaster.

'One article I read, claims, he was forced out from The Gambia due to similar sexual predatory allegations… and Equatorial Guinea before that.'

'Why were we never told? This is a catastrophe. Everything we've worked so hard for will go up in smoke.'

'It seems, this was just the way it was... before the Oxfam crisis.'

'Our corporate and individual donors are going to flee. It's totally unacceptable for our executive leadership, or for any staff for that matter, to use prostitutes, and especially on foundation property. I can only guess the shit-storm that will hit us if any of the girls were underage.'

'Have you heard about the prostitute scandal?'

'No,' Eric lied to his wife. He'd been told exactly what went on at Josh Scott's house by Steven; he'd been quite envious of his deputy when hearing the lurid details.

'It's privileged white men exploiting impoverished young girls; it's despicable, a disgrace!' Sylvia declared. 'This is not do-gooders using prostitutes, as that implies choice; this was exploitation. It's filthy men taking advantage; sex work for these women is not a lifestyle choice. The use of power by the powerful to get what they want is abuse. They didn't even pay the girls, but just got them drunk so that they are more compliant to their perversions; it's vile.'

'Girlfriends, "girlfriends" and prostitutes,' Eric started to reply once his better half had finally run out of steam, 'are inter used words depending on the talker and the target. If the girls were under the age of consent, it's a criminal matter, much as the Jimmy Saville abuse at the BBC was. If the girls were in any way linked to Brits for Afronia, either as staff or beneficiaries, then I agree, it was an abuse of power... just like the Catholic priest scandals. If it was neither criminal in nature nor an abuse of power, then it's a contract issue. If the men in question had signed a code of ethics which detailed repercussions for having paid sex or inviting unknown guests onto the foundation's property, this could be punishable by termination of contract.' Eric knew this argument very well; it was the same one that Steven had use when he'd explained to his boss how he'd got caught up in the controversy, the pair giggling about the whole episode. 'Not all aid workers are altruistic... there are good, bad and in-between... just as there are in every strata of society. Aid, development workers, whatever you want to call them are not a homogeneous group of saints. There are war junkies who chase adrenaline. The disaster specialist who wants to be at ground zero to help re-build. The development worker who lives for capacity building and in other circumstances could morph into a business manager or civil servant.'

'I suppose so.'

'The development sector can be likened to the Military Industrial Complex. Countries ensure they meet their global financial obligation... but much of the money ends up in the pockets of companies that the same governments tax; it's a financial merry-go-round.' Eric had come to this realisation from his numerous meetings with Charlie Daniels. 'Why do you think HydroDevelop are the darlings of the British Embassy... we help both their commercial and development arms.'

'Oh,' came the almost silent response, Sylvia ashamed of how her family benefited.

'The truth of the matter is this, if rich governments and media say often enough, that Africa is poor and the west is there to help, Africans, as much as the British public, will believe the lie.'

'Africa is not poor?'

'Sub-Saharan Africa is a net creditor to the rest of the world to the tune of about £30 billion annually, this several multiples of total development aid. And this doesn't even start to calculate the damage done by climate change, largely caused by the west and which is one of the main reasons fuelling the migrant rush to Europe. Multi-national corporates, HydroDevelop included, hire fancy lawyers and accountants, many of whom are based in London, to dodge taxes or repatriate profits. Then there is debt.'

Eric paused not willing to explore all the dirty secrets of his employer. 'I digress. If the women involved were older than the age of consent, then shagging is not a sackable offence! I think it's a lot of hullabaloo, and unfortunately, organisations that do much good will potentially lose significant funding from the UK government and private donations due to the damage to their brand. On another note, local staff at these development organisations or global private sector companies, have salaries, benefits and allowances that dwarf their peers... and so are often the worse sexual harassment offenders due to their relative wealth and having a better understanding of cultural and social norms. It is not just a white, middle-aged, foreign male issue! As for there being a cover up... from what I've read, Brits for Afronians did what they could. If their Chief of Party didn't make a contract breach and there was no evidence that it should be a police matter, there is little they could have done other than ask for a resignation. The unfortunate thing is, that in this age of suing for anything… if someone resigns and they are asked for a reference by a future employer their previous organisation is not legally allowed to say why they resigned but only what role they previously had was and for what period of time they did it. Only if it was a criminal matter is the former employer legally required to be fully transparent. In summary, Sylvia, did the staff commit a criminal act or break their moral contract? If yes, was this reported to the appropriate officials and what remedial actions were taken? If the contract was not broken and no criminal act committed, then it was consensual sex, end of story. The reality is, that if you offer free food, alcohol, a swimming pool, a comfy bed and taxi money, my bet is that seventy-five percent of unattached girls who come from poor backgrounds would take up the offer whether that is in Afronia or Aberdeen. Is this reprehensible, some would say so, but this is a morality issue and should not be the source of pontification by those in the media who have no idea what it's like to live in a developing country.'

On the steps of the Foreign and Commonwealth Office, a statement was read by the Chairman of the independent watchdog, the Charities Commission.

Afronia is recovering from the civil war and several British charities have received millions of pounds to help in this noble effort. However, while many organizations and individuals do sterling work, a minority of senior male aid workers have abused their positions with those most vulnerable in society and who they were meant to be helping.

Allegations were made that the Chief of Party of Brits for Afronia Foundation held sex parties at his British taxpayer funded villa with girls under the age of consent and who he liberally plied with alcohol. Sources have indicated that the British Embassy in Umoja City was aware of the allegations but that the report was put in a locked drawer as the adverse impact on British commercial and diplomatic interests were considered too important to jeopardise by making the allegations public. As such, we find the Department for International Development failed to show moral leadership and should be held accountable to the British and Afronian public.

Chapter 28

F ARAWAY FROM THE salacious front pages of the British press. 'We must act now,' the CEO of Europe Gold Mining Company said to the assembled members of the Jobuja Group while on retreat in the Swiss Alps. 'Blaise is out of control with his nationalisation of our business-es. Our share price has dropped eight-percent in the week since he put a block on exports. With the imposition of new laws, raising taxes and the renegotiation of contracts, I have ordered our head office in Antwerp to suspend all Afronian operations until there is clarity around the presi-dent's proposal to completely renationalise the gold sector.'

'It's the same for oil,' another CEO spoke up with an equal amount of indignation. 'We have been forced to stop offshore drilling... though are falsely citing health and safety concerns. Once money stops filling the pockets of corrupt ministers we will see how much support Blaise has to continue his crusade.'

'Now is the time to act,' Sir Hillary Chapman secon-ded. 'We have significant ownership in the utilities and the bankers amongst us have extended their credit lines to breaking point; we can call in the debt when we wish. The construction of the Southiland Renaissance Dam has led to local opposition and we have been forced to assemble a minefield of checkpoints to access the construction site. Police informants tell us how villagers are planning to sabotage the project.'

'Maduhu is sabre-rattling at the impact of the dams on the water flow into Taberia. And Igor Victov, who we know covets Afronia's land, water and minerals, has recently approved the lease of two Russian long range-strike battleships to Taberia. We have to move now before it's too late.'

In Umoja City. 'You were in the political wilderness for several years,' Innocent Shembles stated to the man opposite him in the Hillview Coffee Emporium, the renowned café that had seen so much history in the making.'

'It's true,' the grizzled political beast Robert Yohan answered his inquisitor. 'Coming here, to this institution,' Yohan admiringly looked around, 'on its fortieth anniversary and knowing how many patriots have enjoyed the wonderful coffee and pastries is a real honour. Walter Blaise has given me a second chance to help move this great country towards a prosperous future… the Hillview Coffee Emporium encapsulates this hope.'

'Is economic prosperity for the few coming at the expense of the many?' the journalist quizzed before taking a mouthful of the café's famous strawberry cheesecake.

'If you drive through Umoja City,' a thoughtful Yohan started to answer, 'you'll come across all socio-economic strata. There are investment bankers in gleaming office blocks and who reside in high rise condos and five-star hotels… but there are also slums just a short walking distance away. Umoja City has always been this way and will likely remain so for the foreseeable future due to urbanization and a fast-growing population. And the undeniable fact is, that Afronia is starting the process of getting back on her economic feet. However, Afronians need to remain patient. Without adequate urban masterplans that have a sense of reality that take into account informal businesses and residential realities rather than proposing a mini-Dubai, then safety, public services and the industrialisation of the economy will be difficult to achieve. Indeed, it will create a ticking time-bomb as the poor will rub shoulders with the new rich and which won't sit well with many.'

'What's your solution?'

'All levels of community must be involved in redevelopment initiatives. We must prioritise the use of technology to facilitate and manage growth. The electorate must be able to vote out those who don't meet the wishes of the people. And most importantly, there needs to be sustained political will to make hard and contentious decisions for the greater good.'

'Can the landfill tragedy or the rivers of sewage many in Little Wahili cross daily to go to work in the houses of the nouveau-riche be considered economically or politically sustainable? Is it reasonable to expect the poor, who in some cases live with their livestock in flimsy homes made of discarded wood, iron sheets and tarpaulin, be asked to be patient?'

'Umoja City is economically expanding and unfortunately some will be left behind as space needs to be found for housing, factories and even rubbish dumps. City administrators need to construct schools, transportation networks, latrines and many other public services—'

'Does this justify city officials forcing residents, young and old, whether with families or single, able bodied or infirm, to leave at short notice and with few options of where to re-locate before bulldozers arrive and smash their dwellings to smithereens so a new high-rise can be built?'

'Growth places a strain on social services, but the president's choices are stark: investment or stagnation.'

'What about the recent clampdown by the security forces?' a voice in the café questioned. Both Innocent and Robert Yohan looked around, neither realising that nearby patrons had started to eavesdrop on the private conversation.

'Blaise is nothing but a wolf in sheep's clothing,' another voice opinionated to a round of muted applause.

'Peaceful protest is enshrined in the constitution in the Second Republic. Every citizen has the right to question their government,' Yohan calmly replied with a twinkle in his eye as he got ready for that which he most loved—a verbal joust.

'There are harrowing accounts of police intimidation and shots being fired into crowds of unarmed protestors; is that justified?' Innocent was referring to an incident two days earlier in Nyala where there was a protest against HydroDevelop for the increased deaths from Malaria.

'We need foreign investors in Afronia if we are to economically grow. Do their methods always work? No. And when that happens, they lose millions in their investments. But Afronia can't go it alone—'

'Afronia is doing a deal with the Devil?' a slim, astute, bespectacled customer in her early 20s who'd been sipping coffee while listening intently, interrupted the president's special advisor.

'If we want economic independence. If we want free healthcare. If we want world class universities and, yes, if we want safe water, then we must decide how to move collectively forward. Afronia's population will double in the next thirty years and so we have to make the hard choices now to guarantee the future for our children...' Yohan looked round the room with a beaming smile, 'great-grandchildren in my case,' he got the ripple of laughter he was hoping for. 'Afronia is one of Africa's star economic performers—'

'At the cost of incarceration, detention and violence?' the youth with glasses interrupted a second time.

'It is Somalitreans who are causing the unrest,' a visibly agitated Yohan replied as he looked the young woman in the eye.

'The government is dominated by Wahilis and Southis. They are expanding the city into Somalitrean traditional lands; it's a land grab. Farmland is our culture, our identity. We are now marginalised in everything: jobs, business opportunities and the armed forces.'

'What would you rather?' Yohan queried. 'Only ever being one minor stumble away from economic catastrophe and which could set the country alight again or, move the WHOLE country from poverty to prosperity? I am a Somalitrean,' Yohan reminded everyone, 'and I will do what is best for my people and which means what's best for the country.'

'Can democracy and development ever co-exist?' Innocent provocatively asked.

'We are following the same political and economic model as that of Ethiopia and Rwanda. They went through crises but have a thriving economy now.'

'Many say, they are repressive, authoritarian and centralized administrations. Democracy in those countries is not a reality. Their model is dependent on their citizens accepting reduced freedoms in return for more wealth in their pockets.'

'Critics can say what they like, but the truth is they are leading economic lights as they pull their countries back from the brink. Afronia has created more millionaires since the end of the civil war than over the lifetime of independence, and this with greater transparency than ever before. Poverty levels have declined by five-percent; we are moving in the right direction!'

'But at what cost if the economy has a foreign foundation?' An economics lecturer who'd recently entered the café after seeing his favoured coffee shop crammed to the rafter, wanted to know. 'That is not the model Rwanda, Ethiopia or China follow.'

'We have a system of government based on the needs of the people. The number of migrants leaving Afronia is at its lowest in our history; this must be construed as making significant headway,' Yohan deflected the question. 'We have support from developed nations that want to see Afronia prosper. The Second Republic is an economic revolution that's considered our politics, democracy, historical ethnic divisions and, the need to collectively move in the same direction; Afronia is rising!' There was a loud round of nationalistic whooping at what had become an impromptu political rally... with a few well-timed interventions from patrons who had been told what questions to ask as earlier instructed by Yohan.

'But let me warn you, there are some who don't want to see Afronia surge. There are some conspirators, cabals and cliques, who are attempting to undermine from within. Traitors who want to return to the dark days of civil war for their personal ambitions to be realised. But under strong leadership,' Yohan, deliberately didn't mention Walter Blaise, 'I reassure you, that Afronia will not be a house of cards. We must not bury our heads in the sand and think there are no problems but rather be aware of those who want to make trouble and are raising funds through corruption or gifts from foreign governments for nefarious reasons.' This was an undisguised dig at the president.

'Do you still have ambitions for the highest office?' Innocent pondered after noticing the change in tone from the man opposite.

'I'm happy to serve my country in any capacity and to the best of my abilities. I was just pointing out that not everyone is content to see Afronia rise like a phoenix from the ashes, and so every patriotic Afronia must lookout for malcontents. Walter Blaise has done a wonderful job; I'm honoured to serve at his side.' At this Yohan stood up and started shaking hands, the interview over.

'You didn't answer my question,' Innocent re-asked the disappearing back of the political veteran.

No, I didn't, Yohan chuckled as he started to mentally prepare for a potentially defining meeting.

❧

'At least there are still some people who are more concerned about money than ethics,' Robert Yohan guffawed half-an-hour after walking out of the Hillview Coffee Emporium. 'What are you going to do?' he asked, these the six words he'd been eagerly waiting to utter.

'That's up to you,' Ulrich Müller answered as clam as you like; he was an excellent poker player.

'I'm all ears,' Yohan, not budging an inch in this game of chess.

'Afronia is one of the fastest growing economies in Africa and a current darling of the West—'

'But there is no way Blaise's vision will become reality through internal resources alone.'

'Quite.'

'What are you missing?' Robert pretended he didn't yet see where he fitted in.

'Maduhu,' the Swiss answered. 'Maduhu wants re-unification.'

Chapter 29

A s Yohan was meeting Müller, Julius Stewart walked confidently through Umoja City International Airport, his passport claiming him to be a Chilean. *Hopefully this will be my fifth and final time to Afronia,* he considered as he swiftly passed through the diplomatic channel while other passengers sweltered in the low-ceilinged immigration arrivals hall and went through the laborious process of applying for visas and showing their Yellow Fever travel immunization card and which if they didn't have they had to pay $50, that being that it was no longer possible to give a $30 bribe for a stamp and forgo the jab.

In Little Wahili there was a Taberian refugee who went by the street name Soros. He was born on Black Wednesday, the 16th September, 1992, the day that the United Kingdom unceremoniously fell out of the Exchange Rate Mechanism. Soros was from humble beginnings, though like his namesake, he'd also become extraordinarily rich.

It was twenty-five degrees Centigrade in the shade, an unusually mild day for the time of year, though Soros was wearing a thick coat as he stood in the stockroom of the wholesale business he'd been running very successfully since the end of the civil war. Three years earlier, he'd taken a $100 loan from a moneylender (who charged 100-percent interest every thirty-days) but when Soros heard Sheila Solomon declaring a ceasefire, he'd decided, *It's now or never.* With his first loan he'd bought four cartons of biscuits, five crates of Coca Cola and twenty multi-packs of crisps. With Afronia at peace, Soros kept reinvesting his profits so that he now had several warehouses full of all sorts of household stock and which ranged from cereal, powdered milk and sacks of maize to shampoo, cans of insecticide, plastic kitchenware and packets of sugar. It was ordered positively Amazonesque for operational efficiency, the net result being a profit of $20,000 in a bad month.

But Soros was troubled as he'd been tasked with an unusual order. It wasn't for food or household items, nor money—he'd become a successful money lender—it wasn't even for girls, at least not of the sexual favours type. 'I need two gunmen,' the man had demanded rather than requested. 'Two females who are not afraid to die if their families will be well looked after.'

'That is not my business,' Soros answered and not at all sure who the gentleman was. 'Your information must be mistaken.'

'I'm never wrong. You have one of the best networks in Umoja City and know where anything can be found.'

'You're asking someone to commit suicide?' Soros wanted to clarify.

'Two people.'

'Jesus!' Soros who was not normally one to blaspheme couldn't help but let slip. 'For what reason?'

'None of your business. Your answers suggest that you do indeed know where such people can be found; I pay handsomely.'

'I don't need money,' this as Soros looked up and down the shelves of his fully stocked warehouse.

'I take a dim view of anyone not helping me,' the gentleman said in a menacing voice while surveying the stockroom, the implication being that either Soros or his business would be in dire jeopardy if he didn't fulfil the order.

Soros came to a quick conclusion 'There's a man named Mustafa and who can be contacted through the Second Embassy.'

'Thank you,' Julius finished the impromptu conversation.

Three days after Julius had met Soros, the president was touring a renovated secondary school, this the keystone project of his education policy. He was standing in front of the school assembly with a beaming smile, his security detail some distance away, Blaise admonishing them earlier when saying, 'If a president isn't safe at a school, how can the youngest and most vulnerable of society feel protected by the state?' Two female teenagers walked towards the head of state, each holding a bunch of flowers. They approached shyly, their heads bowed until three metres away when they suddenly rushed at Walter and thrust the flowers in the president's face. Quickly manhandled by the surprised presidential bodyguard, the young women spat and fought their assailants, all the time trying to push the flowers on any of Blaise's exposed skin. Eventually subdued, and while being led away, they simultaneously said, 'We made an oath to ISiSS and willingly die as martyrs in the name of Allah.'

The president immediately started having difficulty swallowing fluids and breathing and was rushed to Umoja City Central Hospital his health deteriorating rapidly. He went into a coma three hours after exposure to the toxic element in the flowers and never regained consciousness. President Walter Blaise was pronounced dead ten hours after the audacious ambush, his family in head-to-toe anti-contamination getup by his bedside.

Hamza Leso handed a statement to Vice-President Professor Rashid. The Minister of Economy had a benevolent look on his face as he sat sombrely dressed in front of TV cameras.

> Afronia is under attack. Our leader, His Excellency President Walter Blaise has been assassinated. In this time of national grief, the three vice-presidents will form a government of national unity and ensure the day-to-day business of running the country as we enter seven days of national mourning and prepare for presidential elections in four-weeks-time.

Chapter 30

WATCHING THE NATIONAL address was General Mutoni. He'd been mid-conversation with fellow senior officers when the TV was turned up, the group listening in astonishment to Rashid. 'Blaise made this country a leftist kleptocracy. His levity has left this country in the calamitous cultural and economic morass we see today. There is a moral rot at the heart of Afronian society. We are humiliated as a nation when white NGO workers prostitute our daughters. The country is living through a political, financial and security catastrophe; it is utterly disagreeable and needs a firm military hand at this time of crisis… rather than leaving it to opportunistic politicians.'

'Are you advocating for a military republic?' the head of the navy wanted to clarify.

'With you at the helm?' this added from the Air Marshall.

'We need changes, big changes. The Afronian people can no longer be prisoners to criminal gangs, gays, or trade union terrorists. We must implement a drastic shakeup to put our country back on the right track and only the army can carry out such a vision; politicians are soft on crime and soft on the causes of crime. Afronia has become a criminal paradise and which encourages civil disobedience. At this time of national crisis, we have no option but to step in,' General Mutoni pleaded. 'This is the third president to die violently in less than four years; the country will go back to civil war if we are not decisive.'

'Are you suggesting a military coup?' this from Brigadier Abel Hussein, one of the more junior officers in the room but who had the personal confidence of Mutoni.

'It is not a coup if we are leaderless. The politburo is disintegrating. The county is rudderless and the security services are no closer to uncovering who was behind the assassination.'

'I'm in agreement with General Mutoni,' this from an admiral. 'The armed forces must take control for a limited time until a civilian authority can peacefully step in.'

'This afternoon I'm taking a flight to Moscow and meeting their military leaders and defence minister to discuss deepening bilateral cooperation in a post-Blaise world. Russia is one of Africa's largest investors as they search for natural resources and agricultural products. They will bankroll a military coup in Afronia.'

While it was true Mutoni was going to the Russian capital, the Kremlin connection was a red herring and he would not be having the meetings described, instead, he would be spending the majority of his time in the Radisson Blu Hotel meeting a number of people who resided in Europe.

'Who was behind the assassination?' Hamza Leso asked as he looked around the politburo table. 'Who convinced those two stupid girls to murder President Blaise?'

'We can't let this abomination derail the successes we've achieved over the last two years,' the Minister of Health spoke up. 'In the memory of Walter, we must continue his policies of development for all.'

'Fingers must be pointed towards ISiSS or Russia,' Hamza suggested. 'What of the two suspects?'

'They had the same VX Nerve Agent symptoms that killed the president,' Dr Ralph Lisoyga informed the grouping. 'They are undoubtedly guilty. They have also died.'

'How could such a chemical weapon enter Afronia?' Professor Rashid thought aloud.

'We simply don't know. We expect it was either smuggled in through our borders in connivance with a local criminal gang or through diplomatic channels. If the former, I suspect ISiSS, the later, Victov.'

'We have to be very careful who we accuse Hamza. Any investigation has to be airtight before we go public with our findings. If it was ISiSS, we can assume they will claim responsibility. Victov has sent a letter of condolence,' and which Rashid proceeded to read aloud.

The Russian people express our outrage at the use of such despicable chemical weapons. If this is the work of a foreign state, we consider it a declaration of war and will stand shoulder-to-shoulder with our Afronian friends.

'What balderdash,' Ralph thundered.

'Victov wants back into Afronia and would conspire with the devil if needed,' Hamza ruminated before pouring himself a water to calm down. 'What do we do?'

'Constitutionally, we have to hold presidential elections within four weeks,' Professor Rashid, the de-facto head-of state confirmed. 'We must run government and conclude the investigation in that time.' There was no dissent to the elderly gentleman. 'We have to be wary of a military putsch,' Rashid stared at the Minister of Defence. 'There are elements in the armed forces who have stayed in close contact with their Russian counterparts since the civil war. It's a certainty that the Denga Chemical Massacre was caused by Russian weapons but deployed by sympathizers in the Afronian Air Force. Now is the time to clear the armed forces once and for all of those involved in that abomination but never tried, and I include Yohan in this list.'

'Is there corroborating evidence? Punitive measures will guarantee retaliation from the military brass and Robert still has extensive networks. We will be the ones forced into exile if we move too quickly,' Hamza cautioned.

'Robert Yohan has no position in this country,' Rashid emotively said of the notable absentee. 'He must go and so to any other remnants linked to Altimus Solomon or Isaiah George. Now is the time for revolution. We can change the country the way Walter Blaise was never politically able to for fear of a second civil war. A true republic derives power from the citizen and not economic elites or military cliques.'

Chapter 31

Two days after the respective late-night discussions between the politicians and military men, General Mutoni addressed Afronians via the military radio station.

> The country is in deep mourning for His Excellency President Blaise, but now is not the time to expel or suspend members of the opposition or military because they have different opinions. Walter Blaise made Afronia a progressive country and the faults of our past were dealt with during the Truth and Reconciliation Commission. Now is not the time for politicians to purge the armed forces but to unite behind a progressive vision. Squabbling and positioning of politicians must stop while a unity government is formed.
>
> It is of no use to Afronia if our innocent top military minds flee into exile for fear of reprisals. The removal of military officers or veterans of the Independence Wars for political purposes is treacherous shenanigans and will not be tolerated. If there is need to protect the Republic from those with evil thoughts the military will step in.

❧

'The armed forces believe they hold the balance of power,' Jacob said to Sam on their weekly phone call.

'How worried are you?'

'Very. And Yohan is back in the picture; this can't be a coincidence. Everything is finely calculated with that man.'

'Do you think he had something to do with the assassination?'

'I don't know, but he has close ties with Russia and Taberia, and their tears are of the crocodile variety.'

'You sense a conspiracy?'

'I always sense conspiracy when it comes to Afronia. What are you working on?' Jacob asked to move the conversation away from the recent spate of troubles in his adopted homeland.

'Do you remember a report some months ago about a British fishing company in Zarusha playing fast and loose with tax avoidance?' When there was no acknowledgement from Jacob, Sam continued, 'I've been doing some digging—'

'Here we go,' Jacob laughed done the line. 'Have you got your Deerstalker and pipe ready... Sherlock,' he mocked.

'Yeah, yeah, say what you like,' Sam taking the jibe in good humour. 'The company's registered office is not where it should be... it's at a London based law firm that provides offshore legal services including the registration of foreign companies.'

'That's not illegal.'

'True. However, the business has no economic activity in Mauritius. It is taking advantage of double taxation agreements, treaty shopping to avoid paying tax for their clients… and that is illegal.'

Chapter 32

THE SOMALITREAN VICE-PRESIDENT, an Independence War veteran known as The Eagle, a nickname well-earned for his ruthless attention to detail when carrying out Altimus Solomon's orders, was holding a rally in Presidential Square. 'Afronia is like a man in a suit who looks good on the outside but underneath the fine silks is fat, stressed and seconds away from a heart attack. Walter Blaise saved Afronia from implosion, but now is the time to let entrepreneurs thrive. Our wonderful country needs a born winner who has managed many businesses, not a frail loser professor who only has theories,' the Eagle said in the simplistic manner of the American President. 'Afronia needs real change, real leadership and not a business-as-usual attitude. If Rashid is so loved by the people, why does he resort to dirty tricks to try and silence me? If he was truly popular he would engage me in a televised debate. He claims that Afronia has one of the highest percentage of women in parliament, but what authority did they have under Blaise?

'Is it going to be Rashid's luxury mansion that will be under twenty metres of water when the dams are completed... or your villages? How many of you will be moved from your house, your castle, into a tin roof shed with no garden for planting maize? Is this not just one more cynical way to change voting boundaries to his corrupt ways? Why do you think the World Bank has pulled their funding from the National Water Project if they don't have serious doubts as to the transparent bidding process for contractors? Rashid wants to keep the poor and destitute at the bottom of the economic pile while simultaneously degrading the environment; he has no morals. Do you really want him, or would prefer a Somalitrean brush to get rid of the rubbish? Walter Blaise's effort at sustainable economic transformation has failed, but now his Minister of Economy wants to manage the country... and lead Somalitreans into ruin. International partners have assured me that if I'm elected president they will provide technical assistance and policy advice to maximise investment when implementing an industrialization renaissance strategy which will prioritise sectors with the highest growth potential such as tourism, light industry and natural resources.'

'Afronia has recorded impressive rates of economic growth in the last two years,' Professor Rashid started his rally. 'We can't afford to take retrograde steps and be pushed off-track by threats from the military. Walter Blaise set us on the right course and it is for all Afronians to keep up the hard work as we move towards a prosperous and progressive society. Afronia is showing signs of successfully diversifying away from our reliance on natural resources, and while we must be wary of sovereign debt, we should continue to work hand-in-hand with our international partners and supporters as we go through the needed structural transformation to achieve development for all based around social cohesiveness and sustainable industrialised development.

'Half our population is under the age of nineteen, and it is this youth dividend that must be encouraged into economic earners for our country, rather than 1) being unemployed as the policies of the Eagle would make happen, 2) become militia under military rule as General Mutoni has threatened, or, 3) think their only option is to migrate to Europe. We can't afford to lose this generation's potential. The youth need the tools and training to get the skills and experience to become entrepreneurs and decide their destiny.

'As for Yohan, he was a henchman for Solomon. He carried out ethnic massacres. He led the feared Intelligence Services and played a key role in imprisoning political opposition throughout Solomon's reign. He does not respect human rights. He has close ties with Taberia and Russia. These are undisputed facts. Afronians, do not vote him into the Presidential Palace.'

Chapter 33

WHILE POLITICAL RALLIES were taking place, the Southiland Regional Administrator died in mysterious circumstances. A second death in unexplained events was that of an Afronian millionaire businessman who exported fruit and was a major contributor to Rashid's campaign. The Afronian Ambassador to the United Nations died after becoming ill during his fiftieth birthday party. The untimely death was reported as food poisoning though the strain of the virus was never officially identified. The day before his demise... he'd been lobbying the international community to back Rashid. The Afronian Ambassador to the UK suffered an apparent heart attack during a break-in to his apartment, though when his wife was questioned what items were missing, she couldn't see anything out of place. The autopsy proved inconclusive as to the cause of death. The Regional Administrator for Wahilistan was found unconscious having suffered severe head injuries after tripping and falling down two flights of steps and breaking his neck in the process; he died in hospital after three days in a coma. The Minister of Internal Security died from a gunshot wound to the head during a carjacking.

The deceased all had one thing in common. 'My supporters and key allies are falling like flies,' the professor said to Hamza.

'And the Eagle is catching you in the polls; these two facts must be connected. Equally worrisome, a senior member of the Electoral Commission has resigned and fled into exile, her last reported words being, I have received death threats and fear for my safety; Afronia can't hold credible elections.'

'We're turning into a mafia state where you are assassinated or blown to pieces for wanting to lead the country,' Rashid sadly said at a loss. 'What does it mean? Who's doing this?'

Chapter 34

IN THE POLITICAL LIMBO, Umoja City was tense but calm amid the uncertainty, that was until eleven days after President's Blaise's assassination, when General Mutoni—escorted by four Armoured Personnel Carriers—was driven to the Presidential Palace. At intersections, troops on tanks and other armoured vehicles saluted the convoy as it made its serene way to the seat of power. There, General Mutoni flanked by senior officers, gave a televised address to the nation.

> My dear Afronians, we are in a period of turmoil the likes of which this country thought was in our past. To retain peace, I have ordered troops to secure the airport, parliament, government offices and other key sites. Afronia will remain peaceful. Do not fear that our united country will split along ethnic lines. The army will never stand idly by and let our republic descend into civil war.
>
> We suffered a great blow with the murder of Walter Blaise. His slaying was no ordinary happening but a direct attack on all Afronians. This was a declaration of war. The armed forces are sworn to protect this wonderful country and our

constitution; we will not rest until justice is done and the country is safe. I will not accept an investigation by the Presidential Guard or the Commissioner of Police into the death of President Blaise as both can be considered suspects as there has been a culture of impunity in recent years with crimes not investigated much less punished. The Military Police will lead the investigation and report directly to me.

We are living through a time of political, social, financial, administrative, and most worryingly, security catastrophe. Our beautiful country is being attacked from the inside by kleptocrats and communists, and from the outside by liberals. There is a calamitous morass and moral rot in the heart of Afronia that Walter Blaise let fester. Afronia needs a hard and drastic shakeup, and only the army have the will to push through the changes to stop those plotting against us including the Taberians who are massing on our border. As such, my first order is the reinforcement of the northern zone and the building of a wall to keep out the heathens.

Blaise was soft on crime and Afronia has become a criminal paradise. He decriminalised drugs and allowed guns on the street. Corrupt individuals have thrived for years while amassing fortunes, living in mansions and buying yachts in connivance with the upper echelons of government; they will be brought to account. I will tighten the laws and give the army the right of shoot-to-kill criminal elements. So, if you insist on carrying a gun, if you are a drug pusher, if you are a criminal of any kind, don't complain when you are in the morgue; I will no longer permit drug use or homosexuality in our country.

Prisoners will work day-and-night as their repentance to society. Lazy inmates will face solitary confinement. Criminals will farm their own food rather than be a burden on honest taxpayers. They will no longer have conjugal visits. They will mould bricks to build houses for their guards. I will reform prisons to make detention feared.

I will withdraw Afronia from the jurisdiction of the International Criminal Court, a western conspiracy that tells outrageous lies to neuter the sovereign power of its leaders for the sole purpose of economically colonizing the continent.

With no visible civilian leadership, I will not let Afronia fall victim to the vindictiveness that is directed between presidential candidates, a feature of all past elections. I will not allow our democracy to indulge in smear campaigns or have personalities prioritised over governance at the expense of the national interest.

At 12 PM today, there will be a government of national transition headed by the military. Patriots will run this great country on policy issues rather than self-interested opportunists looking for personal gain.

The military led government will follow four guiding principles: political neutrality, strong but transparent leadership, social cohesion and, economic development for all. Ministerial posts will be headed by senior soldiers. I will amend the constitution so that the vice-president automatically becomes the incumbent if the president dies in office so that we do not enter such a state of limbo again.

My fellow Afronians, there are going to be changes, big modifications as I make Afronia great again.

The cameras turned off, General Mutoni walked over to the twenty-foot-high bay window which looked over Presidential Square. 'We need a spectacle to unite Afronia... a military parade,' he thought aloud. 'Splendid looking soldiers, airmen and the navy all in dress uniform and being flanked by tanks, APCs, mobile artillery and missile carriers. Military hardware will roll down Umoja's boulevards while helicopters and fighter jets scream overhead, and the navy fire window shaking ordinance. I will bring pride back to the people and exemplify that the military is always for them. It will be the greatest parade ever seen on the African continent.'

'We welcome the army stepping in to ensure peace and order,' the Russian Ambassador proclaimed at the United Nations Security Council meeting. 'We call for a transitional authority made up of competent and loyal Afronians whose mandate will be to put in place measures to run government until a new president is elected. Russia will send advisors to Umoja City to help with preparations for free and fair elections; no one wants chaos.'

'General Mutoni is driving Afronia back to the dark ages. He is reversing all the progressive policies of the Blaise presidency,' this from the British Foreign Secretary. 'As an international community, we must not stand idly by when military coups take place otherwise we will give free reign to every despot wannabe.'

'He's publicly stated that he will commit human rights abuses, imprison journalists, sanction assassination and re-introduce mandatory national service conscription,' the American Ambassador gave his country's official response. 'We will immediately impose an arms embargo, freeze all assets of the coup leaders and impose a travel ban on the ring leaders.'

Following the withdrawal of Afronia from the International Criminal Court, President Maduhu spoke at a special hearing of the United Nations General Assembly. 'The international community must hold General Mutoni to account. He is an African Hitler and is driving the region towards mayhem. Afronians are starving and their economy is collapsing. Democratic institutions revived under President Blaise are being destroyed and progressive policies wilfully dismantled. This is completely unacceptable.

'We have to be judicious. Afronia is stumbling from crisis to crisis. We must engage rather than push the country over the edge... but as the President of Taberia I will not allow our cousins be subjected to indiscriminate and unlawful subjection nor allow the region to descend into war. I am prepared to take further action if the government of General Mutoni persists to impose its authoritarian rule rather than hold democratic elections as promised.'

Chapter 35

'IT'S NOT ALL TOGETHER UNEXPECTED,' Hamza commiserated as he bear-hugged Professor Rashid. 'The British Foreign Secretary's pathetic statement of mild opprobrium and with no tangible consequences is utterly inconsequential; no wonder he's called a lame goat by Fleet Street.'

'It's a betrayal of Afronians, to the memory of Walter, to all who died in the civil war. This is a junta. The generals don't privately pretend it's anything but a money grab. Patriotic Afronians who want a vibrant democracy must not stand for it.' The intellectual calmed down and reflected on the current situation with a more refined mind. 'How sure are we that it wasn't the army who plotted to kill Walter? He was voracious in his quest to root out corruption, not forgetting that it was the former Minister of Defence, a general, that was his first victim.'

'Undoubtedly, there are many men in uniform who want to protect their financial interests... but killing Blaise, I don't think so. I have very good relations with the army and I never heard of any conspiracies.'

'Nevertheless, the appointment of the military into the politburo is worrisome. That move doesn't represent the new Afronia. We have to regroup and insist on an elected civilian authority within one month.'

'I fully agree, but how?'

'Unbelievable... if it were anywhere other than Afronia...' Sam didn't need to finish the sentence.

'I smell a rat,' Jacob concurred. 'Blaise being assassinated just before he was about to launch a very public probe into the influence of foreign owned business in Afronia... it's too much of a coincidence. And then out of nowhere, General Mutoni somehow sitting on the presidential throne... there must have been a lot of planning for that to happen—'

'Something is fishy.'

'Mate, aren't your investigative antenna twitching?'

'I'm done with Afronia and Afronia's done with me. I'll come and visit you and Tigist one day on holiday, but I'll not work there again.'

'I understand, Sam... but aren't you curious?'

'You've great contacts. What does Innocent say? Tigist is the queen of uncovering the word on the street. You must get plenty of titbits of information through the incubator, and with Stella and your friend Brigadier Abel you have access to the military inner sanctum. If anything comes up in London connected to Afronia I'll be sure to let you know.'

'Do you think the recent spate of negative stories about Blaise had anything to do with anything? Death by a thousand cuts? And that's not forgetting the previous assassination attempts at the food fair and Jay Peters unsuccessful coup.'

'Potentially there could be a connection.' Sam paused to gather his thoughts. 'If I was to plan a hostile take-over of the Presidential Palace, then the corruption stories would have been a good strategy to soften up the public by diminishing Blaise, and so when killed by the school-girls, while it was surprising it was not totally out of the blue.'

'You might be onto something,' Jacob's voice belying that he was not convinced. 'Do you think Leso or Yohan had any involvement?'

'A Manchurian Candidate?'

'It's just a theory—'

'But for who? That pair of scoundrels have been relatively quiet in the last weeks.'

'Follow the money,' Sam reminded his friend. 'What do we currently know?' Though he hadn't planned it, he could nevertheless not help but become interested in the country that had so shaped his recent past. *I have unfinished business in Afronia and a new investigation might, just might shed some light on Jessica's murder?*

'For starters, what about the UK's increasing influence in Afronia? At all levels in the private sector there are Union Jacks waving and the Brits are helping the Afronian government with foreign investor friendly policies. Whitehall authorised the supplying of armaments to the armed forces… and a Sandhurst educated army man is now in the Presidential Palace.'

'No. I don't think so. Mutoni visited Moscow a few days before he made his first pronouncement—'

'True, though he was surely meeting other people there as well. Think about it. Whitehall mandarins and city financiers must be watching developments closely, and it's been noticeable how quiet the Foreign Office has been about the military coup. The UK's private and public sectors have invested billions in Afronia. There is huge sovereign and private debt. British companies largely control the Afronian utilities and wouldn't want their investments put in jeopardy. The UK is the largest export market for Afronia. The British Embassy never closed its doors during the civil war and is looking to purchase nearby properties to expand, with a new building specifically to support British businesses to invest in the region. In short, Afronia will be castrated if British interests pull out or the cumulative private and sovereign debt needs to be repaid in a hurry.'

'A British led conspiracy? Come on Jacob, this is not a John Le Carre novel. We both have a few leads to follow up so let's keep in touch, mate,' and with that Sam put the phone down.

Chapter 36

'GENTLEMEN,' GENERAL MUTONI addressed his cabinet twenty-four-hours after he had taken office. 'I have a mandate to create Afronia in my vision. My first order of the day is to crackdown on dissent,' this as he brought his fist crashing down on the conference table. 'We cannot let pesky bloggers, opposition politicians or activists spread vile words; we must have an iron grip to control Afronia at this inauspicious time.'

'You promised a free media,' a junior minister, and one of the few non-military men in the meeting, reminded the president.

'Who are you, my friend?' Mutoni sweetly asked the civilian, the rest of the room staying silent, the generals, admirals and air marshalls knowing better than to question the chain of command.

'I'm—'

'YOU ARE WHO I FUCKING SAY YOU ARE!' the president thundered. 'Get out of my sight. It is only your naivety that's saved your life.'

The trembling woman stood up and was swiftly escorted out of the room by Presidential Guard. *Will I be picked up by the secret police? Should I leave Afronia and seek asylum?* She asked herself as she was unceremoniously pushed out of the locked gates of the parliament building.

'I will not tolerate impudence. Afronians must respect law and order and that starts from the top. I will repeal the Sexual Rights Law as carnal knowledge against the order of nature is not God-fearing. Sexual deviancy will be punishable by twenty years in prison.'

'That is intolerable,' this from Ralph as he slammed his sheaf of papers onto the boardroom table.

'Have you ever seen a gay pig or a bi-sexual cat?' Mutoni joked.

'What about a transgender rat?' The Eagle grinned. 'A lesbian fish?' he was really enjoying himself. 'Homosexuality is not in the Torah, Bible or Koran; it's not normal; there is no place for it in Afronian society.'

'Resign… and you and your queer friends will no longer be protected by ministerial privilege,' the general threatened.

Ralph was speechless for ten seconds, the whole room staring at him. 'Adults should be able to engage in consensual and mutually desired private and intimate means of self-expression,' he argued as he tried not to rise to the bait.

'Minister of Health, resign if you feel so strongly.'

'It's unconstitutional.' Ralph looked around for support but only saw an ominous bowing of heads.

'This has nothing to do with the values of democracy and equality,' Professor Rashid said as he stood up for his friend.

'Accept it or leave; both of you.'

'Cowards!' Ralph shouted accusingly at those who were in Blaise's politburo but who now stayed silent. 'You are all cowards and are desecrating Walter's vision of an Afronia for all.'

'Go or I will have you arrested as a bum-boy.' This quip from the general earned a snigger from a few in the room though many remained uncomfortably silent.

Ralph had no option and left the meeting fearful for his friends once the edict had been rushed through parliament and made into law.

'The second order of the day,' Mutoni, all smiles re-started, 'is to introduce God-fearing, socialist-nationalist policies that have family values at its core. We will ban breastfeeding of loose girls in school. There will be no abortions, both the woman and doctor sentenced to life imprisonment for the deaths they cause. Divorce will become legally convoluted and a social disgrace. But families who are patriotic and produce many children will be financially rewarded. Single-parent mothers who are a burden to their families and the state will not be tolerated. Those who are weak of mind, the alcoholics, gamblers, whoremongers, drug addicts and psychologically ill, will be imprisoned to keep them from their vices. Their medicine will be hard labour to rebuild the infrastructure of this great country. The handicapped shall be kept at home so as not to impede the able. Criminal responsibility will be reduced to ten years of age. I will put an end to the national decay of young dreadlocked men and cheap women selling sexual services and spreading diseases; they will serve time in forced labour camps. The sooner we are free of all these vermin the sooner our society will be civilized.'

My God, a flummoxed Professor Rashid thought after the meeting concluded, *Afronia has a Nazi monster. Even Altimus Solomon at his most radical, or Isaiah George at his most psychotic wouldn't introduce half these policies. If he encourages religious conservatism, mosques and churches that have sat side-by-side in every neighbourhood peacefully for decades could enter conflict; thank God, Afronians are observant rather than devout. The general must be stopped.*

Totally unaware of the seismic policy changes or Ralph's dismissal, Charles Ontag, and Innocent Shembles were enjoying a happy-hour Gin and Tonic sundowner at Beaches, a newly opened and quite popular seaside bar in the Afronian capital. They calmly watched the turquoise waters lap onto the shore and a Sea Eagle soar on the tidal vortex. Looking down the shorelin, they saw hawkers scraping a meagre income from selling fruit juice, horse rides, hair braiding… and themselves. Dreadlocked muscular young men, colloquially known as bumsters, offered their company to middle-aged female tourists whose bared breasts had turned pink in the equatorial sun. 'Hey, nice lady,' they would say, 'what's your name? Where are you from? You like dancing?' There were also young, mainly petite girls, who walked around skimpily dressed as they sought the attention of older, grey hared, pot-bellied, Arabic, Russian and Western men; sex tourism had become a boom industry for Afronia. And together with the variety of mountains, forests, flora, fauna and wildlife, it was easy to understand why Afronia had been drawing holidaymakers in ever greater numbers over the past few years.

'Hi,' Charles and Innocent heard a familiar voice approach from behind. 'I've come from one of the most terrifying meetings in my life,' Ralph informed his chums.

'What's happened?' Innocent wanted to know why his friend had such a furrowed brow.

'Our community,' he said referring to Afronia's LGBTQ family, 'are going to be persecuted; Mutoni has re-authorized anal and virginity tests.'

'As Minister of Health can't you stop him?' Charles asked. 'This last year it has been possible to wake up, brush teeth, eat breakfast and go to work, without the fear of summary arrest; we will live in fear once more. Just walking the street or having a drink in a bar, and we could be arrested for being who we are.'

'I was forced to resign... otherwise he would have fired me; he knows I'm gay.'

'How?'

'He just knew.'

Chapter 37

WITHIN FORTY-EIGHT HOURS of Mutoni taking charge he was imprinted on the national conscience. Three politburo members and a dozen high-ranking soldiers he'd considered threats had been publicly executed. Corruption investigations against seven former cabinet ministers had started. A legal framework to change the constitution allowing indefinite military rule was being drafted... and a distant cousin of the general's had been appointed Chief Justice. Judicial beatings were legally introduced, public demonstrations were violently ended and the police had been given a licence to kill. Many of Blaise's more progressive policies had been reversed and/or removed from Parliament's order of business. There was constant haranguing against the media from the presidential palace, and religion, the social glue that had not splintered even during civil war was referred to as, a divisive tool of fundamentalists. The term, terrorism, was liberally used to describe anything which did not conform to Mutoni's world view. In all way, Afronia was in an authoritarian spiral, the president only interested in his own agenda at the expense of the people who were shocked and investors who saw a faltering economy and whose conversations had rapidly turned to talk of divesting.

'Afronia was going in the right direction under Blaise,' Emmanuel, said to Jacob as they sat in a recently opened café near the incubator, the owner now wishing she hadn't spent her life savings to get the business up and running. 'He was democratic, a progressive beacon that allowed coffee shops to open and flourish. Mutoni is turning the country back to destitution with his paranoia. Next, he will purge civil servants who support Professor Rashid. There will be no teachers or doctors as they will be in prison. He's stated, that he's on a drive to make Afronia's natural resources assets and key infrastructure, such as utilities, open to foreign investors; he is selling the family silver and I expect he will personally keep much of the proceeds.'

'We need foreign direct investment in certain sectors, but sovereign debt could lead to hyper-inflation; Afronians won't be able to afford essentials. From the farmer to the city entrepreneur, all will suffer if control of the economy is lost.'

'Trade investment has to be on fair terms. If it's exploitative, it will bleed Afronia dry and drive the country back to civil war,' Emmanuel voiced his fears. 'Something has to be done, and quick... the crisis has led Moody's to downgrade Afronia to Ba1 and, Standard and Poor's to BB+, both are non-investment grade; the economy is in freefall.' Emmanuel took a sip of his coffee—it was cold, one more thing to dampen his usually sunny disposition. 'Why else do you think the British Foreign Secretary is here?'

'Is he? I didn't know. Are the British launching a new aid package?'

'Nope. He is inviting Mutoni to the Commonwealth Heads of States meeting in London.'

'Seriously? They're endorsing him?'

'We live in a world of realpolitik and not ethics my friend. If the British economy is on the line, the rule book of who to do business with gets thrown out the window!'

As Emmanuel's latte went cold, the British Foreign Secretary was meeting his junior Minister for International Development in readiness for their conversation with Mutoni. 'The problem with Afronia... it was never colonised. If we had been in charge during the times of Empire, at least there would have been some infrastructure we could build on... no pun intended.'

'Bloody hell Jonas, you can't be so openly dismissive,' the Foreign Secretary admonished. 'There might be listening devices.'

'I'm only saying what the politically correct in Whitehall are afraid to utter.'

'You're meant to be a senior diplomat.'

'And this I tell you; colonialism was no bad thing. In other countries we helped develop coffee and cocoa plantations, build roads and hospitals, develop education systems and democracy; just imagine where Africa would be if we were still in charge.'

'We are dumping hundreds of millions into Afronia to support British businesses win contracts.'

'Giving direct budgetary support to Mutoni, is that wise?'

'Don't be naïve. Direct aid is a small percentage of our total spend. We channel most funds through purposefully opaque routes. Why else would taxpayer money go to The World Bank and the like? Aid money doesn't have to be spent efficiently of effectively, but only to help us reach our desired goals. So, what if a blog post costs north of £10,000?'

'As long as it's a British blogger,' the junior minister interrupted with a grin.

'And trust funds with unwieldy processes and no clear objectives are little more than a slush fund for projects the British government, World Bank or United Nations can't be seen to be involved in. We are in the business of regime change through weak accounting practices!'

Chapter 38

'I'M USED TO ABUSE, but Mutoni has me generally worried,' Innocent told Ralph when they met at Geronimo's Café on the Umoja City promenade. 'The Editor of the Daily Afronian News was sentenced to 1,000 years in prison when he published findings that funds worth $60m to buy helicopters for the army were unaccounted for. He was thrown in with hardcore criminals, notorious murderers, rapists and armed robbers. He will be murdered as an example to all journalists to keep their noses out of where they're not wanted.'

'Aren't you afraid?'

'Of course, I am… but I can't back down, give in. I have to keep exposing the corruption, the mindless stealing of the nation's wealth. I will keep investigating corrupt officials wherever they might be, whether they are referees, officials or players in the fledgling football league, civil servants conspiring with foreign investors for visas… or dubious arms contracts. Furthermore, I shall never be silenced unless I'm resting in peace. Mutoni is afraid of the truth and the people know it. That's why I must continue. To give hope and light after the blackness of this army coup.'

'But why do you always have to provoke with your articles? You must tone down your inflammatory rhetoric.'

'My words are all I have.' Innocent paused. 'I might have to go into exile.'

'What the hell did you say?' Ralph asked with concern in his voice.

'I wrote a post on Facebook… here, read it,' he said as he passed Ralph his smartphone.

Corruption link between General Mutoni and the Popovs.

Afronian marchers in London say they are disgusted with the way President Mutoni is moving the economy. "There must be a vote of no confidence," they demanded. "Our democracy is under an unrelenting attack."

The demonstration followed public outcry over leaked emails which exposed an unusually close relationship between the president and his Russian billionaire friends the Popovs. Afronian commentators in exile declared, "The Popovs have extraordinary influence over the president. They work hand in corrupt glove to enrich each other through murky deals. There is a conspiracy of money laundering and kickbacks. The Popovs fund General Mutoni in return for winning multi-million-dollar government contracts that the president has personally awarded since taking the reins of power."

But who are the Popovs? They are two brothers and a sister who moved to Afronia in 2001 as small gem traders, but who now have diamond and gold mines, a bank, a technology business, a number of transport companies and a media house in their business empire. They were on the periphery of politics during the Solomon years… but their wealth multiplied many times during the civil war where they supplied all sides with arms. They recently elevated Felix Mutoni—the oldest son of the president—onto the board of directors at a number of their companies. "The Mutonis and Popovs lives and business interests are intertwined."

'You're mad!'

'What else could I do Ralph but write the truth? When the army stormed the Supreme Court and arrested Chief Justices who refused to implement Mutoni's laws, what else could I have done other than expose the reality? If there is not an independent judiciary the rule of law is worthless; I had to say something.'

'And what do you expect will happen now you've pulled the tiger's tail?'

'The ministry of propaganda will spit homophobic vile. They will request the president to put a noose around my neck for inhumane behaviour. They will probably put my face on a crude online beat'em up game, my digital ego will be a blooded victim who is attacked with baseball bats, bottles and machetes. It will not be subtle; it will be open season. They will publish my address and tell patriots to visit me. This happened in the days of Altimus Solomon and I expect Mutoni will do the same.'

'Are you leaving Afronia?'

'Never! I'm a journalist. It's dangerous seeking the truth in a totalitarian state so I will be disciplined. I will self-censor and double-check for unintended insults as I wobble on the tightrope between reporting the news and not getting arrested. I might flinch every time the doorbell rings unexpectedly and wonder when I leave the house if I will safely return… but I will not be cowed.'

Two days later, Innocent was arrested as part of a nation-wide crackdown, his crime: seditious remarks. 'This is intolerance at an unprecedented scale,' Ralph said to Charles when they met after learning of their friend's arrest, their pizza left untouched the oil from the cheese slowly solidifying.

'What did he hope to achieve?'

In the Central Police station. 'I'm not a criminal,' Innocent protested. 'Press freedom is the right of the people,' he started to argue until donkey-punched in his midriff. 'I'm not a thief or terrorist,' he spluttered. 'Mutoni is a tyrant who is expunging the progressive initiatives of President Blaise.' He was hit on the side of the head with a gun butt and knocked unconscious and then thrown into a cell.

Bloody, bruised and with no legal representation, he however did have the sympathies of a guard who gave him a sheet of paper and a pencil.

Dear Sir,

I have followed the mother of all democracies across the years with admiration. I admire the British iteration, that all the peoples of the world should have the basic freedoms of expression and opportunity no matter their skin colour, ethnicity, sexual or religious preference. As an Afronian, I'm now denied those human rights and not able to question the legitimacy of my president.

There was a genuine, thriving democracy under the leadership of Walter Blaise, but now there are death squads that terrorise our city streets. There is unrestricted violence by the police and army at political rallies. It is the lack of democratic truths that is driving many Afronian patriots to migrate to your great country.

In the depths of Umoja City Prison I have been beaten, electrocuted, humiliated and interrogated, but I will not incriminate my people for having the same ideals as your country. I'm imprisoned without reason and I have no hope for a fair trial, this denial of freedom of expression being against all that makes us humans. And so, I beseech you to stop supporting and arming the illegal regime of General Mutoni. Let your actions *in regards freedoms of speech, expression and opportunity speak louder than your words.*

Yours sincerely
Innocent Shembles

In the cell next to Innocent was an even louder and arguably more influential dissident, the musical genius Rasta BobbyAfro. He'd composed and sung a lament at Walter Blaise's funeral and which had poked fun at the junta. The lyrics were rich with visualisation of protestors tortured for voicing their democratic rights, off economic inequality, police brutality and social injustice. He'd even named General Mutoni in his gangster rap video— I die. Another song, Rebellion, urged Afronians to take up arms; guns and bullets, was the crowd's refrain to this tune. He'd been charged with criminal conspiracy and membership of an illegal organisation, charges that amounted to treason and the death penalty. He'd been a hunted man for weeks until the police discovered him after an impromptu basement concert.

Innocent's letter had been smuggled out of the prison and published on the Cell156 website by the time Charles and Ralph next met. 'Who will protect press freedoms?' asked the doctor and who'd earlier in the day had his medical licence revoked.

Charles shrugged his soldiers. 'Who knows? Who cares? I mourn our friend.'

'As do I,' Ralph said as he put his arm around his friend. 'I also mourn democracy. I'm afraid for our friends in the LGBTQ community. I'm afraid of the Presidential Guard. I no longer recognise this country where surveillance and censorship are the main themes. Speaking the truth, like Innocent did all his life, is as good as committing suicide.'

'I thought the digital revolution was meant to have ushered in a golden age of media freedom, everybody with a smartphone able to freely share their opinions and experiences for the benefit of all.'

'That was the hope, but data analytics in the name of national security means those who investigate corruption and abuse at the highest levels of government, are at huge risk. Censorship is one of the main tools of authoritarian states; it has always been that way. Digital surveillance means that the internet is not the anonymous platform that encourages whistle-blowers many thought it would be.'

'What are we going to do?' Charles half-heartedly asked.

'Whatever we can,' came the answer, the conversation of their friend's death confirmed by a police statement in a national newspaper.

General Mutoni critic, Innocent Shembles shot dead in Little Wahili.
"The killing appears to be targeted. He was shot at his home in the slums of Little Wahili where he lived with his gay lover," the police spokesman stated. "This high-profile murder was a ho-

mophobic attack and had nothing to do with his antagonistic style of reporting."

"Shembles was shot twice in the back as he walked through the slum area, this after leaving the notorious Frank's Bar which is a known hangout for perverted and deranged gays who don't follow the laws of nature. He was found bleeding by a fellow homosexual deviant and died in the ambulance on the way to Umoja City Central Hospital," a Ministry of Health official confirmed.

Chapter 39

S AM WAS IN AN INTERNET café on Coventry Street in London, this road between Piccadilly Circus and Leicester Square. He waited ten minutes before a swivel chair—in a row of twenty squashed together—with a wobble became free, this discomfort though a price worth paying so that his browsing history would remain anonymous.

With an extortionately priced coffee steaming to the side of his monitor, Sam typed: business, conspiracy, Jobuja, into Google. Within milliseconds the search engine returned over 10,000 entries. He started to scroll down the list while looking for familiar words, names, places and phrases: Altimus Solomon, Presidential Square Massacre, Denga Chemical Attack, Lesotho Street, Hamza Leso, civil war and mercenaries were the most common. He paused when he saw to his surprise, Jessica Webb's name come up. He clicked on the link and went to a website that commemorated journalists who'd died for their profession; Innocent's name was the most recent entry.

Sam went back to the search engine and followed a link to a Wikipedia page that had earlier caught his attention.

The Jobuja Group is a secretive clique of powerful, influential, connected and wealthy individuals who have an interest in the African Continent, their objective to have unrestricted access to open markets.

Less than ten-percent of members are of African descent with the majority from either Europe or North America. Historically, membership was evenly split between the worlds of politics, business and aristocracy, though in the last decade the percentage of private sector attendees has noticeably increased.

Meetings are conducted under Chatham House Rules and are held twice yearly. They provide an opportunity for participants to freely speak their mind during the enclave. The group resembles the Bilderberg Group, in that there are no votes, resolutions or policy statements issued.

Partly because of the Jobuja Group's strict adherence to secrecy, the undisclosed nature of proceedings has led to many conspiracy theories in regards genetically modified crops, the failure to eradicate Malaria, the limited mitigation on climate change and the rise of Islamic State in Sub-Sahara.

Sam started a new search. He typed: Afronia, Jobuja, Switzerland.

Former British Minister for International Development now a consultant to Swiss hedge fund.
Many a former public servant with an impressive network of contacts, whether politician, army

general or university Vice Chancellor, finds that the private sector are willing to pay grandly for the opening of doors to win government contracts. But your stock rises exponentially when the global capitalist hegemony wants access to your little black book and it is for this reason that AfricaInvest, a Swiss hedge fund willingly pays the current Chancellor of the Exchequer, Andrew Sinclair an astounding £30,000 a day, excluding share options, for a non-executive directorship. The question that needs asking, is, whether this is the epitome of business rationality on the part of the hedge fund or a gross conflict of interest.

It's not much of a push to understand how the Chancellor, despite his very busy public schedule, can squeeze in time on weekends or evenings to work for AfricaInvest—but is he worth it? "A high price tag, but from a business with such massive assets, he can be considered value for money, good business," one hedge fund manager claimed. "Understanding global policies on poverty reduction, the intricacies of the United Nations' Sustainable Development Goals and, access to the highest levels of decision makers in Africa, South East Asia, the Caribbean, Latin America and the Middle-East is priceless."

AfricaInvest conspicuously claim, "He doesn't lobby governments or manage investment portfolios, as that's forbidden; his value is his perspective and insights on the global repercussion of climate change and the impact of changing weather patterns on the Bottom of the Pyramid," this in reference to those living on less than $2 a day.

"The private sector recruiting public figures is an age-old strategy; politics and business have been in each other pockets for millennia," a minster with a considerably lower profile than the Chancellor stated. "As a serving Member of Parliament and contributor to a renowned national newspaper Sinclair will be under intense scrutiny. It will be very difficult to simultaneously ride three stallions and not have the whiff of conflict of interest."

Interesting, Sam considered, *but nothing I couldn't have guessed.* He did one more search.

Several major European oil companies and commodity traders headquartered in Switzerland have been accused of exploiting weak fuel standards in Afronia through exporting high polluting fuels with Sulphur levels hundreds of times higher than in Europe. Sir Boris Taylor, Chairman of UK Fuels PLC, a major donor to the ruling Conservative Party and recently appointed Knight of the British realm, has been directly implicated.

AfricaInvest, a Swiss Hedge fund is a majority shareholder in UK Fuels and other companies that export to the African continent. While there is nothing illegal about the practice of blending fuels, it is ethically dubious. In the case of Afronia, it is a little-known fact that Ulrich Müller and Isiah George went to university together in

Geneva. It is rumoured, that Sir Boris Taylor and Ulrich Müller are members of the Jobuja Group.

Finishing his second coffee, and after paying his £9.50 bill and walking into the crisp London early evening air for a smoke, Sam thought aloud, *The same names and companies keep coming up. It's a spider's web of connections and intrigue, but who or what is at the centre of it?*

Returning from the internet café Sam settled on his Ikea sofa and picked up a glass of red wine from the Ikea coffee table and which was populated with the TV, ceiling lights and surround sound system controls. After a long slurp of Claret, he dialled. 'What do you know about the Jobuja Group?'

'Who?' Jacob answered, this after being interrupted by the shrill tone of his mobile phone. He'd been watching an episode of the first ever Afronian soap opera while receiving a foot massage from Tigist. What the TV programme lacked in editorial and filmmaking quality it did however cover important social issues such as public housing, education and the role entrepreneurship was playing in the Second Republic, the last of the plot lines being the main draw for the manager of the business incubator.

'They're a neo-liberal elite that has its claws in Africa. Members think nothing of exploiting men, women, property, land, natural resources, or any other asset class to further their profits. James Buchanan is their Messiah.'

'Who's he when at home?'

'He developed public choice theory, and which argues that democracy should bow before the altar of freedom to make huge profits. He went so far as to say: despotism may be the only organisational alternative to the political structure that we observe. He lived his master plan in Chile when helping Pinochet draft the constitution, his raft of policies exacerbating social inequality and making the poor poorer and the wealthy even richer.'

'And the Jobuja Group want that in Afronia, Africa writ large?'

'Think about it. What is Mutoni doing other than reversing all of Blaise's progressive policies—'

'Conspiracy theory!' Jacob bellowed down the line. 'Mutoni is Russia's henchman; he went to Moscow shortly before entering the Presidential Palace. Besides, he's destroying the economy and frightening investors not welcoming them with open arms.'

'Buchanan said, and this is a quote: conspiratorial secrecy is at all times essential. If all fingers are pointing in the same direction, then rumours and supposition might be more than mere conspiracy.'

'Maybe?' Jacob now sitting up. 'But conspiracy of what, who and how? Do you have anything solid, reports? Affidavits?'

'Not yet.'

Five kilometres from where Sam was puffing on his Cheroot, Stacy Adams was once more entering The Shard and making her way to the offices of Walterson and Partners. 'Hi, yah,' she cheerily said to Daryl, the guard on the front desk and who she'd gone out for a drink three nights earlier.

'Hi, dear. I didn't know you were working today.'

'Neither did I. Zero-hour contracts means I can never be too sure where or when I might be given a job.'

'Don't I just know it,' Daryl admitted ruefully. He'd landed his permanent job in the lobby six-months earlier after being given the opportunity by a cousin, the security manager. 'Will I see you later?' he asked with a Cheshire cat smile.

'If you buy the first round,' Stacy replied with a glint in her eye as she swept her hair back, pouted and purposefully exaggerated the sway of her hips as she shimmed towards the elevators.

Fifteen minutes later and with the vacuum cleaner in hand and the kettle brewing in the janitor's room, thoughts of flirting were far from Stacy's mind as she started cleaning the expensively furnished offices. Stacy always followed the same routine when on a cleaning job, *Start at the opposite end of the floor to any employees who still happened to be working and do the private offices of top management last as sometimes meetings go on late and/or a manager comes back after a few drinks in a nearby pub to collect their briefcase.* She learnt this routine the hard way as on one occasion, and with her headphones blasting, she had embarrassingly walked into a private office to see a man on his knees in front of who she guessed was the boss; she never cleaned at that company again.

One-and-a-half hours into her shift she'd completed the hovering and wiped down and polished desk surfaces. She had also cleaned the kitchen area. *No one is in the office and in ten more minutes I'll be enjoying a pint with Daryl,* she smiled at the thought as she entered the Chief

Financial Officer's room, the last space that needed her attention.

It was an imposingly large office and the only part of the whole floor which had solid walls and a wooden rather than glass door. Stacy started to organise the loose bits of paper and notebooks into some semblance of order on the eight-foot-long desk that housed two thirty-inch Apple monitors and a laptop docking station. Next, she went to the cupboard where several hundred lever arch files in a multitude of colours were stacked. Starting from the left she straightened up or aligned all the disorderly folders, this taking a little over a minute. About to close the cupboard doors she saw a yellow Post It Note which had errantly found its way on to a shelf. She picked it up knowing that she wouldn't be able to help herself from not reading it. *Curiosity killed the cat,* she gently chuckled.

Thank you; it's the little details that count.

It would've been nice if that was for me, a small appreciation but these sorts don't even know people like me exist! The lives I've seen destroyed by the recklessness of self-serving lawyers and the financial sector. If only Joe Public knew what conversations really took place in the boardrooms of these City Goliaths and the internal controls that are wilfully flouted so that grotesquely large bonuses can be earned.

It was at this admonishment that two familiar words on the spine of a black file caught her attention. With a furtive glance over her shoulder she reopened the cupboard and picked up the file marked RED FLAGS.

Chapter 40

'EXTERNAL DEBT?' Yohan questioned from the plush surrounds of his Umoja City villa.

'Yes, my friend,' Ulrich confirmed. 'Afronia will borrow more than it can afford. I can ensure there's cheap credit... as when Afronia can't pay state assets will become mine!'

'And why should Afronia borrow from Swiss banks?

'They are not officially borrowing from me. No business associated with me is investing in Afronia; that's the beauty of offshore accounts... they are very difficult to trace. I have an account which is financed to the tune of $20 billion for the express purpose of regime change. I have sole discretion over investment decisions. I won't disclose the identities of my funders and I only have to give basic updates to my board on the investments I make. I have a free hand to do as I wish.' Yohan stayed quiet. 'After Mutoni's economic rampage Afronia will be in more debt than it can ever repay. And if he doesn't resign he'll be forced from office; it's already been arranged.'

'Will I be the next President of Afronia?' Yohan asked directly. 'A wise older statesman and acceptable face to the people? Someone who they can trust.'

'Robert, with control… anything is possible. We can change economic objectives and follow the regional strategy that we talked about all those months ago. Victov wants someone in the Presidential Palace who will unify Taberia and Afronia, but not Mutoni; he is too… unpredictable; power gets to some people and makes them go crazy.'

'I'm ready to be president once Mutoni stands down,' Yohan implored the Swiss. 'I have the support of the citizens, the military, businessmen and international partners. I can use the Southiland Renaissance Dam controversy as a pretext to attack Taberia, and then you and your backers would be primed to invest in the reconstruction of a unified Greater Afronia. Are we agreed that I'll be the next president of the Second Democratic Republic of Afronia?'

'Yes,' came the response as the two men clinked champagne flutes.

Chapter 41

JEAN-MARC LASTRADE, a French national based in London had received an anonymous tip to go to an address in South-West London. With the smell of a good story, he did as instructed. A little over an hour after opening the anonymous envelope that had been hand delivered through his front door, he looked up and down a suburban street and didn't see anyone or anything that looked suspicious or paying him undue attention. He swiftly walked up the flight of seven concrete steps and trying the front door of the cream coloured, semi-detached Victorian house found it to be unlocked. He entered.

'Hello?' he quietly called out, not that he expected anyone to answer. There wasn't. He opened the nearest door, to his right, and immediately found his surprise. In the middle of the drawing-room was a wooden pallet on top of which were three cardboard boxes. He approached it with undue caution half expecting it to be some kind of a bobby-trap. *What is inside and why would such a gift land in my hands?* Gingerly lifting the lid of the box on the far left of the row, he saw a collection of tapes and disks. *Video and sound recordings?* The middle box was neatly filled with lever arch files. He picked up a blue one at random and flicked through it. *Africa? Commercial contracts? Afronia? Water?* The third box had an assortment of photographs. He picked up a handful and leafed through them. He didn't recognise anyone, *Though there is one person who was prominent in many of the surveillance shots; who is the man?* Jean-Marc took out the magnifying glass he habitually kept in his leather shoulder bag and hovered it two inches above the black and white image. He pulled his hand back a little bit to a better focus on the face in the middle of the convex glass. 'Zut alors!'

Lastrade picked up another photograph to check if it was the same person in the collection; it was. *What's the story? Where's the connection?* He went back to the middle box and pulled out a yellow folder inside of which he found a stack of confidential letters, the contents of which concerned the transferring of millions-of-dollars to an offshore account. The letters had no signature or indication whatsoever of who had sent it but the implication was unmistakable, it was all to do with the man in the photographs.

Five sleepless nights later and after the facts had been checked, cross-checked and checked once again by a team of researchers his news organisation had hastily put together to ensure the authenticity of the material, Jean-Marc had the pleasure to press the send button on his email, the article flying through cyber-space to his editor who'd already got approval from the proprietor and legal department to run the exclusive if all the facts added up, and which they did.

Prince James implicated in £60m corruption scandal.

Second in line to the Royal throne, Prince James in his capacity as a British Trade Envoy, is at the centre of a growing controversy in relationship to his involvement in helping HydroDevelop win the lucrative water infrastructure and irrigation project in Afronia, the impoverished East African country that is currently in the grip of an army coup.

HydroDevelop won the £500 million Afronia water project, though there has been a swirl of troubling allegations that not all was above board with the awarding of the contract. Specifically, it relates to the Prince's dubious business connections with the regime of former Life President Altimus Solomon and being a personal friend of the international fugitive Isaiah George. In an email to the Afronian Minister of Natural Resources, the Prince wrote:

Dear Minister,

HydroDevelop is a world leading British company in the arena of engineering water solutions. I believe they have put together a world class technical, environmental and financial proposal and are primed to start work should they win the contract. I would be honoured to host a meeting with the decision-making committee and the Chairman of HydroDevelop at Buckingham Palace to discuss any outstanding questions.

Logs of phone calls, photographs and emails, show that in the spring of 2018, three months before the awarding of the contract, the Prince used his global network to ensure HydroDevelop won the first-phase, five-year contract of the transformational infrastructure project to build water channels, irrigations schemes and sewage plants in Afronia. Over the next 25 years there is a reputed budget of £6billion for follow on projects.

An anonymous source within HydroDevelop confirmed, that the Duke of York received a finder's fee of £5 million for facilitating the meeting (with the Afronian procurement team) and arranging a personalized tour of Buckingham Palace. "We felt a one-percent commission for the life-time of the contract was fair. By winning the first phase of the project we will be in prime position to win further contracts; the Prince could net up to £60 million."

This is one more in a slew of controversies for the Prince and which has included the sale of his marital home to a Saudi Prince for double the market value and, selling his five-percent share in an offshore business to a Russian Oligarch for triple the share price, this shortly after being photographed in an intimate embrace with a Russian supermodel twenty-years his junior and whose family is said to have connections with the Russian mafia.

Without a doubt, the Afronia Waterways contract has been a great success for the British economy as it helps to solidify the commercial services that the UK can provide to Africa and enshrines the government's combined business and aid strategy. However, the way the deal was negotiated appears to be in clear contravention of the Foreign Corrupt Practices & Bribery Act, and if the British government had tacit knowledge of it, this raises serious questions about the legality of the Foreign Office's strategy to get embassies, and in this case the royal family, to be involved in commercial discussions.

Richard Price, MP and former International Aid Minister, was quoted as saying, "These findings raise serious questions not only about the impartiality of the British Crown in matters of politics and business, but also the use of taxpayer-funded tours of Royal property and the ethics of winning business through opaque methods. This is another example in a litany of accusations that Prince James has cashed in on his royal connections to develop dubious relationships with questionable personalities. He is enriching himself rather than acting as a trade envoy for the UK. He shows scant regard to the government's public stance on human rights and anti-corruption initiatives. He is an embarrassment to the Royal family and a national disgrace."

Buckingham Palace released the following statement: "Claims that Prince James acted out of self-interest are erroneous and defamatory. Any documents referenced are a breach of the Prince's privacy and the Editor's Code of Conduct. Royal lawyers are being consulted."

General Mutoni read Jean-Marc's article about his friend the Duke of York with considerable interest. *Bloody hypocrites. The thing with the moralizing west… is they are moralistic rather than realistic when it comes to the human instinct of wanting more. Now I must live up to my end of the bargain.*

The new Minster of Health had called a press conference at which he read out a statement written by his boss.

The Bible teaches that every life is sacred and that only God the Almighty can decide when someone can sit at his right-hand. Afronia is a God-fearing country and we must respect our traditions. We will follow our great partner, the American President's lead in that abortion will once more be outlawed. As such, a list of all the country's gay men will be published. All have been subjected to anal tests and found guilty of unnatural acts. With immediate effect, twenty HIV/AIDS facilities that provided lubricants and condoms for sodomy activities will be closed.

Chapter 42

'What's happening to our country?' Prince asked Adela on one of his rare visits to Umoja City, the business of hunting down Jihadis having become all consuming. 'How have we ended up with another tyrant?'

'It's a travesty; I don't know how Mutoni managed it—'

'What are Afronians thinking? How can we allow our hard-won democracy to slip away so easily?'

'Sometimes the price of democracy is bad leaders; look at America.'

'What can we do?'

'Afronia can't go back to armed struggle. Reforming the United Opposition and highlighting Mutoni's destruction of the constitution is the only option,' this from Tom Finch who'd escorted Prince to the capital so that he could have a frank discussion with Brigadier Abel Hussein about the worsening situation in the mountainous border area between Southiland and the region of Harari.

'We should reconvene the rebel war council for their input.'

'We can't risk that Adela. We can't countenance another civil war.'

'It would be a red flag to a bull in these times,' Tom agreed with Prince.

'Soon there will be no option but direct action; it's the only language people like Mutoni understand. But why has the Hero of Nyala, the General who defeated ISiSS changed so?'

Prince put an arm around the shoulder of his girl-friend. 'Since he came to power, I've been restricted to barracks. ISiSS is getting a toehold in Southiland and that's why we're meeting the Brigadier to see if he can exert some influence.'

'The outside world has not grasped the severity of the crisis. If ISiSS gets back in, they will open old wounds and Russia will get itchy feet to intervene—'

'Do you think Victov has something to do with the actions of the general?' Adela interrupted the Englishman who was more than twice her twenty-two years of age.

'I can't claim to know what's happening,' Finch responded, all the time thinking, *Why has Charlie Daniels been so unusually quiet since the coup?*

Chapter 43

'THIS IS A DISASTER, HAMZA,' the elderly Professor Rashid stated. 'The economy is in free fall. We're highly dependent on imports and there is no liquidity. A parallel black market is dollarising now that the Shilling is almost worthless. Our debts must be repaid in dollars and which the government doesn't have. Bonds have junk status. Inflation is spiralling out of control. There are food shortages and to top it all, Maduhu is threatening military intervention.'

'Mutoni can't blame the chaos on Walter Blaise's policies forever; the people know what is happening and who's responsible. There are rumours, that the huge crematoria Altimus Solomon built and Isaiah George used during the civil war are being re-activated.'

'How do you know this?' Rashid questioned as he paced the room.

'I have my sources.' It was Charlie Daniels. 'There's aerial photographic evidence of daily lorry loads of prisoners going to the site. Many are already dead but those who are not will be hanged at the newly erected gallows. Mutoni is crushing dissent and burning the evidence.' Hamza hastily added, 'No pun intended.'

'What can be done? We can't risk pushing Afronia

towards civil war.'

'We must identify who was behind the assassination of Blaise.'

'Could it be the same person, country or group who assassinated Altimus Solomon and Khalid Omar?'

'Why do you ask, Rashid?'

'While the two schoolgirls were the perpetrators, who put them up to it? I have a contact in the Army Intelligence Unit who confirmed they were forced into signing a false confession about being members of ISiSS.'

'Anything?' was the first word out of Jacob's mouth.

'And how about... how are you, my old mucker?' Sam laughed down the phoneline.

'How is sunny London?'

'Fine. And, yes, I do have something, sort of, I've uncovered a network of dark money which is managed through AfricaInvest a Swiss hedge fund managed by Ulrich Müller.'

This is going to be good, Jacob thought.

Sam, referred to his notebook. 'One of the companies the fund invested in is UK Fuels—'

'It's the same names and companies that keep coming up.'

'Exactly. Sir Boris Taylor of UK Fuels received a Life Peerage in last New Year's Honours list. AfricaInvest gave a £1million donation to a controversial think-tank that specialises in consolidating corporate interests and lobbying on their behalf, including, The African Institute for Justice, Free Trade Africa and The African Migration Institute... three Pan-African organisations which have the aim of a one government continent. It seems that the Jobuja Group is looking to buy political power while simultaneously consolidating their commercial supremacy; they are what links everything. And Müller seems to be the semi-public face of their continental ambition.'

'What's their end goal?'

'Controlling Africa's natural resources. Though the question that needs to be asked, Jacob, is whether Mutoni becoming a dictatorial president is part of their master plan or something unforeseen and out of their control?'

'And the Russians?'

'Whatever game Victov is playing, I'm fairly certain it has nothing to do with the Jobuja Group.'

As Sam and Jacob discussed the Jobuja conspiracy, in the Forests of Wahilistan villagers from Bangadu had other concerns. 'I'd rather die than lose land,' the 73-year-old head village elder—and who was dressed in sarong, sandals made from discarded rubber from truck tyres and a Manchester United football shirt—spoke up at a hastily arranged meeting.

The group of elders was huddled around a map and saw that their traditional land bordered the plantation formerly owned by Solomon Enterprises and which had recently had a large investment made by Ibex Investment. 'This is a battle for our very future. We cannot surrender our traditional land like the Somalitrean herders and fishermen did.'

The villages that made up the traditional area of Bangadu covered an area of 500 square kilometres of pristine forest. The Wahili River silently flowed through the forest until it reached the gorges which led to the Great Afronia Falls and then onto the Taberian capital of Rapoli. Fishing and hunting wild pig were the two primary sources of protein for the villagers; there were only a few slices of land cleared for crops. The smallholder farmers grew coffee for income, selling the premium quality bean, to amongst others the Hillview Coffee Emporium, though with the business incubator as a shareholder there had been high hopes to start exporting.

'Was it really a surprise our coffee factory burned down?' the village headman rhetorically queried as he looked to his left and saw the smouldering ruins. 'We were getting close to breaking even but now have nothing left. Our new neighbours will come in and take ownership of our land; we'll have no choice but to sell.'

'An all-out war is the only option,' a grizzled elder said as he took the wooden goblet from his neighbour and drank the green liquid, this being the tradition in such meetings of the elders. 'Indigenous rights are in the constitution of the Second Republic—'

'No one is standing up to Mutoni, so we must. If they take our land, they will cut down our forest that has stood for eternity so they can plant maize or palm oil.'

'There is no respect for our traditions. The police and army burnt outlying villages three days ago. When that didn't intimidate us they set alight our factory. We are already in a war. They have not yet started to kill us but they are burning, chopping and poisoning our land.

When the water is polluted from their factories and we have no more food we'll be forced to move.'

'Can we lease our land to the British company?' a female voice suggested. 'We should not put our children and grandchildren in harm's way if a peaceful solution can be negotiated.'

'Their business will flatten our forests. We'll lose our livelihoods when they come with their yellow monsters,' the headman was talking about heavy-duty land clearing machinery. 'Their companies are decimating our forests and clearing lands for plantations; soon we'll be like the barren lands in Harari region. It will end in disaster. When all the trees have been cut down it will not be possible to plant during the rains and there will be no shade in the dry season; it's a self-fulfilling prophecy of ecological destruction. The whites will make their money, live in grand mansions and, when Mother Earth has died, will leave us with the brutal consequences.'

'We complained to the new Regional Administrator—'

'We wasted our time; he is one of Mutoni toads. He tried to bribe us with cell phones and cheap clothes; he showed us no respect; we can't trust that man.'

'Last week, when peacefully protesting in Lirobi, we endured teargas and truncheons,' a grey bearded grandfather uttered, his voice trembling as he gesticulated wildly at the indignations he'd experienced. 'The government lies, it's what they've always done best. The land is our identity and that of our ancestors. As long as I'm alive, I will fight for our survival,' he concluded before passing the goblet onto the next speaker.

Chapter 44

'BUSINESS IS BOOMING,' Henshaw informed Ulrich. 'Our partnership is very good. Human life has never been more expendable,' he asserted with a smile. 'Looking at history books, I see that I make 25 times the return on my investment than my counterparts, slave traders, did in the 18th and 19th centuries. My average profit per person across all businesses is $4,000 but sex trafficking, moving bitches, is disproportionately lucrative, each girl earning me $35,000 a year,' he chuckled. 'I personally take charge of activities that involve your requests.'

'I need you to stoke up trouble in the regions; you will be well compensated.' Ulrich's plan was that disquiet in the regions would lead to increased military spending and which he would facilitate negotiations with British manufacturers; he'd earn a handsome commission for such introductions.

'Consider it done.' After shaking hands Henshaw handed Ulrich a box of the finest Cuban cigars to cement their partnership.

The following day and twenty kilometres to the north of Umoja City, in Zarusha, recent storms had eroded ten metres of land the beach washed out to the ocean. 'Not only has the general stopped all social payments but he has extended the 5,000-acre plantation owned by Hydro-Develop to the coast,' Abeker, on personal instruction from Henshaw, started to rabble rouse. 'Traditional land is being given for nothing to the wealthy British.' This was a complete fabrication… but there were many true examples of such land seizures by large foreign corporates as rural retreats for their executives.

'It's outrageous and we must fight back,' said Desmond the fisherman. This was the same reaction pastoral cattle herders who lived in a sparsely populated region of swamps and dense scrub some twenty-five kilometres to the west of Zarusha had reacted when Jamil sold them a similar story, his leading to outbreaks of unrestrained violence against foreign business interests. In the subsequent retaliation, dozens of villagers had been killed and hundreds more imprisoned in clashes with the security forces.

Sir Boris Taylor called Afro Safari Lodge home when in Afronia. The property consisted of six stone and wood bungalows perched on the edge of an escarpment. The sumptuous view took in three acres of pristine gardens, the flora and fauna irrigated from a nearby river. There was a large watering hole visited by all size of mammals and reptiles during the blazing hot days and which became a key ambush site for predators after the sun had set. In the middle-distance giraffes, elephants, buffalos and smaller wildlife could be seen walking through the acacia bush and through to the savannah grassland which rolled into the far distance.

Prior to the tycoon taking ownership of Afro Safari Lodge it had been derelict for three years having previously been run by a conservationist until the civil war when marauding soldiers had murdered the naturalist and slaughtered nearby wildlife for bush meat. After Sir Boris had bought the property he'd restocked the wildlife by importing animals from South Africa. He would crow to visitors this is the property jewel in my African crown.

Three nights after the visit of Abeker, five fishermen from Zarusha crept through the bush in the dark of night towards a point in the bend of the river less than a kilometre from the lodge. At the rendezvous they met five herders who had been arrested when they protested about the loss of their land. While in prison, the security forces went to their homesteads and shot or stole over 100 of their cattle.

'That bastard will pay tonight,' a crouching Desmond whispered. Nine heads nodded in union.

'My ten-year old son was imprisoned,' one herder informed the others. 'What could he possibly have done to deserve that?'

'My niece was arrested,' another herder reported. 'A prison is no place for young girls. She was released this morning but could barely walk, her body and mind tormented. I could smell the stench of male sweat on her.'

'I was arrested three weeks ago,' a fisherman joined in. 'I was protesting the building of the hotel... but now want them to complete it so I can laugh when it falls into the sea.'

'Last month I was placed in a police dungeon. I lived in a hole in the ground with over fifty others. We shared one bucket toilet. We were only ever given bread and water. We were always hungry and dehydrated and never knew if it was night or day. I was interrogated about who our leaders were but didn't say anything. I was kicked and slapped, electrocuted and had my wrists tied behind my back before they hung me on a hook and beat me with sticks and their fists until I lost consciousness. Three ribs were broken and my hands turned into mush.' He held up his disfigured fingers. 'Thanks be to Jesus for the doctors who put me back together.'

'It was Taylor who paid the police to be so vicious. We herders have lived here peacefully for many generations; we did not start this fight.'

'We serve justice tonight,' Desmond articulated what all the others felt. 'We will approach from the ravine; herders, come through the gardens,' this as he sketched out a map on the dust with his machete, the metal blade sparkling in the moon.

After the two groups shook hands, wished each other well and agreed to start the attack in fifteen-minutes time, Desmond started to lead his fellow fisherman to the wall of the ravine. He looked for a route up and which was not hard to find, it having been used by animals of all shapes and sizes to either go up to the lush grass plain or down to the refreshing water for years.

Peering his head around a boulder, Desmond who carried a recently crafted blow pipe—the other fishermen armed with machetes—saw lights coming from the right of the six bungalows. The group leopard crawled forward in a single line until they were just ten metres from one of the eight armed security guards. Desmond put the home-made weapon to his lips and gave a forceful blow, the dart smeared in poison from a Stonefish pricking the neck of the unsuspecting guard and causing near instantaneous paralysis and death. Three more guards were dispatched the same way before the fishermen and herders charged the property with adrenaline, hatred and vengeance flowing through their veins.

A startled Sir Boris was woken by gunshots. 'What's that?' he asked his wife who was half-asleep. 'Poachers?' When two more shots were fired, he instinctively knew it was not rustlers and that his family and guests were in real danger, this confirmed when a bullet splintered the bay window of the master-bedroom and buried itself in the rare Knobwood timber that had been used to decorate the property with little thought of environmental sustainability. 'We have to escape,' the business tycoon screeched, but it was too late the house and outbuildings having been set on fire, the fishermen and herders guarding all exits of the property and not caring if the women and children inside burned.

'I will not be hacked to death,' Boris said to his wife before he put a shotgun under his chin and pulled the trigger.

His wife did manage to get out of the inferno. Coughing and spluttering as she reached fresh air, 'I'm a mother,' she pleaded, 'my children are inside.'

'And you will all die as martyrs,' came the uncompromising reply as a machete came down on her neck. In total, twenty-four were slaughtered.

'Opposition politicians have incited hundreds of herders with racially charged language to start unprecedented and unprovoked attacks. They attacked Afro Safari lodge and murdered in a horrific act of unbridled violence a friend and investor in Afronia, Sir Boris Taylor and his family, this as the pretext to stealing thousands of cattle,' an enraged General Mutoni thundered at a press conference. 'I ask, who is exacting penance? Execution with God's blessing will act as a deterrence to these terrorists. I authorise the army and security services to retaliate against these barbarians. I will bomb them until they have no legs to stand on. I will send the Counter Terrorist Unit, Paratroopers, the Presidential Guard, whoever is needed to drive these uneducated herder sons of bitches off the land. I will bring back death squads if that's what is needed to stop the wave of kidnappings and murders. I will not let Afronia become lawless. I have advised the police to step up their operations. Landowners, you have every right to defend your property in any way you see fit. I have set this country on the path to economic recovery and will not let some disgruntled former politicians pervert farmers into causing violence as they try to derail our move from poverty to prosperity.'

Chapter 45

Is there influence beyond Afronia's borders?

As Afronia lurches towards another catastrophe, one largely of its own making, the question on many lips is whether General Mutoni is purposefully collapsing the economy, and if so, why?

The military junta has been in power for a little over two months, and in that time more bombs have exploded than in the run up to the civil war. Professor Rashid accuses the military of, "Gross negligence of human rights, freedoms and the economy. Afronia is being pushed back to the days of Altimus Solomon where power was in the hands of a few, and free market economics attractive to foreign investors was but a theory. Afronia has too much sovereign debt and is in danger of becoming bankrupt. The current war footing between military loyalists and unnamed revolutionaries is putting Afronia on a cliff edge. And inflation is running out of control and the tax-base evaporating. The hard-won wins under Blaise have largely been lost; economic output has fallen to pre-civil war levels. Whoever is next in power has the thankless task of reinvigorating the economic mess from this corrupt regime who have been shamelessly stealing from its people and laundering funds through offshore accounts with complicity of the international financial system."

Taking a back seat to the economic carnage is the fate of Isaiah George. It is hypothesized, that he has a base in Geneva where he has many connections from university days. "He is our rightful president," so claims a 32-year-old man who stands in Presidential Square and looks admiringly at the tanks on the adjoining roads. "We need a strong man who understands business and foreigners; not Red Rashid."

"There are strings being pulled from Switzerland. No one knows where Isaiah is. He is a pariah and can't return to public life, but still exerts influence," this spoken anonymously from an army source.

What is undoubtable is that the prevalence of bribery, torture and murdering of opponents has once again become commonplace and that some of the best, brightest and commercially astute have left the country. Generals, colonels and even majors have become insanely rich overnight through granting lucrative contracts in exchange for kickbacks. Whether its tanks or potatoes, whisky, beer or cigarettes, anything that needs to be brought to keep the army running is being exploited.

"Revolution is life. We are a nation of poor farmers; the Professor understands that. The army has betrayed the people," so said one disgruntled former rebel leader.

'Why is Mutoni driving the country into the ground?' Charles rhetorically asked Ralph. 'And why has he adopted a ridiculous string of titles and claim magical powers to cure AIDS? Why has he set loose death squads against the opposition, human rights groups and gays? He is an anti-Christ and crushing everything that made the new Afronia worth living in. If vulnerable Afronians miss out on vital social security payments they will starve.' This last point was about one of Blaise's proudest achievements.

'As long as soldiers are paid, we can sleep soundly. Mass demonstrations are planned. Teachers, journalists and other professions are joining. Lawyers, pharmacists, you name it, everybody is going to the street against Mutoni's economic policies,' Ralph updated his friend. 'The Afronian Medical Association has called on its members to stop work and only treat emergencies; outpatient clinics are postponing all appointments.'

'Daily assassinations, imprisonment of political prisoners, censorship of the press... Afronia has fallen to a textbook dictator,' Charles re-asserted.

'There will be a popular uprising when our most impoverished neighbourhoods protest unemployment, food shortages, a lack of medicines and textbooks, and all at a time when inflation and crime are soaring.'

Not far from where Ralph and Charles had been chatting, two days later a protest marched on Parliament. "Mutoni go!" the demonstrators roared as they waved placards in the faces of the heavily armed police. "We will die for democracy!"

The rally was in response to the increasing scarcity of many basic household items. Fuel had more than doubled in price, drivers were forced from the forecourts to the black market to get petrol or diesel. Those who did buy at the pump waited hours in queues that stretched many hundreds of metres. When one did get to the head of the line, arguments would break out between attendants and anyone wanting more than the government imposed ten-litre limit. Cash machines which previously could disperse $500 per person per day had been restricted to $50. The queues around bank branches were like those at the petrol pumps as desperate Afronians tried to withdraw their savings before their hard-earned money became worthless. In short, everyone was getting frustrated and worried at the worsening situation. As one wag commented, Afronia is now a country of economists.

As the demonstration started to get more heated, a three-ton truck was being driven through the streets of the capital by Japheti, a nineteen-year-old Chadian who had lived in Afronia for the past three years after becoming intoxicated by Mustafa's outrages in Nyala during the civil war. However, while Japheti was a loyal jihadi he was not convinced by Mustafa partnership with MH-16. 'It can't be right to be working with infidels?' he had protested.

'Allah shows the true light; we dare not question his wisdom,' was Mustafa's stock reply, one that he used if anyone questioned him.

'But the Koran teaches us—'

'Do you know the Koran better than me? Or military tactics?'

'I was just—'

'You were just... what?' Mustafa bulldozed away the argument as he stared at the young Chadian daring him to question his authority. 'We have to be flexible in our tactics when we serve Allah and his messenger Mohammed,' Mustafa continued in a conciliatory tone. 'Your mission is of vital importance; you will be greatly rewarded in heaven.'

And it was thus, that Japheti drove towards the well-fortified Embassy Row with a truck packed with explosives. What he couldn't have known was that Mustafa had held a similar conversation with another jihadi and who drove to Embassy Row in an equally packed ten-ton truck thirty minutes after the Chadian had blown himself up, this as the emergency services were attending to the wounded from the first blast.

Chapter 46

S HOCKED EQUALLY BY the brutality of the police at the demonstration, the first protest he had been to, and the twin terrorist explosions, the young entrepreneur Kamdonyo Wanjubi had much on his mind, but it was other matters which he was currently considering as he walked through Little Wahili. *Where is Amina? We can't screw up our pitch.* They were due to present his Afroloo business at the monthly Afronian Wolves Lair Pitch Night.

Arriving at the business incubator Kamdonyo's nerves were rattling. 'Every woman wants to look good,' Helena pronounced as she held up a range of skin lightening cosmetics and supplements. 'If you want to make money this is the business to be in. Men look for light-skinned, petite women who are big in the hips; it's a symbol of wealth.' She did a twirl on the stage to show the effect the pills had on her curvaceous behind. 'These,' she held up a small bottle, 'are fattening pills, I've branded them, Hips Don't Lie.'

The three investors locked at each other, none sure what to say. Emmanuel finally spoke up. 'Are these products regulated? Do trained pharmacists disburse them?'

'It's a sure-fire winner; I can't keep up with demand,' Helena replied as she deliberately didn't answer the question.

'What about the side-effects? I've heard they can lead to kidney failure and blocked arteries.'

Helena didn't have an answer... so kept smiling.

'I'm out,' Emmanuel said to Helena's disappointment. The two other potential investors quickly followed suit, all alarmed at the dangerous social trend; it was not the type of investment they would ever make nor in all honesty expect to be pitched.

Next up was Samuel. 'I'm an artisanal coffee maker. I source fresh coffee beans from the farmers in the Wahili forests. Through adding a secret combination of spices I have come up with AfroCoffee Express. I currently supply ten coffee shops in our towns and cities. I'm looking for an investment of $250,000 to help me get Fair Trade certification for export.'

'Wow!' this from an impressed Eric. 'I love your enthusiasm. Well done for getting clients... but that level of investment is more than I'm willing to make for such an early-stage business; I'm out.'

'It sounds a good opportunity, but I would have a conflict of interest as this incubator is an investor in Wahili Coffee.' Emmanuel also dropped out.

Next up was midwife Isabelle. She had a brightly coloured backpack which had three solar panels on the outside. 'My pregnancy was ok. I had no complications and was able to attend all my ante-natal classes, but many women in Afronia are not able to afford public transport to go to a clinic. In the village, pregnant women largely rely on volunteer health workers or traditional birth-attendants, most of whom have only rudimentary training and little equipment. I have developed a hi-tech backpack that can dramatically improve the level of access to primary care through using portable health technology that can monitor the vital signs of mother and baby as well as a resource for the volunteers to directly contact trained doctors through a recently launched telemedicine service.'

'How does it work?' an intrigued Eric asked.

'In the backpack, there are a range of medical gadgets that are designed to monitor the mother's and baby's health, including a portable ultrasound screen, a wind-up foetal Doppler, thermometers and other medical instruments. The solar panels power the equipment and data is sent to Umoja City Hospital where a diagnosis can be made in a matter of minutes and verified by a doctor or midwife.'

'What a fantastic idea,' Eric enthused. 'How much investment are you looking for?'

Isabelle rattled out the numbers impressively and within five minutes had received three offers, the wolves deciding to split the deal equally, each agreeing that Isabelle was an inspiration.

'An Afroloo looks like a Western toilet—'

'From high-tech to loo-tech,' Emmanuel quipped.

'There's a plastic seat and a flushing handle,' Kamdonyo carried on once the laughing had stopped from the audience and his beating heart had gone back to a more reasonable rate, 'but instead of water moving the waste down a pipe and into a sceptic tank it goes through a trap door and is captured in an air tight bio-degradable bag which is stored under the toilet until the service team collects it on a twice-weekly basis. Are there any questions?'

'What is the cost to build an Afroloo?' Eric enquired.

Where the hell is Amina? She knows the numbers better. 'It costs $40 per unit to assemble. The household pays a deposit of $10 and a monthly fee of $5. We breakeven on the unit after nine months. The business is projected to sell 1,000 units in year one, 10,000 units in year two and 30,000 units in year three. This will lead to a loss of $5,000 in the first year, profit of $10,000 in year two and a profit of $50,000 in year three, by which time we hope to start licensing the business to neighbouring countries,' Kamdonyo nevertheless confidently rattled out the commercial projections. 'I'm looking for an investment of $15,000 for a twenty-percent equity stake. I will use the money to rent a warehouse, buy components and train the field team.'

'Well done for the comprehensive financial projections; this is the area that often trips up entrepreneurs,' Emmanuel congratulated.

'Other than money, what other value are you looking for in an investor?' Eric enquired.

'I'm looking for support in raising future funds and how to decrease my cost of production.'

'I'll make you an offer,' Eric came to a sudden conclusion. 'I will offer you all the money for twenty-five percent of the business. For that, I will ensure HydroDevelop finds storage for you. Where possible, you can purchase components at cost price from our warehouse.' It was a generous offer.

'I'll also make you an offer,' Russell Jackson, the founder of Ibex Investments spoke up. 'I will offer you all the money but I only want ten-percent... though this is ten-percent of all your businesses. I have been following your progress in the business incubator and love how you are so entrepreneurially driven. I'm particularly impressed with your drone business... and which I will also invest the required amount to get ten-percent equity.'

'I'd like to accept both offers,' Kamdonyo immediately and enthusiastically agreed, not bothering to hear what Emmanuel might offer, this the only fault in his near perfect pitch. Handshakes exchanged and a meeting set up for the following day to get the partnership started, an overjoyed Kamdonyo sat in the audience and listened to the next entrepreneur.

Once the pitches had finished, Kamdonyo started walking back to Little Wahili. There was a lightness in his step and he couldn't wait to tell the exciting news to Amina all recriminations of why she had not appeared forgotten.

Reaching home Kamdonyo didn't find his girlfriend. He knocked on his neighbour's front door half expecting Amina to appear with baby Irene in her hands as she would often babysit, but there was no answer.

'Have you seen Amina?' Kamdonyo inquired from an old school friend who was passing by, his joy from earlier in the night turning to curiosity as to where his business partner and lover might be.

'There you are; I've been looking for you—'

'Why?' Kamdonyo asked, his curiosity turning to dread from the distressed look on the face of his old compadre.

'We must go to the hospital, Amina is hurt.'

'Jesus!' the religious Kamdonyo couldn't help but blaspheme.

The pair got in a taxi and fifteen minutes later were at Umoja City Central Hospital's Accident and Emergency department. 'Oh my,' Kamdonyo uttered as he put his hand to his mouth when he saw Amina swaddled in blood-soaked bandages. 'What happened?' he whispered as he watched his drug induced girlfriend breath with the aid of a ventilator.

'No one knows,' answered Aunt Beatha. It was clear from the stains on the blooded dress which lay limply on a nearby wooden chair that Amina had most likely been brutally raped.

'We'll track them down; Little Wahili looks after their own,' Uncle Joseph reassured his wife and future son-in-law. 'Someone knows who did this to our lovely daughter; there will be street justice.'

'She's so strong; a survivor,' Beatha tried to console the tearful Kamdonyo as she wrapped her arms around the shocked man before burying her head in his shoulder and started wailing.

It was three days before Amina started to get over the shock. The mental and physical pain still raw as she described to Aunt Beatha what happened; she was too ashamed to tell Kamdonyo or any other males the intricate and horrifying details. 'I was so excited to be presenting Afroloo at pitch night and was rehearsing my lines as I walked through Little Wahili. I passed a guy who was sitting on a broken piece of wall and whistling a Bobby-Afro song. I turned and smiled at him, and that's when I was grabbed. A cloth was put over my mouth and I was manhandled into an abandoned building. It happened so quickly.' Amina paused for a drop of water, her throat drying up with the memory of what happened next.

'There were three men inside, the one with the lightest skin had a ring through his ear, dreadlocks and cracked teeth. I could smell weed on his breath as he ran his tongue up my face. He pushed me onto a grubby mattress on the floor. I tried to scream but the cloth made me choke; all four men laughed. Be quiet or we will kill you, the one who abducted me threatened before punching me in the stomach.

'They took turns raping me and I was certain I'd be killed once they finished. I fought as hard as I could and caught the short bald one with my fingernails, blood coming out from the scratches. He hit me with a tyre spanner and knocked me unconscious; I don't know anything after that.'

'When you didn't show up at the business incubator Kamdonyo called me,' Beatha informed Amina. 'It was two children playing football with a sock filled with newspaper who told someone that they'd seen a woman being pushed into a derelict building. By the time we rushed there the men had left. You were curled in a ball murmuring incoherently. Your dress torn and raised over your hips. You face swollen and a big gash on the side of your head. We thought you were going to die but God intervened. We called an ambulance.' Beatha couldn't stop the tears coming to her eyes as she looked at the young woman who had been like a daughter to her, she herself not able to conceive. 'You have been given anti-retroviral drugs to protect you from HIV and the morning-after pill. Your body will fix itself and your family will be here to help mend your mind. The police haven't caught anybody yet, but Little Wahili is on the lookout for the monsters.'

Neither Kamdonyo nor Amina could have known about a meeting two weeks earlier, 'You must start a violent crimewave over the next month,' this requested of Mike Henshaw by Ulrich Müller.

'Not that it's a problem, but why?' Henshaw enquired while tucking into a plate of fish and chips at Geronimo's Café on the promenade.

'Afronians must think the public institutions are failing… including law and order.'

'No problem,' Henshaw cheerily replied as he dipped a chip in ketchup.

Amina was unfortunately in the wrong place at the wrong time, but when it became street gossip that it was four members of MH-16 who had gang-raped her, talk of revenge quickly died down, no one willing to cross swords with the White Devil.

Henshaw was enamoured by how he was feared, reviled and admired in equal measure. 'Make an example of a known rapist,' he ordered. The identified man had no connection to Amina's ordeal, though when his headless body was found with his genitals cut off and hanging by the ankles out of a window from the building where Amina had been found, no one dared question the veracity of what they could see with their own eyes.

Chapter 47

HAVING GIVEN HIS instruction to Henshaw to stir up merry hell in Umoja City, Ulrich Müller flew into London and the less rarefied surroundings of a London Soho strip club. 'Thanks to MH-16 the crime rate is soaring,' he started, 'and there is hyperinflation and food shortages. Bombs are going off daily. Gross Domestic Product is shrinking fast. The Shilling is almost worthless, the black market is king, and soldiers are now patrolling the streets. The country is imploding and cries for civilian rule grow louder by the day. There will be revolution if Mutoni doesn't step down—'

'And when that day comes, the British will be there to pick up the pieces with a massive aid initiative and low interest loans,' Charlie Daniels said with a grin on his face. 'You've played a blinder—'

'And the crown will have a twenty-first century commercial colony… like the Chinese have in Zimbabwe.'

'Quite.' Zimbabwe was a sore spot for Charlie, it was his former station before Mugabe's Land Distribution Program. 'When debt has built up to such an extreme… we move into phase three.'

Less than a kilometre from the strip club, 11 Downing Street to be precise, 'We must freeze development aid to Afronia,' the Chancellor of the Exchequer advised.

'Mutoni is riding roughshod over human rights; we can't endorse him,' the Minister for International Development concurred. 'Stories of police brutality are enough to revoke our commitments. Besides, the press is scenting blood following the Prince James revelations so soon after the prostitute scandal. The aid budget is a political hot potato and my department doesn't need more controversies. There should be an independent audit that looks at all contracts that have anything to do with Afronia.'

'You've seen which way the wind is blowing; the Prime Minister wants money diverted from the aid budget to support private sector investment; Afronia is the canary in the mine for this change in strategy—'

'But... your job is safe, for now Minister for International Development as long as you show the UK is making lasting positive impact to those in the world's poorest countries.' This threat was from the Foreign Secretary and who'd been waiting to strategically intervene. 'Otherwise, your responsibilities will become subservient to me. Remember, the onus is showing that we spend our zero-point-seven percent international commitment for development... not how we spend it!'

Chapter 48

ROBERT YOHAN WAS IN his usual haunt, the bar of the Golden Tulip Hotel. Within minutes of ordering a Double Jonnie Walker Blue Label, one of his chubby hands was cupping the bottom of a teenage prostitute, his libido energised by a mixture of the power that was soon to come his way and young flesh.

Also in the bar was Julius Stewart and who had returned to Umoja City a little under a week earlier. He had surreptitiously watched the septuagenarian for over an hour before following Yohan and the underage whore to the former presidential advisor's complimentary suite.

Five minutes after entering his room, and for what he expected to be two hours of kinky sex, the teenager who'd dressed up as a schoolgirl and was willing to be exploited in every known way, the pair heard a knock at the door. 'Room service.'

'That must be my celebratory champagne. Let him in,' Yohan ordered the young woman.

The naked girl whose sixteenth birthday was in two months' time opened the door as ordered. Leaving it ajar she nonchalantly walked back to the lecherous grin of the aged man with the expansive girth, mullet, and luxuriant moustache, *What a pig!* She didn't hear the door close, her mind trying to block out the thought of what she was going to be forced to do for the coming hours. And she didn't have time to turn round when the ice bucket holding a bottle of Armand de Brignac crashed to the floor, as by then a Ruger 22LR silenced pistol, and which Henshaw had personally handed to Julius, had risen in an arc, centred on the back of her teenage skull and been fired; she was dead before her lithe body crumpled onto Robert Yohan's blood and brain splattered hairy chest.

Wiping his face and pushing the youngster onto the floor, Yohan stared at the gunman. 'That double-crossing bastard,' Robert uttered as he thought back to his last meeting with Ulrich Müller. 'I've been played like a fool, a pawn to misdirect, for others to think I was conspiring with Maduhu and Victov.'

'You're a loose end who will sleep with God tonight,' Julius said in a calm voice as he approached the seventy-three-year-old before pulling his finger on the trigger, a hydro-shock bullet passing through the forehead of the man who had done so much wrong to the people of Afronia.

Chapter 49

S TACY ADAMS GOT OFF at London Bridge and walked to the offices of Walterson and Partners at the Shard for a third time, this a month after her second visit. It had not been a good period of work for her as more and more people were entering the world of zero-hour contracts and the fight to get any work became more intense.

Stacy took the elevator up to the twenty-sixth floor, gave her greetings to the receptionist—whose hairdo had transformed from blonde beehive to chestnut bob—before making her way to the janitor's closet to hang-up her coat and prepare her cleaning trolley. Going desk-to-desk and then office-to-office she finished as always with the CFO's office. She started hovering and then put anything that looked messy into what she hoped was its rightful place. That done, she took her duster and polishing spray and started cleaning the wooden surfaces, first the desk and once that done the cupboard with the files of many colours. The only job left to do before she could put her trolley back in the janitor's closet and go to meet Daryl for a pint was to empty the trash. She picked up the bin from under the CFO's desk and saw a solitary piece of paper; she bent down and picked it out. As she was in the process of depositing it into the black bag that hung on the end of her trolley, a few printed words caught her attention. She furtively glanced around before reading the memo.

> This deal legally represents an extraordinarily strong conflict of interest. If reported to the regulator, uncomfortable questions may be asked. I strongly recommend Ibex Investments should not make the money transfer. If its essential to finalise the purchase, an offshore company should be used as a special acquisition vehicle for any transactions.

Oh my! Who are Ibex and who are they sending money to? If this is page two... what's on page one? Looking around to double-check no one had come back to their desk, Stacy went to the file cupboard and pulled out the brown coloured Ibex file; it was wafer thin. *That's unusual; maybe a new client or just some meeting notes? In for a penny in for a pound,* Stacy decided as she opened the file. There were only five sheets of paper, the top one being a transcript.

Russell: Can you set up the offshore company?

Walterson: An offshore account is perfectly legal; we are not a rogue law firm.

Russell: Can the transaction be traced?

Walterson: Everything can be traced if someone wants to look hard enough... but no one has highlighted any payments you've made to Henshaw. The two payments were for dividends; to the casual eye, he is an investor in Ibex Investments; I wouldn't worry.

Russell: And what about the $950 million investment from Ulrich?

Walterson: He's well known for equity investments in Afronia. What's strange about a hedge fund investment for a sovereign wealth fund that wants to ensure a steady income for future generations. No one will ever know the money will be used to grease palms in the military or secure public private partnership contracts; it is just a transfer. No one can know what happens to the money once it is out of your account.

Russell: How much can I draw down from the fund?

Walterson: Normally, a fund this size would be spread across asset managers to reduce risk. But having sole responsibility is not unduly suspicious so long as we hide the source of the funds. I know you have already pulled down fees of $85 million.

Why are there no alarm bells from the compliance department? If whoever this Russell is had declared his interest in a board meeting then questions must have been raised; no bank would approve this type of transaction much less from a law firm... unless all stakeholders are in on the scheme.

Again, checking that no one was in the office, Stacy photocopied all the papers in the Ibex file before hightailing it to the lift.

'What should I do?' Stacy asked her boyfriend Daryl after telling him the rudiments of what she'd found.

'Keep well out of it!'

Stacy didn't take this sage advice, instead that evening she entered: Afronia, conspiracy, journalist, UK, in Google. The first result was an article Sam had written two years earlier. Using his Twitter handle at the end of the article Stacy contacted him and two days later they met in the Starbucks at London Bridge Station.

'What do you have?' Sam asked after hands had been shaken and lattes ordered.

'I have looked through a number of Walterson's files and they show an unrivalled number of complex arrangements to facilitate opaque investments on behalf of their clients. There is a bewildering array of acronyms for companies who are registered in a wide range of offshore jurisdictions to guarantee secrecy. The arrangements all seem above board but are far from transparent. All contracts that I've seen have confidentiality clauses that are intentionally obscure to disguise intention, influence and the movement of money... this a common tactic to ensure plausible deniability when laundering money.'

'How many clients do they have?'

'I don't have a precise number, but its north of 10,000.'

'Can you get files out of the building?'

'I don't want to do anything illegal.'

'Stacy, it's too late for that,' Sam said looking at the file. 'It's Walterson and Partners who are in the wrong. If they are involved in Afronia then they are up to no good and most likely somehow facilitating corruption, probably worse.'

'What could be baser?'

'Arms sales, funding terrorism. If my hunch is correct, they might have a leading hand in the civil war and who knows what else.'

'You really think so?'

'Yes! All indications are that there is an international conspiracy, the citizens of Afronia paying the ultimate price.'

It was a week until Stacy next had a job with EazyClean. She arrived at The Shard half-an-hour later than usual. 'My bus was cancelled; what-can-you-do?' she lied to the receptionist who was impatient to leave. Five minutes after going through her routine of making a brew and getting the cleaning cart fully prepared to clean desks, computer screens and empty bins, Stacy pushed the trolley through the offices. Seventy minutes later, and with no one entering the office for over an hour, she made her way to the CFO's office, closed the door and started to rifle through the files until she had a clearer picture of how illegal money flowed through London. She photocopied documents and inserted the external hard drive she stored in her handbag into the computer; by midnight she had over 50GB of data.

'Good luck hunting,' Stacy said to Sam as she handed over the information cache.

Chapter 50

Sam had only scratched the surface of what Stacy had given when he realised, *I need a collaborator; who wrote the Prince James expose?* After swapping emails, the two investigative journalists met.

'Jean-Marc?' Sam enquired in the Horse and Hounds pub.

'Yes. Sam?'

'Hi.'

Jean-Marc saw a questioning look come over Sam's bearded features. 'You were expecting someone else, non? My parents are French and worked for a health charity in East Africa during the 70s and 80s. They adopted me from the Second Chance Orphanage in Umoja City when I was ten-months old,' he said matter-of-factly and in such a way as to deter any further questions about his heritage. 'We lived in Afronia for five years after independence before moving to Marseille; what's happening in Afronia is very personal to me.'

'Can I get you a pint?'

'London Pride, thanks. I've lived in the capital for the last seven years, though other than my Afronia links I don't know why I was the chosen recipient of the Prince James dossier.'

'Was there other information you didn't publish?' Sam asked after coming back from the bar with a pint of dark brown ale in each hand.

'I specialize in big business corrupting politics and have worked on stories regarding big tobacco, petroleum and pharmaceuticals. I detest lobbyists, dark-money, think-tanks and fake-news agencies... all of whom corrupt public perception for commercial greed. I loathe politicians who purport to represent the man on the street while simultaneously cosying up to big business. In short, I think politics and business is incestuous and must be kept apart.'

Sam nodded his head in complete agreement as he shovelled a handful of honey roasted peanuts into his mouth. 'I too believe there is an unholy alliance between business and politics. Have you heard of the Jobu-ja Group? They are the European elite and are trying to economically colonise Africa; I think Afronia is their first domino.'

'I've heard the rumours but never seen any concrete evidence; what do you know?'

'Big business has always pushed the edges of getting away with what it can. Similarly, lobbyists are in the process of turning the British Government into a glorified conglomerate; the Foreign Office is facilitating British business expansion. The Jobuja Group want Afronia to come under their sphere of influence. Shall we pool our resources? What do you have?' Sam, enquired through raising his extravagant eyebrows but not yet willing to share his information without first seeing what Jean-Marc knew.

'After a crisis the private sector fight over government development contracts. Think of Iraq and Afghanistan. Grenfell Tower and Hurricane Katrina. Government is under pressure to act quickly and has the power and mandate to circumnavigate national budgets and procurement oversight. As such, right-wing politicians foster an atmosphere of crisis, chaos and disaster, as this opens the cheque books to their corporate buddies. Think of any devastating event and then of the contractors who make millions, billions at a time when thousands of the poorest are abandoned or treated as criminals as they scavenge for survival—'

'And it's the very same politicians who whipped up a storm who are appointed as non-executive directors of the benefitting companies. It's no coincidence that retired military brass get offered directorships from weapons companies, or former health ministers onto the boards of big pharma.' Sam paused and indicated to the barman to bring another two pints. 'I have a mini Paradise Papers from a legal company located in the City of London that specialises in African affairs. There seems to be a link between Ulrich Müller, Isaiah George, Russia, Switzerland and the Jobuja Group. I don't have all the pieces of the puzzle, but one company, Ibex Investments seems to be a central player. After Mutoni staged his coup and during the public chaos, he started a firestorm sale of government bonds to European and American investors, rushed through privatizations and accelerated deregulation to force open national markets to foreign trade and capital. He claimed this was to grow the economy, pay off lingering civil war debts and fund the national infrastructure plan, though in reality it was free market economics trumping democracy. The result… Afronians will forever be subservient to foreign owned businesses.'

'Do you think Mutoni is a smokescreen?'

'Possibly. The economy is a basket case. There are daily protests about the lack of food, medicine and many other basic goods. Power cuts are longer, inflation is moving towards being hyper, and crime is rampant. The country is in chaos. Utilities are in large owned by foreign companies and the Afronian Government is in huge debt to City of London financiers. With the revised contractual law, if there was any government default there would be a change of ownership from a public private partnership to privately owned. Its the same in the tourism sector and most concerning, much of the extractive industry. Agriculture is the last piece of the jigsaw to give British companies and finance houses almost complete control of the Afronian economy. And then there is the spectre of a second civil war and which would drive the share price down of all companies. The Afronian elite and government would likely sell their remaining equity at cut price.' Sam paused and supped his pint. Licking his lips he continued, 'If Mutoni was a strawman, then it's very much a case of mission accomplished. Consider that the Islamists have their Caliphates, and Communists had the Soviet Union—'

'And neo-liberals want Africa,' Jean Marc interrupted as he raised his pint of beer in mock celebration.

'Afronia will have no choice but to kowtow to the financiers if they want to stave off implosion. Foreign companies owning key sectors and infrastructure is a singular vision based around free market principles. British politicians have been welcoming the world's rich to London with open arms for decades. There are few questions of where money comes from or where it goes to. The mere fact it goes through the City of London's accounts means it's good for the British economy. If more companies are listed on the Stock Exchange, more jobs will be created and more tax paid to Her Majesty's Revenue. Why should anyone look under rocks when everyone benefits?' Sam rhetorically asked. 'Everyone can make their thirty pieces of silver as long as there are no hard questions or forensic audits. Money laundering, blood diamonds, buying arms, everything is possible behind closed doors. If the regulator doesn't aggressively search for dirty money, start formal investigations into the financial sector, and largely leave it alone, then nothing untoward will be found—'

'Regulations that concern the origins of money have been consistently watered down. A reduction in regulatory oversight is exactly what's been happening in London for the past four decades, and that's why the financial services sector makes up nearly twenty-percent of the economy. London is the global centre for dirty money,' Jean dismissively said, anger clear in his voice.

'Have you come across anything on an Ulrich Müller or the Jobuja Group?' Sam asked, Jean's response being an upturned mouth and a Gaelic shrug but no reply. 'According to the Afronian Central Bank, officially there is a £100 million financial flow surplus to the UK, i.e., more forex is coming into Afronia from the UK than going out, this primarily from the British government's budgetary support. However, I calculated there is a net balance of negative £0.5billion. For a country with Afronia's battered economy that is a huge discrepancy. And these amounts don't include what comes or goes via third party countries such as Switzerland or offshore tax havens where most crooked finance passes through.'

Jean stayed silent as he received a lesson in international finance; he'd even forgotten about his second pint.

'Looking at companies who had some level of investment in Afronia and made or received payments through third countries but whose transactions could reasonably be linked to Afronia, the gap trebles. The wealth does not stay in these offshore centres… registration is simply to obfuscate the origins of the finance. For instance, a public official whose wealth is wildly disproportionate to their salary can put the excess into a London bank account and withdraw when they please, no one any the wiser. The fact is, there's a tidal flow of liquid capital from every corner of the globe that pours into and out of the City of London every day, and thanks to the best accountancy brains it is indistinguishable from legitimate transactions. In short, it is global fencing on an unprecedented scale. The really worrying thing is that the regulator must know what's going on, and thus by politicians denuding them, it would suggest the motivation for weaker regulatory supervision is for personal gain.'

'Where does all the money go?'

'A lot will have gone into property and luxury goods. However, what's more revealing is not so much where money goes but where it has come from. The Swiss fund manager Ulrich Müller runs a fund which has investors from Russia and the business elite of Europe. Some of his transactions can be linked to corrupt Afronian politicians. The law firm I mentioned before and who seem to be in the middle of this global conspiracy, Walterson and Partners, fiddles the books of their clients to claw back hundreds-of-millions in taxes that are meant to go to the Afronian government in corporate taxes... and directs some of this money into Müller's fund.'

'Really?'

'Yes! I traced dubious transfers exposed by corporate finance whistle-blowers and cross-referenced them with criminal cases in France, the US, Canada and Germany... but not in Britain. Investigations were always stopped before they got to court. I believe there is a conspiracy between MPs, lawyers, bankers, businessmen and accountants; they are collaborating in a Faustian pact.'

'Is this the Jobuja group you mentioned?'

'I think so. When you cross reference known members of the Jobuja Group with Walterson and Partners clients, there is a very clear correlation. If Afronia went bankrupt, and which is a very possible risk, then these foreign businesses would suddenly own a large percentage of critical national infrastructure—'

'What evidence is there?'

'There's so much dirty African money embedded in the UK financial systems that identifying it all would be a Herculean task. The guilty have influence, power, political connections and money. They will not hand over incriminating documents easily and can afford the best lawyers to create insurmountable hurdles. And I strongly doubt the British government would set up an independent enquiry as you don't kill the cow you drink milk from,' this an Afronian proverb. 'It's never going to happen; dodgy money would disappear from financial institutions faster than an Afronian Billy Goat up a mountain.'

'What can we do?'

'I don't have answers Jean-Marc. I'm still trying to figure out the continental puzzle that has Afronia at the centre.'

Three days later, the pair met again. 'What can you tell me?' Jean-Marc asked.

'The Jobuja Group have naturally never revealed their ultimate goal. They talk about a one government Africa at the conceptual level, something that might come to pass in 100 years. African think-tanks, funded by Jobuja Group members, claim there is need for de-regulation across Africa to address population growth, poverty and inequality, the refugee crisis and climate change. Lobbyists say, there needs to be radical reforms to address these fundamental challenges of our times. With a vast network of political power and lethally effective public misinformation campaigns, and backed by like-minded intelligentsia, these pro-business ideas are the siren call for a new global elite. If you look at what individual members and their companies are doing in Africa, it seems like shrewd business investments to placate shareholders, but when taken in the whole, you can see incremental and coordinated steps. For example, the National Water project started under Walter Blaise—'

'While a much-needed infrastructure project, HydroDevelop pulled out all the stops by involving Prince James to make sure they won. If national debt is driven up to unsustainable levels,' Jean-Marc continued the logic, 'and government can't pay their bills, no pun intended,' the two men smiled at each other, 'the water utility will go into the hands of HydroDevelop—'

'And this project will stoke tensions with Taberia. If Afronia is a de-facto British colony, they will pour weaponry into the country to ensure victory.'

'Sam, it's a great conspiracy but how can we reveal the madness?'

'Hmmn,' Sam, was annoyed at being stopped in his tracks, *But he has a point; we need solid evidence to base our narrative around.* He started ruffling through his copious notes until he found a piece of paper where there were lots of arrows, words underlined and the occasionally name circled. 'The Walterson and Partners documents show that Russian investment bank IGB, and which is known to be pivotal in managing Victov's global business interests and has links to Russia's intelligence agency the FSB, bought $480 million worth of stock at a social media company's Initial Public Offering.'

'I thought Victov would be the Anti-Christ to the Jobuja Group?'

'Publicly, at state level, you are correct… but Victov is also a billionaire and so may have been invited into the inner sanctum.

'You think that's why he very publicly courted Mutoni?'

'It's one theory. And his name appearing in Walterson and Partners files raises more questions than gives answers. Consider this, HydroDevelop was given a $250 million loan from IGB, and which just happens to be the guarantee amount they had to provide as part of their proposal for the National Water project. That has to be more than coincidental.'

'Hmmn,' It was Jean-Marc's time to brood. 'Is there any direct link between the Jobuja Group and Mutoni?'

'Not that I can find, though there's a set of payments from Ibex Investment to an unknown recipient. What's interesting is the transfer dates; they are all in or around the dates of seismic events in Afronia—'

'Such as?'

'The Assassinations of Altimus Solomon and Khalid Omar. The ferry bombing and King of the Mountain Hotel fire. Walter Blaise's death. The introduction of mercenaries into the civil war.' Sam paused. 'The murder of Jessica Webb,' he said in a quiet voice.

Jean-Marc put a consoling arm around Sam's shoulder. He'd read about Sam's former girlfriend before their first meeting. 'Paying an assassin?'

'That or a middle-man who paid the assassin.'

'You think it was this Ulrich Müller, on behalf of the Jobuja Group who set Afronia on fire?'

'Everything points in that direction. It fits the neo-liberal theory of needing chaos and state bankruptcy to have the ideal conditions for a private sector take-over. It all makes sense in a fucked-up sort of way... if we could only find out who these payments were to—'

'Where do we start?' Jean-Marc enthused.

'Jessica might be dead, but her spirit lives on. Just before her death she was following up on leads which led her to Geneva—'

'Whoa! That's very significant when taken into context of everything else we know.'

'Exactly! Just before her death, she posted a blog about corporate crooks in London and Geneva. She didn't go into details, but from her tone I sense she was close to something big. Her laptop and notebooks were stolen when she was abducted, and her online accounts in the cloud where she backed everything up were wiped. But I do know she was focusing on Isaiah George who was the catalyst and ringmaster into starting the civil war. She found corroborating evidence from the Panama Papers. I think, it was because she was getting close to uncovering the why and how the war started that she was murdered.'

'But what about Mutoni? Is his, a puppet government?

'He's certainly committing economic Hara-Kiri, and making it more likely that foreign corporations, finance houses and hedge funds will own Afronia. I'm reminded of a quote by President Franklin Roosevelt: The liberty of a democracy is not safe if the people tolerate the growth of private power to a point where it becomes stronger than their democratic state itself.'

Jean-Marc suddenly held his hand up, the pair stopping mid-conversation. They saw a photo of the man at the centre of the conversation suddenly appear on TV. The two men left their table and took their pints to the bar.

'Mate, can you turn up the volume?' Sam requested the landlord.

General Mutoni has made a snap resignation amid the political and economic unrest that has engulfed the East African nation of Afronia, a staunch ally in the fight against Islamic terrorism but which has been in a state of turmoil since the assassination of President Blaise.

Mutoni said: three months ago, at the start of the state of emergency, I promised to change the constitution so that the vice-president would automatically step into the shoes of the president rather than the country forced to go through divisive elections; I have achieved this promise. I have submitted my resignation in a bid to ease the political turbulence as Afronia moves from military to civilian rule. As my last act, I signed the authorisation to release hundreds of political prisoners, including prominent former rebels and opposition leaders so they can be part of a lasting political solution to our great nation and partake in the upcoming presidential elections. But Afronians, be wary who you elect. In the last weeks there has been hundreds of deaths at the hands of Rashid inspired rebel forces who are trying to plunge Afronia back into civil war. Under my personal supervision, the army has captured terrorist suspects who were making bombs more powerful than the twin Embassy Row attacks. Explosives were recovered and a bomb-making laboratory destroyed. The army stopped jihadists and radicalised Southi separatists from carrying out further atrocities. Suspected militants have been rounded up and interrogated in the assassination of Robert Yohan.

Thanks to the army intervention, Afronia is a safer country than at the time of Walter Blaise's untimely death. The army will continue to ensure security at all polling stations so that you, the people, can hold peaceful democratic elections as is your constitutional right.

'What does that mean? What next? Where does that leave our theories?' Sam rhetorically asked Jean-Marc.

Chapter 51

POLYGLOT HAROLD ALTIMUS NZEBILI, a nephew of Altimus Solomon, had been a spoilt playboy during his youth. He'd considered the president his personal bank and that wealth and privilege was his birth right. He'd schooled in the finest halls of learning in Europe on his way to earning an economics PhD. However, after the Presidential Square Massacre in 2013 he'd become an outspoken reformer and entered politics in 2015. Despite his at times disrespectful language towards his uncle, he was nevertheless given the position of Minister of Agriculture, Altimus seeing in him a potential successor that he could groom.

While the Solomon family were en-masse accused of state capture there was never evidence that Harold had benefitted from ill-gotten gains. And he'd wisely not been part on Isaiah George's ticket in the election before the civil war, in fact he'd been a staunch supporter of Sheila Solomon and a junior cabinet minister in Walter Blaise's administration. In short, the 49-year-old was by-and-large a unifier and democratically legitimate.

As Harold was being pampered with a massage he was strategizing. *There is overwhelming pressure from the foreign business community to leave Afronia; I need Sir*

Hillary Chapman to be my running-mate in the upcoming election if I want to finally become president. He can't be a threat as the vice-president role is largely administrative and, as a foreigner, he can't hold the highest position in the land. Once I'm in power I will get rid of Chapman and his cronies. I'll take a leaf out of Uncle Altimus' playbook and only have men around me I can put the fear of God in.

Elsewhere in Umoja City… 'You're the obvious candidate,' Hamza tried to persuade Professor Rashid. 'We can't let Harold,' who had announced his candidacy earlier in the day, 'and Chapman rule this country.'

'I don't know, Hamza, I'm too old. The country needs a young buck who has the energy to keep implementing Walter's vision.'

'The country would put their trust in you. You are a safe pair of hands and that is what the country needs after Mutoni's madness. You would have the support of most of Walter's cabinet; I've made enquiries.'

Chapter 52

'HOW'S LIFE IN AFRONIA?' Sam enquired of Jacob at the start of their weekly phone call.

'No one expected Mutoni's sudden resignation. No one knows what's going to happen next, but there's now opportunity for a fresh start.'

'I hope so, Jacob, I really do, but everything I've found in recent weeks suggests there is a conspiracy being played out. I admit, Mutoni leaving office is a bit of a curve-ball, but I have a gut-feeling it's all part of Ulrich Müller's masterplan.'

'Who's Müller?'

'That's a simple question, Tigist, but one with a hugely complicated answer. Where does one start?' Sam rhetorically asked before summarising what he and Jean-Marc had uncovered. 'It's on public record that he is the founder of AfricaInvest, one of the world's largest hedge funds and which our beloved Chancellor of the Exchequer is a non-executive director—'

'Is this a coincidence?' Jacob butted in.

'Müller is a known associate of Isaiah George, the two of them buddies from university days. That they connived to loosen regulation allowing the importation of toxic petroleum into Afronia for many a year to earn both men a mountain on money is also a known fact.'

'Are they still in contact?' Jacob asked.

'No one knows but we can assume so. The former president has not been seen or heard from since his run into exile, but if he'd taken refuge in one of Müller's residences it wouldn't be a great surprise.'

'What is the conspiracy?' Tigist wanted to know.

'I was passed an intriguing dossier from a source who works at Walterson and Partners, a legal company operating in the City of London and which has a who's who of dubious clients based in the Square Mile. Additionally, I met Jean-Marc, a French Afronian journalist who wrote the article on the shady dealings of Prince James—'

'I remember reading the story,' Tigist interrupted. 'The Prince got a commission for making introductions that led to HydroDevelop winning the half-billion-dollar contract.'

'That's the one. He has a whole host of recordings, reports, photographs and other information in the boxes he was anonymously tipped-off about.'

'What joins the dots?' this from Jacob who then paused to take a sip of water. 'FUCK!' he swore, as some of the liquid spilled onto his keyboard, the moustache he'd been cultivating—much to Tigist's disapproval—getting in the way.

'At the moment, I'm not discounting anything. When there are mutually beneficial interests nothing can be ruled out. One must consider who will benefit the most from the anticipated outcome.'

'Sam, what are you trying to get at?' Jacob's voice betraying his impatience.

'In Jean-Marc's stash of incriminating evidence, a house in Dar es Salaam—the capital of Tanzania—was under surveillance; for what purpose it's not currently clear. Back in 2012, Ulrich was photographed entering an expansive house ten kilometres north of the city. There were five guards at the entrance gates each with a Kalashnikov rifle; this was a serious meeting. Anyway, Ulrich was travelling with two members of a Columbian drug cartel and Isaiah George.'

'Whose house?'

'One of Isaiah's,' Sam informed Tigist. 'The cartel was looking to ship cocaine through the port of Dar es Salaam and Isaiah would then use his diplomatic immunity to import the drugs into Afronia. If you can remember, there was a drugs link during the civil war. The British used a slush fund to import cocaine for the rebels who then sold the narcotics to fund the purchase of weapons. And I'm sure, Ulrich would move in the same circles as arms dealers as he is in the very centre of irregular commercial investments, money laundering and arms trading. He is the man with a very extensive network of contacts who can secure meetings with, or make introductions to, presidents, drug cartels, politicians and powerful corporations. He has enough political and financial backing to destabilize nations!'

There was silence Jacob and his fiancé staring intently at their friend's face on their laptop. 'For the last three years, we have assumed it was the Russians who set in motion the civil war through the ferry bombing and King of the Mountain hotel fire,' Tigist finally breaking the quiet. 'Might we have been wrong? Could it have been Ulrich all along who was pulling the strings? Is he the paymaster of Julius Stewart?'

'I think he might be,' Sam said in little more than a whisper. 'And I'm certain now more than ever, that he is working on the behest of the Jobuja Group.'

'That would be an enormously long strategic play,' Tigist, as ever, giving her opinion. 'To manoeuvre a country into a position where it is acceptable for a private sector entity to run the state would be decades in the making.'

'Altimus Solomon,' was Jacob's riposte. 'It's on record as historical fact that he was recruited by the CIA. Do you think it's possible that he was deployed with the express remit to fail after independence? How many presidents has Afronia gone through in recent years? Isaac Muriithi, Isaiah George,' he started to make a list, 'Sheila Solomon, Walter Blaise, Mutoni and now… who knows. For two Solomons and Blaise to die in office… can this really be coincidence? Just think of how the economy has tanked in the last few months and thus making the promise of economic stability through a captain of industry being vice-president appealing to Afronians?'

'And with the changes Mutoni made to the constitution, if anything untoward happened Chapman would automatically become president no matter that he's a foreigner!'

'Good point, Tigist,' this from Jacob as he stood up and started pacing the room. 'But how likely, nay rational, is our train of logic?'

'We know from meeting Charlie Daniels, that it was Julius Stewart who was responsible for many of the events leading up to the civil war and now we have a direct link between him and Müller. Has this Jobuja organisation,' Tigist spat out the name, 'been behind every catastrophe to have plagued my wonderful nation?'

'It's a working hypothesis, and it is British companies who are holding the Afronian economy to ransom through debt. So, Tigist, my dearest, my one true love,' Jacob smiled, 'I think we need to employ your special talents.'

Chapter 53

Swiss immigration records obtained from Jean-Marc's contacts confirmed that Ulrich had landed at Privatport Geneva three days earlier. ATM withdrawals indicated he was most likely staying at his 10 million euro flat on the left bank of the River Rhône opposite the Jardin Anglais Parc and only a short walk to the Old Town. Hacked credit card records showed he was a regular at the nearby elegant indoor-outdoor Restaurant Gusto at the Hôtel Métropole Genève.

Tigist, dressed to impress, was quite the sight as she elegantly wore a head-turning Marchesa Floral one-shoulder silk evening dress. Arriving at the landmark building and taking her seat in the restaurant, she pretended to be very embarrassed by the man on the other side of the table, Jacob, and who was flamboyantly dressed in a cocktail of colours, the ensemble making him look like a playboy; he'd dressed to be noticed.

'Over there,' Tigist motioned with her eyes as she saw Ulrich enter the three-star Michelin restaurant. Müller was dressed in a dashing hand tailored white cotton suit with an underplayed mahogany shirt and bright pink cravat. *On anyone else it would look ridiculous,* Tigist considered, *but on him, it's suave, regal. He's one of Geneva's princes... and he knows it.*

Ulrich attention was briefly compromised as he glanced in Tigist's direction, much as many a man had done that evening, but he was the only one who had caught her eye; he received a sly but obviously bored smile. *What a splendid bitch,* he considered.

Twenty-minutes after Ulrich had entered Jacob abruptly stood up. 'You fucking cunt!' he yelled before storming out and leaving Tigist alone at the table with her glass of NV Pol Roger Brut Réserve champagne and a barely touched plate of grilled chicken breasts with grapefruit glaze.

Tigist acted shocked, saddened and highly embarrassed by the scene. 'Charge the bill to the pig and give yourself a $500 tip,' she instructed the maître de before making her way to the reception.

'Can I buy you a drink, miss,' Sam politely asked. He was slapped across the face for his troubles, the crack strong and dramatic enough for heads to turn, including that of Ulrich.

'Is there a lounge?' Tigist asked the barman hoping she'd said it just loud enough for her quarry to hear over the hum of satisfied eaters.

'The MET Rooftop lounge, madam.'

Tigist took the elevator up to the trendy hotel rooftop bar & lounge with stunning panoramic views over the lake and city. Nursing a double Johnny Walker Blue Label it was not long until Tigist saw Müller appear from the direction of the lifts; he'd followed her up after swiftly finishing his meeting.

When Ulrich saw Tigist's dazzling smile, he confidently sauntered over to her. 'Africa, as a continent, has two types of economy,' he paused to see what reaction he would get.

'And?'

'The corrupt… and state led,' he clarified. 'The less politics and the more state benevolent development there is the more the country moves in the right direction. They prioritise mobilization of savings in government owned development banks so they can reduce external corporate finance while investing in key infrastructure like roads, network connectivity, hospitals, schools etc. This helps to keep the masses happy as they see their lives getting better.'

'Who are you and what do you want?' Tigist asked as she acted not at all impressed by the financial showmanship.

'An investment banker that specialises in African affairs,' Ulrich honestly answered with his million-dollar grin.

'And what do you think about democracy and free speech? Tigist asked as she turned in her seat to face her suitor.

'Overvalued. The ordinary African wants access to credit to invest in their house or business and to be financially independent from corrupt governments. Africa will work if there is suitable financial regulation. This is not a sexy answer, but it is the truth.' Ulrich took a sliver of smoked salmon from a passing platter and deposited it into his mouth. 'Bring us Black Beluga Caviar and a bottle of Blue Label,' he ordered the waiter. 'Where was I, oh yes, take Afronia for example—'

'You presume I'm from an African country?'

'Your beauty and accent confirm that you are,' Ulrich

deftly side-stepped the provocative question. 'Most presidents know exactly what and how to root out corruption in order to reach middle-income status, but they don't have the political will... and are on the whole they are kleptomaniacs. There is plenty of finance available, especially for large infrastructure projects whether it comes from foreign governments, the World Bank or, investment bankers like me,' he had no intention to hide his wealth and self-importance, 'money can normally be found.'

'And development aid to provide technical advisory services to central banks,' a sickened Tigist continued not missing a beat, 'to get the regulation changes that you mentioned? To smooth the way?'

'Exactly, my dear. Controlling the velocity of money in an economy means you control the debt. This is the true nature of banking and what my shareholders want.'

'You want governments to be in your debt?' Tigist asked before taking a spoonful of Caviar.

'Governments take our money and rarely quibble about the terms.'

'And then what?'

'Who are you? You never said.'

'I study at The Centre for the Study of African Economies at Oxford University,' Tigist confidently lied.

'Why learn about economics, when, if you worked with me, you would have the power to change economies?'

'You're very presumptuous... and that is now a second time,' she scolded with a seductive smile. 'I intend to graduate before I change the world,' Tigist laughed.

'Let me ask you, mademoiselle,' the two still not having exchanged names. 'How has sixty years of independence and thirty years of democracy benefitted Africans? Many an independence leader promised they would never rule for more than 10 years… but how many kept their word? Political freedom was the discourse of the independence struggle, and yet only sixteen out of fifty-four countries can reasonably claim to be democratic. Economies favour the elite. Corruption is the enemy of freedom of information and the rule of law. Regional tensions and warlords are fighting for control of natural resources at a time of rising populations, urbanization, mass migration, climate change and food insecurity—'

'And you think that only a business approach can address these challenges?'

'One state at a time,' Ulrich smiled with deadly seriousness.

'A new world order?'

'It's already here, my sweet. Why do you think populist movements are started if not to chase the dollar?'

'And human-rights? Self-determination?'

'Where has that got the world since the end of the Second World War? An overpopulated world where the world's eight richest men have the same wealth as half the planet. This is an unprecedented time for humans. We are at population, climate, financial, technology, ecological and economic tipping points. Civilisation as we know it could implode at any time and so radical solutions must be implemented. Be under no illusions, if changes are not made this is no future for humankind.'

'And business can sort out this unholy mess?'

'Let the market decide. Who the hell is going to explain macro-economic intricacies to uneducated peasants? Besides, when the poor see the social, cultural and economic divide getting bigger every day they will rise up and the world will enter a new Dark Ages; don't you think that its better the inevitable chaos is managed?'

'So, if the true value of banking is the debt that it creates and, if you control that debt through giving loans to build infrastructure and the government can't repay the lender, the financier will take control of the asset and CEOs will be de-facto presidents.'

'Perceptive and beautiful,' Ulrich complimented as he poured Tigist a generous triple whisky. 'For an investment bank it's a win-win scenario; we either end up owning the asset or making a profit. This is the very essence of financing globalisation and the rise of the investment bank. We make individuals, businesses and nations slaves to debt. Do you find this upsetting?' Ulrich was amused by his question.

'Lawyers and bankers in the Square Mile cannot be disassociated with global conflict and death; they are the ones who transfer funds between arms dealers and governments—'

'Whatever presidents and prime ministers might say about eradicating corruption, they know they can't kill the golden goose. Why else are they so slow to deploy anti-money laundering measures? We are not talking about small backhanders and little bribes; this is a national strategy that Europeans have been following since the times of Cecil Rhodes and the scramble for Africa. The Brits are just a bit better and more ruthless than the others. They understand better what the establishment want, nay need to keep the status quo, or the aristocrats, politicians and business elite will face revolution.'

'Why are you telling me this?'

'You're a charming woman… and I assume a journalist.'

'But why?' Tigist persisted.

'Because the world needs to wake up to the conversation that it's been dodging for decades as more and more existential threats arrive. Conversations on the future of this planet must take place now! If the current system of failed democracies and failed states doesn't radically change soon there will be global anarchy!'

'But that is exactly what you're proposing, isn't it?'

'In fact, the opposite. I'm a realist and tough choices must be made for the benefit of the majority.'

'For the wealthy at the expense of the poor?' Tigist couldn't hide her sarcasm. 'And you think business leaders are more effective than elected politicians?'

'Business leaders are proven winners. They find solutions in the most cost, time and resource efficient way; this is how markets work. Business is transparent, the goal is profit. Government is opaque, they have no incentive other than to get re-elected and that's why they push tough choices down the road while they concentrate on winning the next election. Politicians are egotistical and selfish people whatever their idealistic intentions might be.'

'What is she doing here?' an out of breath and genuinely flabbergasted man uttered.

'Our paths cross again, Isaiah George,' Tigist calmly replied as she finished the newly arrived glass of whiskey in two gulps.

'You know each other?' Ulrich seemed delighted. He raised his arm to catch the attention of a passing waiter.

'Don't trust that bitch; she's poison!'

'And you are the dead.'

'Really?' Isaiah guffawed as he looked around his surroundings like a Caesar. 'I don't think so!'

'How was Müller?' Jacob asked as he, Tigist and Sam started their sixteen-hour night-bus to Cortona, a hilltop Italian town in Tuscany in the Chiana Valley, this where the bestseller, Under the Tuscan Sun by Francis Mayes had been set.

'Müller worked out I was a journalist fairly quickly, but he still explained his agenda and rationale for economic colonization. He never mentioned the Jobuja Group, but he hinted at such a network and almost admitted that it was British and Swiss banks who fund global conflict—'

'You're joking me?' Did he mention a second civil war being a likely outcome in Afronia? Anything else?'

'Their strategy is to control national assets through debt. If there is conflict, by its very nature it will create more debt as the state becomes less economically productive and more is spent on weapons—'

'And which no doubt is being sold by Jobuja Group member companies! I expect they hope for regional contagion, the next domino to be sucked into the quagmire, Taberia… the HydroDevelop dams could be both the gasoline and the fuse!'

'A quite brilliant if totally amoral strategy,' Jacob summarised what all three felt.

Chapter 54

A S THE JOBUJA GROUP'S vision started to become clearer, Sam went back through the documents Stacy had given him. 'Jean-Marc, I've got evidence that links the Russian bank, IBG to Ibex investments. Walterson and Partners provided offshore services to both entities. They set up a Virgin Islands holding company for Afronian European Bank and have been their agent since 2012. The paperwork shows money laundering, fraud, international crime and terrorist financing. The file has repeated red flags but it seems none were acted on by the City of London regulator. I believe this is the tip of wilful connivance, a Faustian relationship between regulators, government, auditing firms and financial institutions. As Upton Sinclair succinctly wrote: It is difficult to get a man to understand something, when his salary depends upon his not understanding it. There are extensive financial incentives for neither regulators nor government stooges to ask awkward questions.'

'Do you think all potential stakeholders are in league?' Jean-Marc queried as he got up to go to the kitchen to turn on the kettle, they were meeting in his flat rather than the pub this time. 'Cuppa of builders?' he asked, this the most loved version of tea for many Brits.

'Thanks. A little milk and one sugar. How else can systematic financial fraud be achieved? It's a long con, and Joe public who lives in wilful ignorance of how his country is run, is the mark. So long as he has a job and can pay his mortgage and car finance, he lives in blissful ignorance of the millions of lives that are ruined for the sake of a few old men becoming even richer. It is fraud on a national scale. Confidence men taking advantage of deliberately weak systems with insufficient checks and balances—'

'And with friends in high places to protect them.'

Sam took out papers from his shoulder bag. 'These are transfers between the Afronia military and Geneva. There are also multiple transfers to a London account and which I believe is MH-16's. Six-months ago, The Financial Crimes Enforcement Network, part of the US Treasury which analyses financial data, alleged AEB provided financial services to terrorist organisations and should be blacklisted. Walterson and Partners, acting on behalf of AEB, denied the charges and took action to contest the findings. The case was suddenly closed three months ago in the name of British National Security!'

'But to what ultimate purpose?'

Chapter 55

IN THE INFORMAL SETTLEMENTS of Little Wahili and far from the glitzy malls, imposing office blocks and grand hotels in Downtown, was thirty-four-year-old Kwano. Housing conditions in this part of the city ranged from decent to calamitous and just the previous day there had been a storm which had flooded the neighbourhood leaving floors covered in slime and children playing in sewage-tinged water. Out of their one window, a visitor would see a deep ditch filled with green sewage and the glittering half-finished National Stadium in the distance, the latter being just one vanity project of many that Altimus Solomon had started though not completed, the funds being squandered on corrupt kickbacks. However, what the small home lacked in amenities was more than made up by the welcome guests received as they entered the communal area where walls were covered in religious paraphernalia and family photographs.

The colourfully braided Kwano had excelled at school and earned herself a scholarship to Umoja City University where she studied physics and later became a lecturer. She was one of four friends aged between thirty-two and thirty-eight who lived in the three-room dwelling, all having been residents of the Second Chance Orphanage and which housed children who were conceived through rape and abandoned by their traumatized mothers.

Afia, a strikingly elegant woman who was born HIV positive, lived with Kwano. She was just one of hundreds-of-thousands of child victims and was only three-months old when her mother had tried to force feed her ant poison. It was a neighbour who pulled the packet away from her hysterical mum, one of countless women who'd been raped by one of the warring factions during the Wars of Independence in the 1980s. Men on a murderous warpath who'd seen their families brutalized and comrades killed had no compassion when they saw something they wanted.

The two girls lived with Markoi who was tall and toned, a strapping man who daily pushed his bicycle laden with plastic kitchenware through Little Wahili and down to the central market. He dreamt of one day getting a loan to open a hardware shop. And then there was Nda, the joker and most creative of the friends. He would put his life into poems and songs and was in the process of writing a book about his life.

The friends were part of the so called, lost generation of Afronia, those born in the war years and whose parents had abandoned them or been killed. They were a demographic anomaly, their generation alone bucking the trend of population growth. Many of their number had been killed out of shame, others born with HIV/AIDS had died before their time. The friends had no choice but to embrace their parentless identity and were passionate to defy expectations that their personal tragedies should not define their lives.

The four were sitting in their tin roofed house as sunlight streamed through the plastic sheeted window, a reflection from Kwano's large metallic hoop earrings dancing on the cracked orange walls which had photos of the four having fun… and framed pictures of Jesus in various holy poses. They were drinking coffee with lots of sugar and sharing a loaf of bread amply spread with margarine, this as they huddled around a radio waiting to hear the election results. They expected their neighbours, Kamdonyo and Amina to join shortly and rejoice in a Rashid victory, as they, like almost all in Little Wahili, had voted for the socialist manifesto of the professor.

'Hi,' an uninvited intruder said, as he entered their humble lodgings. The friends looked suspiciously at the bearded man none having a clue who he was. 'Harold Nzibili will win the election; it's been arranged. It's a travesty for democracy,' Abeker crooned. 'This is my number,' he said while writing down his number on a scrap of paper. 'Contact me when I'm right and you're outraged.'

Chapter 56

THIRTY-SIX HOURS AFTER Abeker's unexpected and frankly unwelcome appearance—the counting of votes taking much longer than promised—Nda, Markoi, Afia and Kwano, Kandonyo and Amina, and thousands of Afronians across the land waited with baited-breath to hear the election result from The Head of the Afronian Electoral Commission.

Harold Nzibili has been duly elected President of the Second Federal Democratic Republic of Afronia; Sir Hilary Chapman will serve as his vice-president.

Chapter 57

KWANO HELD HER HEAD in despair. 'Rashid gave us hope. After all that Afronia has been through, finally there was a chance future generations would not have to suffer the mental, physical and economic torture that has been the hallmark of our lives.'

'Can we ever believe in Afronia again?' Markoi lamented.

'The West wants to economically enslave us; they think we are stupid, ignorant Africans,' Amina declared from deep within her soul. 'Their forefathers colonized this continent and now there is another white imperialist in the Presidential Palace.'

'What do we do? We can't have a second civil war where brother fights brother—'

'Revolution, Kamdonyo,' Markoi eulogised. 'It would be righteous; liberty against tyranny.'

'We must depose the puppet,' Kwano agreed. 'With Chapman they will tear down Blaise's progressive fabric. If we, us bastards, unloved by all do nothing we can't call ourselves proud Afronians. These masters of the universe who live in their palaces and penthouses know nothing of the daily struggles for those who call Little Wahili home. They cannot begin to comprehend the beast they have unleashed.'

Chapter 58

AFTER HIS FIRST POLITBURO meeting, Harold had arguably an even more important appointment. 'Congratulations, Mr President.' The smartly dressed man extended his hand.

'Thank you.' *Who is this man and how has he managed to be one of my first guests?*

'The plan has gone as expected.'

'What plan?'

Is he playing dumb or does he genuinely have no idea? Ulrich considered. 'Your election victory.'

'Who else were the electorate going to vote for?' Harold self-righteously declared having turned a blind eye to the vote-rigging and bribing that had taken place to get him elected.

'You are absolutely correct, Sir.' There was a tinge of sarcasm to Müller's words as he casually sauntered over to a side table and liberally poured a double whiskey without being invited.

'Would you like a whiskey?' this said with a sharpness to the president's voice; he was peeved. *The liberties of this man. I had some strategy discussions with his contacts about how to win the election, and agreed to have Chapman as my*

*vice, but I got here under my own steam and with fortune
smiling on me.*

'Do you honestly think…' Ulrich turned aggressively to the man opposite him, 'that the dominoes fell
so perfectly that even with your checkered past and
right-winged manifesto, you could enter the Presidential
Palace without assistance? Don't be naïve.'

The last three words sent shivers up Harold's spine.
In the ensuing starring contest, it was the president who
pulled his eyes away first, this after he poured himself a
generous whiskey on the realization, *I've struck a deal with
the devil.*

'But here we are,' Ulrich continued, his voice now
full of lightness. 'We can now move onto phase two.'

'Phase two?'

'Why else do you think I'm here? Why else would
I put up with that fool Isaiah George for so long if it
weren't for days like today?'

Harold took a seat not sure what would be revealed
next. 'We have much to discuss.' The Swiss took out a
small leather-bound book in which he'd been jotting
down notes over the years as his Afronia strategy evolved.
'First, we,' Ulrich paused, long enough for the new President of Afronia to understand that however much he
thought he was running the country, it was at best in
reality a partnership, 'we…' Ulrich reiterated, 'will get all
sanctions reversed.'

The meeting continued for another two hours, Harold unnerved if intrigued as to what his and Afronia's future held, this before he went to his luxurious office which
during the meeting with Müller he'd been strong-armed

into signing a docket relinquishing a budget of $5 million to upgrade fixtures, furnishings and fittings. Naturally, the procurement order was to a British interior decorating company that had recently established an office in neighbouring Ethiopia. Equally expected, Harold would get $1 million as a backhander. However, it wasn't money he was considering when he picked up briefing papers. The top document had the stamp of his new Head of Afronian Internal Security Services, Brigadier Hussein on it, this after Abel had been handed the document from his good friend Jacob the previous evening, the article having been emailed by Sam and Jean-Marc twenty-four hours before they were going to release it to Reuters.

Ulrich Müller—warmonger and friend of Vice-President Chapman.

Ulrich Müller, a man who moves comfortably in the same circles as financial capitalists and arms dealers, has a past and present that is barely believable. He has amassed a fortune and is one of the most extravagantly wealthy people on the planet, but relatively little is known about this most chameleon-like of characters.

Müller is the man many dare not be seen with. He is the boyhood friend of Isaiah George and was Mr Fixit for Altimus Solomon. He is the go between for businessmen, royalty, politicians and when needed, assassins. On speed dial are friends which include presidents, kings, Hollywood superstars... and the Vice-President of Afronia Sir Hillary Chapman.

In the early part of the millennium, the Swiss channelled money for the United States through AfricaInvest and into the right pockets to secure the release of twenty-three hostages in Baghdad. It's claimed, that he was the conduit for multi-billion-dollar mining deals in Afronia and which brought untold riches to corrupt politicians at the expense of the ordinary citizen.

Mr Müller has been involved in some of Afronia's biggest corporate deals, earning him a reported personal fortune estimated at $3.5 billion. He is not shy with his cash having splashed out on a 215ft super yacht which has a satellite communication system the Afronian Navy would be jealous of and which allows him to broker financial trades and finalise arms deals from international waters and where sovereign restrictions and laws don't apply. One such negotiation involved the promise of a $300 million arms deal between the British and Isaiah George if the former hired 500 mercenaries from Clearwater Solutions—a British registered company—during the civil war... and which the Afronian President did.

Müller is an expert in the art of negotiation and always ensures that all round the table are happy when they leave. This is his gift and explains how he was able to collect funds and convince Harold Nzibili to have Sir Hillary Chapman as his running-mate. But he is also a wanted fugitive in five jurisdictions on charges of racketeering, conspiracy, obstruction of justice and fraud.

However, this dealer in destruction who has been lining his pockets for decades from dubious deals, has contacts in all the right places and so is able to keep moving freely around the world.

What is truth and what is conjecture about this mysterious man remains unclear. However, and without doubt, if there was one person uniquely unsuited to advise Vice-President Chapman, it is Ulrich Müller.

Perfect! The ammunition I need to sack Chapman and get Müller arrested, thrown into a pit of crocodiles like Uncle Altimus used to do, and most importantly… out of my life. I will make the announcement at my inaugural address to parliament.

Chapter 59

Two days after the election result, Kamdonyo and Kwano were pushing a bicycle with a large box on the parcel rack through the streets of Little Wahili and towards Hillview. The package in question measured close to one metre in each direction and had been collected from the business incubator's warehouse the previous day.

Kamdonyo and Kwano walked to the waterfront, and where, with the help of Nda, they unloaded the box and under considerable strain from the weight within, struggled into Geronimo's tea shop.

'In the corner,' Geronimo, also a former resident of the Second Chance Orphanage pointed to a table; he'd closed his enterprise for the morning.

'Nda, keep a lookout for police out front,' Kamdonyo, the ringleader ordered. 'Afia, keep an eye on the beach.' Orders given, Kamdonyo went to the kitchen and returned with a razor-sharp knife and tools to assemble the parts from within the box. Next, he picked up the cutting implement and sliced through the heavily wrapped cardboard container.

It took three hours and much blasphemy before the contents of the box stood proudly on a wooden table that normally had gesticulating and chattering customers drinking tea and eating margarine encrusted slices of bread. Geronimo and the Little Wahili friends looked on with pride at what they had constructed. 'Do you think it will fly?' Kwano asked. 'The fans look too small to move such a heavy… contraption.' He did not know the correct word to describe the drone he'd helped build.

'Off course it will,' Nda said with more enthusiasm than he felt. 'Now comes the dangerous part.'

'Shouldn't we test it first?' Geronimo suggested, uncomfortable now with what had seemed less than a day ago a patriotic action.

'We can't afford to be seen,' a cautious yet bullish Kamdonyo replied. 'Here.' He gave his four friends each two lengths of string while keeping two for himself. For the next three minutes the five very carefully tied one end of each piece of string through a previously drilled hole in the housing of the twenty-five kilogram drone.

'We must test it works,' Geronimo reiterated, his voice now a tone of insistence.

'Ok,' Kamdonyo relented. He turned on the switches of the hand-held control for his prototype agriculture drone that was designed to go where farmers hadn't planted before. He moved the power lever on the left of the console forward and immediately there was a buzz of noise as the fans started to rotate, slowly at first, but as Kamdonyo increased the pressure, quicker and quicker.

'STOP!' Nda shouted above the dim. 'The police will hear us.'

'I told you it would work,' Kamdonyo smiled, even though he'd not dared touch the right directional lever to make the drone ascend, descend and turn left or right.

'Be careful,' this as he gingerly passed two, one-kilogram packages that he'd been given from Abeker earlier that morning to his fellow conspirators. Words were redundant, all knowing exactly what was inside the heavily wrapped parcels.

Slowly the ten bundles were unwrapped until they exposed the metallic oval shaped weapon of death that lay innocently inside the bubble-wrap. The five comrades stared at each other each fully aware this was the last opportunity to abort their mission. There was silence, the tension inside the tea shop building as sweat glistened on more than one forehead. With an almost imperceptible nod from Markoi, the oldest of the group and who had first suggested the plan, the five pairs of hands started the most dangerous stage of the assembly.

It took fifteen nerve shredding minutes, each of the friends in deep concentration as they tied the ten F-1 anti-personnel grenades—each containing 60 grams of Trinitrotoluene explosive—onto the drone before placing them in the cereal bowls which Kandonyo had earlier screwed onto the aircraft, this so that the grenades would not fall out of the contraption without violent movement. With clammy brows and sweaty hands the friends took a collective step back and saw their creation of destruction. 'For freedom,' Afia whispered.

'For hope,' Nda added.

'For Afronia,' Geronimo completed the mantra that in the last few days had become the word on the street for all those were disgusted by the election of Harold Nzibili and his white master, as many assumed Chapman to be.

'We'll strike the first blow of the revolution,' Kamdonyo said, as he solemnly walked towards the inanimate object on the table where normally there was camaraderie and laughter. The other four followed suit, and with a final look of defiance they lifted the metal and plastic drone and walked ungainly towards the beachside entrance of the tearoom.

Afia poked her head out the doorway, and with no police or soldiers in sight, jogged down the twelve steps onto the golden sand and looked up and down the coastline, the surf gently crashing onto the shore on this hot, humid but calm day; she gave a thumbs up.

With utmost care the four men walked down the small flight of stairs as fast as they could before placing the drone on the sand. With one last look in all directions, Kamdonyo ran with the controller in-hand to the waterline where he had a line-of-sight to Parliament, the target Abeker (on behalf of Mustafa and Henshaw) had suggested to the friends, with the words: you will forever be known as patriots for attacking the headquarters of the corrupt.

Kandonyo pushed the left power lever and saw Nda giving a thumbs up to indicate the fans were working, though he needn't have bothered with the gesture, Kamdonyo seeing sand rising into the clear blue sky and which was confirmation enough that his invention, indeed business, was working perfectly. With his friends retreating into the tea shop, Kamdonyo made the drone rise rapidly before the craft was clocked in dust, the danger being sand particles finding their way into the rotors and causing a catastrophic and deadly malfunction. Hovering peacefully, Kamdonyo looked up to his creation and knew his life was about to forever be altered. He pushed the right lever forward and within seconds the drone was not much more than a speck as it made its way speedily towards its final destination.

As the drone headed towards its destiny, Harold Nzibili started his inaugural address to parliament. 'The economy is sluggish. The Afronian Shilling has fallen off a cliff against the US Dollar, and Afronia's debt has been downgraded to junk status. As such, I'm bringing Professor Rashid into my politburo as both a sign of reconciliation and that he was the architect behind the economic resurgence during the presidency of Walter Blaise.' He paused and took a sip of water while planning the exact wording of what he would say next. *My running mate, Vice-President Sir Hillary Chapman is implicated with ne'er-do-wells. I have ordered the head of the Presidential Guard to arrest him and to set up security measures at all ports of entry to apprehend a Swiss gentleman named Ulrich Müller and who is head of an international conspiracy.*

'A report I saw earlier today, and which I will release at the end of my speech, has unmasked a horrifying contempt for the Afronian people. Radical imperialists, colonisers from a forgone age and European bankers, lawyers and lobbyists are trying to plunder the wealth of our nation. My running mate, Vice—'

BOOM! The speech was cataclysmically interrupted by a huge roar as Kandonyo's drone slammed into the roof of parliament, the shock of which dislodged the grenades, the string attached to the aircraft's housing pulling the pins out from the metallic balls of destruction, the ten explosions going off almost simultaneously and rocking the Chinese constructed building, cracks appearing in the ceiling of the atrium as debris fell.

An ineffectual though highly symbolic attack, Julius Stewart considered from his perch in an air duct, this as he looked through the telescopic sight of his Russian-made Dragunov sniper rifle.

As chaos reigned below, he eloquently moved his rifle marginally side-to-side until he could pick out his target. Keeping his aim steady, he sucked in a breath, counted, *Three, two, one,* and squeezed the trigger, the 7.62mm bullet finding its mark, the forehead of Harold Nzibili. *The president is dead, long live President Chapman.*

THE END

Afronian *Revolution*

If you enjoyed reading *Developing Afronia* and want to know what happens during the presidency of Sir Hillary Chapman, you can read the prologue for *Afronian Revolution*.

For freedom. For hope. For Afronia
—Revolutionary Mantra

Following the civil war Afronia rose on the charismatic vision of President Walter Blaise. The country impressively developed and her citizens welcomed the foreign investors and international support to rebuild the country. However, unchecked, this strategy led to unsustainable levels of debt and which was exactly what the Jobuja Group of European business tycoons, prime ministers and hereditary elite wanted in their quest to control Afronia's natural resource riches and ultimately to create a one government continent based on neo-liberal principles.

When Blaise was assassinated General Mutoni conducted a military putsch, his goal: the economic destruction of the country to pave the way for the Jobuja Group's man to take the levers of power. President Harold Nzebili, and who is about to reveal the conspiracy, is assassinated during his inaugural address to Parliament and thus leaving the way clear for Vice-President, Sir Hillary Chapman—the inside man of the Jobuja Group—to elevate into the presidential hot seat.

AFRONIAN
Revolution

Chris Statham

Afronian Revolution follows the fight for the
future of the nation state with foreign investors,
businessmen and politicians on one side and
Afronian patriots on the other.

Prologue

ITHIN A WEEK OF becoming president, the face of
Sir Hillary Chapman was everywhere. On bill-
boards across Umoja City and regional cities his face
beamed benevolently. On the highways that passed the
construction sites of the mega-dams, there he was reminding every citizen that it was his former company
that was going to bring electricity to millions and start an
irrigation farming revolution. School children were encouraged to sing about him as the new hope for Afronia,
a businessman who knew how to cut red tape, stamp out
corruption, drain the swamp of advisors and lackeys, and
stand-up to international organisations who wanted to
impose unfair trade restrictions; in short, he was the man
to get things done. Not a day would pass without his mug
being plastered on the front of daily newspapers or his
name mentioned on radio programs. He dominated the
news. He was omni-present. Indeed, there was a media
and communications team ensconced in the Presidential
Palace that was dedicated to writing flattering commen-
tary outlining the virtues of Afronia's Great White Hope.

Eric Toner, the General Manager of HydroDevelop
was eating breakfast with his family in their lavish com-

pany paid house in Hillview, Umoja City, a Chapman billboard at the entrance to the twenty-house compound.

European businessmen conspire for regime change in Afronia

The term neoliberalism was first coined in the 1930s, the central hypothesis being, there will be full employment through the cutting of taxes and deregulation. It is economic Darwinism based on the belief that humans are rationale and the market will determine the winners. Competition is the leading principle, and for the losers there is no safety-net welfare system.

For neo-liberal policies to take hold a country should be chosen where there is great potential for riches, a weak or recovering political system and one which is ideally at the start of the economic growth cycle. Elections must be closely contested to give an air of legitimacy, but if rounds of political strife led to armed conflict… that is even better. When the civil war reaches a peaceful conclusion much of the infrastructure will be destroyed and the country's coffers empty and thus investment from foreign governments and investment banks will be warmly welcomed. However, the same government must never be able to service the debt otherwise there would be no transfer of state assets to creditors. If there is an inept president who drives the country to bankruptcy this is an ideal scenario as it will allow capitalists to ride to the rescue on the unspoken and undemocratic proviso that foreign business owners will control the country as they are successful and know how to make tough choices for the greater good.

It is with this understanding that Afronia, coming out of a civil war, racked up unsustainable levels of debt. "Developing nations' debt has more than doubled in the past decade and left more than 50 countries facing a repayment crisis," this according to the Jubilee Debt Campaign.

The Jobuja Group has taken the neo-liberal economic philosophy to the extreme, the identified loser, the African continent, Afronia specifically. President Altimus Solomon being politically bankrupt was an ideal target. After the civil war, President Walter Blaise had progressive policies, but in the months since his death and subsequent accession of General Mutoni, British businesses and London based investment banks have collaborated to bankrupt the country and take it to the verge of being a failed state, citizens having little choice but to accept the retreat of democracy for the promise of peace and prosperity. If there is economic regional contagion it would create the perfect circumstances to implement a one government continent in which free market principles in unregulated sectors would run amok. This is the stated long-term goal of the Jobuja Group, the few at the top becoming immensely wealthy while the vast majority economically suffering.

The Jobuja Group claim, that with growing populations, urbanisation, climate change, technological revolution and land degradation, a one government continent is the only practical way to make the tough decisions needed to stop ecological meltdown, mass hunger, waves of refugees heading to Europe and uncontrolled poverty. These are all valid concerns for Africans, but the means to tackle the challenges should be through global cooperation rather than backroom deals, corruption and conspiracy. Their revolutionary model is not with human mules walking through airports with bricks of dollars strapped to their midriffs but rather billions being wire transferred between banks in London, Geneva and Umoja City. They will profit, get a return on their investment from within the ensuing chaos as they buy up state assets, hold the country to ransom and take political leadership positions as they amass unlimited money and power.

HydroDevelop is the tip of the Jobuja's commercial spear; Afronia, the Group's first domino. The east African country has been in a state of continual upheaval ever since the Presidential Square massacre in 2013. Since that fateful day there have been 7 presidents, a civil war, the Denga Chemical Massacre and umpteen other tragedies. There was stability and hope under Walter Blaise but that ended with his assassination.

With unsustainable debt to British companies, the constitution altered to allow a non-Afronian by birth to become president and, the call to reimpose a civilian administration after the military junta, there was little resistance to Sir Hillary Chapman becoming the running mate of Harold Nzebili. With President's Nzebili's assassination, the last obstacle for the Jobuja Group to get their man into the ultimate Afronian seat of power has been removed.

Two days after President Chapman's rise to power, the British Prime Minister, the first foreign dignitary arrived in a show of support. It was a stage-managed public relations stunt for the benefit of investors and hundreds of waiting journalists. "I truly believe that with President Chapman at the helm, Afronia will become the continental leader of how the public and private sector can work together to better the lives of citizens. The British government will strain every sinew to make this a reality. Democracy is in retreat across the world and we will do all that we can to ensure that Afronia stands on her feet and cannot be economically intimidated by Russia and China. The British will stand by Afronia so that she does not retreat to the brutality of colonial times when the weak were devoured by the powerful. We are prepared to be tough on any country that interferes in Afronia's internal politics and will help Afronians take back control of their beloved country and democratic institutions."

Eric finished reading about the Jobuja Group conspiracy. 'If it is true about the British undermining Afronia's democracy over the last decade. If they plotted assassinations of at least two presidents, helped in the instigation of a civil war and multiple counts of election vote rigging, money laundering and the provocation of armed insurrection…' he couldn't finish the sentence so taken aback was he of the revelations he'd just read.

'President Chapman though is clean, he is a knight of the British realm after all,' Sylvia Toner replied to her husband. 'Every morning he can be found outside the presidential palace and about to set out on his morning walk, a brisk daily constitutional where he discusses corruption and patronage, politics and football, economics and the price of bread—'

'He is following the Walter Blaise playbook, hoping for Champhoria rather than Champageddon. If you are business minded, I am sure there will be many opportunities for Afronian entrepreneurs. There will be challenges, but where aren't there? Afronia is moving from a liberal democrat in Walter Blaise to a model of the benevolent dictator in President Chapman; it is difficult to know which way the country will go next—another military coup? Martial law? A booming economy? Revolution? Undoubtedly, the Chapman brand is currently toxic, and so to those associated with it, including me!'

'We can't stay in Afronia, it's just too risky,' Sylvia concluded. 'It sounds as if HydroDevelop is right in the middle of this Jobuja pickle.'

'I agree. You and the kids will be on the first plane out. All non-essential HydroDevelop employees and their dependants are going until Afronia calms down.'

'And you're not?'

'I can't unless my contract is terminated. If what the papers are saying is true, it will be even more important to stay and continue the work that is so important for the country while this mess gets sorted out,' *And my salary will be tripled,* he didn't inform his beloved.

'And what happens when you are killed or kidnapped? What good will thirty pieces of silver do your children?'

'Don't be hysterical; I'll be fine. Besides, I've been assigned a bodyguard.'

'My God, you're mad! Do you not care about your family? Why are you putting money before safety?'

'It's a political crisis and once the dust has settled, the country will quickly get back to normal. I must be here to argue the case why HydroDevelop should continue the Southiland Renaissance Dam project. And besides, the work is a once in a lifetime opportunity.'

'And what happens if President Chapman refuses to resign? It's clear, even to me, that he has no mandate to rule. What happens when his cronies and allies in Afronia and Europe flee as the scandal unfolds? It will be revolution. HydroDevelop and other British businesses will rightly be a key target of Afronian ire.'

'Don't be so hyperbolic. But what I will say, for all the preconceptions I had of Afronia I think I'm going to have to empty my mind and start afresh if I'm ever going to understand this country of contradictions.'